CROSS *my Heart*

USA TODAY BESTSELLING AUTHOR
LEA COLL

CROSS MY HEART

Copyright © 2024 by Lea Meyer

All Rights Reserved.

This book contains material protected under International and Federal Copyright Laws and Treaties. Any unauthorized reprint or use of this material is prohibited. No part of this book may be reproduced or transmitted in any form or by any means, electronic or mechanical, including photocopying, recording, or by an information and retrieval system without express written permission from the author.

All characters and storylines are the property of the author and your support and respect is greatly appreciated.

This is a work of fiction. Names, characters, places and incidents either are the product of the author's imagination or are used fictitiously, and any resemblance to actual persons, living or dead, business establishments, events, or locales is entirely coincidental.

GET THE MOUNTAIN HAVEN SERIES 40% OFF

Get ready for a romance that'll make your heart melt! Seven books, beautifully written stories of rugged men and the women who own their hearts. Off-the-charts chemistry guaranteed! Get 7 books for 40% off for a limited time on Lea's Shop.

CHAPTER 1

❄

FIONA

When I'd agreed to come home for the holidays, I hadn't wanted to stay on my family's farm, so I'd booked a room at a nearby inn. The same one where my high school sweetheart and ex, Aiden, used to live with his parents in a trailer on the property. The trailer had since been removed, and his sister, Marley, ran the inn. I didn't expect to run into Aiden because he was usually deployed somewhere else.

By the time I drove down tree-lined driveway with white lights wrapped around the trunks, my eyes burned from exhaustion. My back and neck were stiff from the long day of travel between the flight and the drive.

The historic inn's columns were wrapped in more white lights. Each window held a wreath with a red bow. I grabbed my suitcases and carried them up the stairs, admiring the tree on the porch that was decorated with red velvet ribbon and gold ornaments. I opened the heavy wooden door to the sound of holiday music drifting down the grand staircase.

A man in a suit rushed forward to take the suitcases from my hands and set them next to the counter.

"Fiona? What are you doing here?" my sister, Daphne, asked, and my attention was diverted to her.

"I came for a visit." That much was the truth.

Daphne's forehead wrinkled. "You didn't say anything to anyone."

My gaze darted away from her. "It was a last-minute kind of thing.

The man behind the counter cleared his throat. "I don't have reservations for you."

When his gaze met mine, it was like all the air had been sucked out of me. Aiden Matthews was standing in front of me. Instead of asking why he was here working at the inn, I said, "I called earlier, and a woman said she had a room for me."

She might have said something about a holiday party in the ballroom, but I didn't think that would affect me. I was here to visit with my family and figure out my life. I wasn't here to take part in the inn's holiday festivities.

Aiden turned his attention to his computer screen at the same time Daphne stepped forward. "Fiona, this is Cole Monroe, my boyfriend."

The name Monroe caught my attention. The family owned a competing Christmas tree farm. Recently, I'd heard my brothers complain that they were eating into our farm's profits.

Cole held his hand out to me. "It's nice to meet you."

I smiled at Cole and said to Fiona, "I didn't realize you were dating anyone."

Daphne smiled up at Cole. "You've missed a lot." Then she shifted her attention to me. "We were just stepping out. Cole has something he wanted to show me. Can we catch up later?"

Even though I hadn't announced my visit to anyone other than my dad, I was a little surprised that Daphne had dismissed me so easily. But then again, I hadn't been a part of my family's life for a long time. I couldn't expect them to drop everything just because I'd come for a visit. The familiar guilt wrapped around my heart and squeezed. "I'm in town for a few weeks, so we'll have plenty of time."

Daphne wrapped a hand around Cole's arm, then frowned. "Are you sure you're okay? Do you want me to stay?"

I tried to smile even though it felt forced. "I'm here for a holiday visit. Dad insisted I come."

Daphne's shoulders lowered. "I'm happy you're here. It would be perfect if Axel and Ryder could visit too."

"That would be lovely. You two enjoy your evening, and we'll catch up later." My smile fell when Fiona and Cole stepped outside, leaving me alone with Aiden.

There was a buzzing in my ears. The last time I saw Aiden, he told me he'd enlisted, and when I reminded him of his promises to wait for me to graduate from college, he'd apologized but remained steadfast. I couldn't think of everything that followed. It hurt too much. He'd ripped my heart out of my chest that day, and I'd never recovered. I'd been young and stupid. Now I knew better than to get close to anyone.

"Marley reserved a room for you." Aiden's voice was carefully controlled.

He grabbed a room key, not the plastic cards used at most hotels. I could appreciate the charm even though I worked for a large hotel chain that specialized in modern decor.

Aiden moved toward me, making my heart rate kick into gear before he grabbed my luggage. "I'll show you up."

Panic clawed my throat. The last thing I wanted to do was be alone with Aiden. "Oh, that's not necessary."

Without responding, he strode toward the stairs. I rushed to keep up with him. "You don't have to do this."

He kept his gaze forward, his shoulders stiff. "I'm carrying your luggage to your room."

My heart felt heavy. He was saying and doing all the right things, but I didn't want to be alone with him. I didn't trust myself not to revert to that nineteen-year-old Fiona who loved him with all her heart. I would have gone anywhere for him, done anything. But he'd turned me down. He hadn't wanted me then, and it hurt to be around him now.

I followed him to the landing on the second floor. "There's a party in the ballroom tonight, but it's on the third floor. You might hear some music, but we make sure it's quiet by eleven."

"That won't be a problem." Ever since I was passed over for a promotion, I'd had trouble sleeping.

Aiden paused in front of a door at the end of the hall where another tree, decorated in green velvet ribbon and gold ornaments, stood in front of a large window. "The inn is beautiful."

"When Gram died, Marley inherited the inn. Instead of selling, she renovated it and opened it for business."

"I thought Marley moved to California to start her own business." I'd looked her up from time to time, wondering if she mentioned where Aiden was stationed because he didn't have a social media presence.

Aiden unlocked the door, then pushed it open. "She still owns a home there but spends most of her time here. She's engaged to Heath Monroe."

He motioned for me to precede him into the room.

I stepped inside, surprised to see a queen bed with a quilt, garland and a candle on the window ledge, beautiful wood furniture, and an adjoining bathroom.

"When Marley renovated, Heath added closets in all the rooms and ensured that most rooms have an adjoining bathroom."

I wandered around the room. "She did an amazing job with the renovations. You can feel the history with the furniture and wood details, yet it feels new."

"She wanted to preserve the history of the inn. She loved the ballroom and refused to convert it into more guest rooms when her Realtor suggested it." Aiden pulled a rack out of the closet and set one suitcase on top and one on the floor. "Will you need anything else?"

My heart jumped into my throat. Was this it? After all these years, we could act like we barely knew each other. I couldn't resist stepping closer to him. "You look good." He sported a closely shaved beard, and his body had filled out since we'd dated.

He swallowed hard. "You do too."

Is that what we'd become? We'd exchange awkward greetings when we ran into each other? I licked my lips and then forced myself to ask, "Are you on leave?"

Aiden shook his head. "I retired from the military."

"Oh? I kind of thought you'd be a lifer." He'd talked about duty and responsibility when he'd told me he'd enlisted. That it was something he had to do, and I got the impression it was a permanent kind of thing.

"I thought so too."

I wondered if there was a story there, but I shouldn't have. Aiden wasn't mine anymore. He'd made that abundantly clear when he'd broken things off. I'd offered to go with him, to marry him, but he wasn't interested.

Pain shot through my chest, but it wasn't as acute as when I was nineteen. I'd get through this just like I had my mother's death. There was nothing I couldn't handle. I just needed to be strong.

I shrugged off my jacket and let it fall to the bed.

Aiden perused me from head to toe. "You should come to the dance. You're already dressed for it."

The promotion was announced at my company's holiday party. I'd gone outside and called my dad. When he suggested I come home, I booked the first flight I could find and told my boss I was taking the vacation time I'd accrued over the years. He'd been surprised but hadn't tried to talk me out of it.

"Are you sure I'm invited?" I asked, wondering if I was bold enough to accept his invitation.

"It's Marley's annual holiday party. She invited all her friends. I think you're a part of that."

I laughed without any humor as I sank to the edge of the bed. I couldn't wait until Aiden left and I could kick off the heels and sleep forever. "I was never a part of your circle."

When we dated, we'd kept our relationship a secret. Aiden was friends with the Monroes, helping at the farm from time to time, and he didn't come from a good family. I didn't want anyone to tell me I couldn't see him. At first, there was a thrill from dating the bad boy, but I quickly realized there was a lot more to Aiden. He was sweet and thoughtful and felt so many things. His mother's toxic barbs ate away at him.

I'd wanted to take him away from his family, and he'd promised to wait until I graduated college. He didn't want to interfere with my education. Then we'd get married and start our lives together.

I'd made him promise me that he'd wait. I'd made him hook his pinky finger through mine and recite the childish rhyme. Unfortunately, he hadn't kept his promise.

"Then I'm inviting you."

Would I survive attending a dance where Aiden was present? Would it bring back the memory of him sneaking into my prom and dancing with me all night? When nothing mattered but him and me?

He moved toward the door, then said over his shoulder, "I'll save you a dance."

I couldn't seem to find my voice as he opened the door and slipped out. His invitation sent tingles down my spine.

I checked my appearance in the full-length mirror. I could easily go to the party and see how it was. Or I could remove my clothes, take a shower, and go to bed where I most certainly wouldn't sleep.

It wasn't a good idea to be anywhere near Aiden. There were all these feelings swirling in my chest. Our relationship felt unresolved, even though Aiden had ended it with no hope for reconciliation.

He told me not to contact him. That he was focused on doing a good job in the military and becoming a better man. Apparently, he didn't see me by his side in that process.

I knew he felt unworthy because of his upbringing, but I never thought he needed something as extreme as a complete break from me. Maybe I was naive back then, but I thought our love was enough.

There was a part of me that wanted to prove to Aiden and myself that I could see him and walk away. That he didn't affect me anymore. I was a confident woman who didn't let any man get to her, especially not Aiden Matthews. He was part of my past, and I wouldn't let him get close enough to hurt me again.

Determined to prove that I wasn't affected by him, I retouched my makeup, and ran a brush through my hair before placing my room key in my clutch. I followed the music upstairs where the party was still in full swing.

There was a band playing, couples on the dance floor, and several bars placed around the room where others congregated. There were a few tables with chairs.

Before I could figure out who I knew in the room, Aiden appeared in front of me. "You came."

"You promised me a dance," I said, sounding breathless when I'd meant to sound strong and unaffected.

Aiden grinned and held out his hand. "I'm glad you came."

I shook my head. "I don't know why I did. I'm exhausted."

He led me onto the dance floor and into his arms. "You had a long day?"

"You could say that." But I didn't want to talk about that now. He smelled like cedar, and his hand on my back felt good.

Aiden dipped his head slightly. "You didn't tell your sister you were coming home?"

There was no censure in his voice. He knew how difficult things were for me after my mother died. "It was a spur-of-the-moment kind of thing. I hadn't had a chance to talk to my siblings."

"Daphne made it sound like you don't normally come home for the holidays," Aiden guided us away from another couple.

"I'm usually working." My gaze traveled around the room so I wouldn't have to look at him.

"I've never seen you when I come home."

I was surprised he'd even thought of me. The way he'd so easily broken things off made me think I'd liked him far more than he had me. "I didn't know you were looking."

Aiden huffed out a breath. "I have a few regrets about how I handled things back then."

My brow raised. "You do?"

He pulled me closer to him so that my body was touching his. The heat of his body enveloped me like a cozy blanket. "I was so eager to get out of town and away from my parents, I didn't see any other way out."

"You could have moved in with me. We could have gotten an apartment—" I didn't want to rehash the past. "It doesn't matter anymore. What's done is done. We've both moved on with our lives."

Aiden let out a breath. "I wish I'd handled things better back then. I wish I hadn't hurt you."

Tears stung my eyes. It was everything I'd wanted to hear, but it was too late. Too much time had passed. Needing to change the subject, I said, "Is it part of your job as the innkeeper to dance with all the single women at the balls?"

A slow smile spread over Aiden's face, reminding me of a time when we were happy and in love. "You're the only woman I've danced with tonight."

I wondered why that was. Did he still feel something for me, or was it merely regret over how he'd ended things?

My mother died, but I still had a loving father and siblings. I had the means to go to college even if it was on student loans. Aiden didn't have any of that support. I just wished he'd realized that I was on his side.

"I usually man the front counter." He looked around the room. "This is more Marley's kind of thing."

"Then why are you here tonight?" I couldn't stop myself from asking.

"I'm friends with the Monroes. I work with Heath in his contracting business, and Marley is close with them. But mainly I wanted to see you."

"It's good seeing you after all these years." I wasn't sure it was good for my mental health. I felt stronger when I wasn't around him. Then I could put him and everything that happened out of my mind.

"I never thought we'd be together like this again."

"Neither did I." Not coming home often was self-preservation. It felt weird being in the house when my mother wasn't there anymore. And I didn't want to run into Aiden.

"Do you know how long you'll be in town?"

I shrugged. "I have to go back after the New Year."

When the notes of the song drifted off, Aiden asked, "Would you like a drink?"

I sighed. "I'm not really in the mood for a party or everything that comes with it."

"Then can I show you the gardens? Marley had Knox add them when she renovated. I think it's the best thing she did to the property."

I smiled at his obvious excitement. "Then I'd love to see them."

Aiden led me around the couples dancing, and into the hallway. "You'll need a coat." We stopped at my room to retrieve mine, then his at the front desk.

He opened the door, and I stepped into the crisp air.

"It's a beautiful night." When was the last time I'd spent any time admiring the sky or the stars? I usually worked long hours where I came home to eat takeout, then worked longer on my laptop.

Occasionally, I went out for drinks or a meal with friends or coworkers, but I didn't feel like I had stopped to appreciate anything in a long time. Maybe this would be a good break for me.

He led me to the side of the inn where there was a line of Christmas trees wrapped in white lights.

"This is gorgeous."

He flashed me a grin before he led me though a gap in the trees. "Just wait until you see the rest."

When the trees led us through a path, I asked, "Is this a maze?"

Aiden squeezed my hand. "It is."

A jolt of electricity traveled down my arm. "I wish this were here when we were kids. We would have had the best time running around."

"You know why that never would have worked," Aiden said tightly.

I spent time at the inn but managed to avoid his parents. Aiden didn't want me to meet them. He said they'd just criticize me and him. He was protecting me from their vitriol. "Have you seen your parents since you've been back?"

I shook my head. "When Marley graduated, Gram told my parents they were no longer welcome on the property, and had the trailer removed. She tolerated my parents, and when Marley turned eighteen, she didn't want them here anymore. It was for the best. I didn't like leaving Marley here to deal with them. I just didn't see any other way around it."

Aiden had abandoned everyone he purported to love. But I'd moved on from him and was stronger for it.

I heard the trickle of water before I saw the source. When we reached a clearing, there was a tree in the center of a massive water fountain. At the base there were small spouts that made it look like the tiny cascades were chasing each other around the edge. "This is gorgeous."

I loved that Marley had renovated the inn, and it was open again. It made me feel like anything could be repaired. It made me hope for something I shouldn't want.

We stood at the edge of the fountain, him looking at the lights of the tree and me looking at him. He was no longer the boy who'd broken my heart, but a man I no longer knew. He wasn't mine and never would be.

CHAPTER 2

AIDEN

I couldn't believe I was standing next to Fiona. I never thought we'd be in the same room again, much less get an opportunity to make things right. I'd resigned myself to regretting my life's choices when it came to her.

I thought I was doing the right thing in pushing her away. The desire to be a man worthy of her love was the only thing I could think about. I needed to do it on my own, and the only way I could be the man she deserved was to enlist.

She'd wanted to marry me and be by my side. But it was something I'd needed to do on my own, and I couldn't be the one responsible for her quitting school. I was shortsighted because I'd made her promises, and I hadn't kept them.

I'd broken her heart. When she realized I didn't want to marry her, she'd pressed her lips into a straight line, her eyes hard, and said I wouldn't get a second chance with her.

I hadn't worried about it at the time. I couldn't see past making myself into a man, but now I had so many regrets. I'd thrown her away, not realizing how lucky I was to find love at such a young age. I assumed we couldn't last, but now I wasn't so sure.

I looked over at her, catching her watching me. "I've missed you."

Her breath hitched, and she looked away. "You can't say things like that."

The only sound was the water in the fountain. Everyone was at the party, and it was too cold for a walk in the gardens. We were alone.

"Why not?" I couldn't help but ask, knowing I was about to get whiplash. Fiona never held back what she was thinking and feeling. It was what I'd loved most about her when we'd dated.

"You don't have that right anymore. You broke us."

I swallowed over the lump in my throat. "If I could go back and change things—"

"What's done is done. There's no need to bring up the past." Fiona's voice was hard and unyielding.

I hated that I had to let it go. That I couldn't make it up to her. I had so many hopes about how this meeting would go now that she was here. I should have known she'd shut me out.

"Can I say I'm sorry for how I handled things?"

Fiona nodded tightly, and I took her hand, guiding her to a nearby bench. I grabbed a blanket that we kept in a container for times just like this. I'd never had a need for it, but it was Marley's idea. She liked to offer small things to improve the guests' stays. I'd never been more grateful for her foresight.

I draped the blanket on Fiona's lap. "I'm sorry I hurt you."

Fiona's face tightened. "It was a long time ago."

"It doesn't change the fact that I'm sorry for how things went down. I was so sure of myself. So clear in my path."

Fiona laughed without any humor. "It's too bad you didn't clue me in."

I sighed. "I was worried you'd talk me out of it."

"You promised—" Fiona's anguished eyes met mine, and she broke off. Then she stood, letting the blanket fall to the ground. "I can't do this."

"Fiona—wait." But she walked away, through the trees and into the maze. The path we'd taken was clear. She wouldn't get lost, but I wanted to talk to her.

I picked up the blanket and put it away. By the time I followed her, she was gone. I went inside, hoping to see her in the ballroom or even the bar, but she was nowhere to be found.

"You okay?" Knox asked me from where he sat on the bar stool.

I gritted my teeth. "I will be."

"I heard Daphne's sister is back."

"Fiona rented a room for the holidays." I resisted the urge to check the dates she'd booked it for. How long did I have before she'd be gone from my life again? Would it be like this every year? She'd drop in for a visit, and I'd hope that I could properly express my regrets, but she'd run from me?

"I think she was hoping all her siblings would visit."

"Are things better between the Monroes and the Calloways?" There was tension between the families because they ran competing Christmas tree farms. Recently, Daphne met and dated Knox's cousin, Cole. When everyone found out about it, they weren't happy. I'd advised Cole to follow his heart, the family's issues with each other be damned. I was pleased to know he'd listened and mended his relationship with Daphne.

I had no idea what would have happened between me and Fiona if I'd stayed or if I'd married her. For all I knew, we wouldn't have lasted. She would have resented the life of a military wife, moving constantly and never being able to finish her education or find a steady job. She could have divorced me within a few years.

She deserved more than I had to offer.

I was never good enough for Fiona Calloway. She'd grown up in an idyllic situation, living on a Christmas tree farm with her parents and six siblings. From what I could tell, they all looked out for each other. The only thing that marred her perfect family was when her mother died.

"I wouldn't say that. Everyone is getting used to the idea of a Monroe with a Calloway. My family doesn't like change."

"I can't say I do either." What I loved about the military life was the predictability. My commanding officers might have yelled at me, but I'd work hard to improve and eventually gain their praise. I could never please my parents.

"Cole bought his own place. He took her out to the new house tonight to show it to her."

"I'm happy for them." I'd started rooting for Cole after we'd talked that one night. It was after everyone found out about their relationship and he'd wanted to give up. He wasn't willing to lose his family for Daphne. But it was clear he was in love with her.

"Cole said he talked to you about the situation with Daphne."

"I told him not to let go of the best thing that ever happened to him."

Knox nodded. "He deserves to be happy. I'm glad he's found his way."

"Me too." I just wished I'd found mine. I'd gotten respect in the military. When Gram died and Marley was alone renovating the inn, I'd wanted to be there for her. It felt like I should come home, that it was time.

"How are things here at the inn?" Knox gestured toward the empty stool next to him.

I sat on it. "It's been hard. Marley's been helping out a lot. I just wish she felt like she could rely on me."

"You'll get there."

"I know Heath wants me to contribute more with his business. I've just been too caught up in everything here. There's the reservations, guests' needs, repairs, maintenance. It's a lot."

"I can give you a deal on landscaping. You should really hire some of this stuff out."

"We have cleaners. That's about all we can afford for now." Marley had offered to infuse her money into the business, but I wouldn't let her. I wanted to make it work on its own.

Knox nodded. "I'm here if you need me."

"I appreciate that." The good thing about my relationship with Fiona was that not many people knew about it. I think her father suspected, but he never said anything to her. Maybe even her brothers now that we were over, but I wasn't positive.

Knox drank his water. "I need to get Addy and Izzy home. It's getting late."

"Thanks for coming. This party is important to Marley. She loves getting everyone together." I couldn't say I had those same desires. I preferred to avoid people, which was why running the inn was difficult for me.

Knox stood. "Always a pleasure to be here. It's nice to have the inn open again."

When I grew up here, I was embarrassed to be a Matthews. My parents' reputation marred the one Gram had created with the inn. I was known as the kid who lived in a trailer on my grandmother's property. I loved Gram, but the situation didn't do my reputation at school any favors. Thankfully I'm not that kid anymore.

I was a grown man, and I was slowly finding my way. I just wished I could dismiss this thing with Fiona as easily. There was something about her coming home unexpectedly. There was a story there, and it wasn't my business to find out what it was. But I wanted to.

I stayed up long after the guests had gone home from the party. Even though there was a cleaning crew that came in the morning, I threw out all the trash, returned the glasses and dishes to the kitchen, and turned out the lights before finally going to bed. My suite was on the third floor, and it was more of an apartment than a room.

When Grandma ran the inn, she slept in a small room on the first floor next to the kitchen. But Marley wanted more privacy for the innkeepers and designed an apartment on the third floor.

I went to sleep thinking about Fiona and all the ways she'd changed. She was curvier, no longer the slight girl she'd been back then. But her fierceness had only increased. I didn't like my odds to convince her to talk to me about the past.

What had she been doing since I walked away? I hated even thinking of her dating someone else. But that was reality. She had a life without me, and if I wanted to get to know her now, I'd have to make an effort. I wasn't sure if I wanted to alleviate my guilt over the breakup, but I had to do something. Maybe then I'd clear away a lifetime of regrets.

~

The next morning, I went for my run onto the Monroes' property. When I returned, I was sweating and only felt marginally better. Nothing would help the scattered sleep I'd gotten the night before. But physical exercise always helped to make me more alert. I showered quickly, then went to the kitchen to start the coffee and make a quick breakfast for anyone who needed it.

Most didn't get up early, and we offered muffins, croissants, and donuts for those people. For the ones who came down early, I cooked. It wasn't something we advertised because I wasn't sure how long I could keep it up. It was a service I offered for now.

I made eggs and pancakes, serving them to anyone who showed up.

Around ten, the breakfast crowd cleared out, and I got to work cleaning pots and filling the dishwasher.

"Is it too late for breakfast?" Fiona asked.

I turned to find her standing hesitantly by the counter. Behind her, the dining room was empty.

"We have muffins and coffee." I nodded toward the platter of muffins and the carafe of coffee.

Fiona smiled. "I smell pancakes."

"We usually offer full-service breakfast earlier, but I can make an exception for you."

"You don't have to go out of your way," Fiona said softly.

"I don't mind." I placed the clean skillet on the burner, then grabbed a mixing bowl. "Chocolate chips?"

Her lips curved into a smile. "Sure."

We'd dated secretly as teens, which meant evenings in the bed of my truck and any stolen moment we could find. The only time I'd risked anyone learning about us was when I'd snuck into her high school prom.

I never took her out for dinner or a movie. I'd never had the opportunity to cook for her. I hadn't minded back then, but now I was wondering if we'd missed out on a primary part of any relationship.

Fiona sat on the stool while I mixed the batter and poured it into the pan.

There was so much to catch up on, but at the same time, it was nice to just be together.

"Now that you're back, are you running the inn?"

"And working part-time with Heath. I think he'd like me to take on more, but I'm trying to get the hang of this place."

"That makes sense."

"There's a lot to do. Breakfast, cleanup, checking in guests, fixing anything that's broke, and landscaping."

"You could hire someone," Fiona said.

I shrugged. "We can't afford to do that yet."

"Daphne recently started selling her pies. I know it's tough to get a business started."

"Especially since this one was closed for so long. The long-term guests moved onto other accommodations, and others don't trust that we'll stay open."

"Consumer trust is a big part of business."

"I didn't know anything about business until I started here. Luckily, Marley's good at it. She helps when she can, but she has her own online consulting business. I like to figure things out on my own." I wondered if that was where I went wrong with Fiona. I'd taken things into my hands and decided the future for both of us. I'd thought I was protecting her from the life of a military wife. But I took that choice away from her.

I wasn't sure how to broach that subject over breakfast, so I stayed silent. When the pancakes were done, I stacked some on a plate and handed it to her.

"This is great. Thank you."

"You're welcome." Watching her eat the pancakes with obvious pleasure satisfied something deep inside me. I liked taking care of this woman. The years had done nothing to lessen my feelings when it came to her.

The fact that I'd never felt anything similar with anyone else was also telling. Nineteen was too young to understand what I was giving up and that I'd never find it with anyone else. In order to move forward, I'd need to deal with our past, and I wasn't sure that was possible.

CHAPTER 3

❄

FIONA

After breakfast, I headed to my dad's house. I couldn't avoid it for much longer. He'd expected me to stay with him. But I couldn't stay in that house. I'd barely been back in all the years since Mom died.

I worried the memories would be too much. That I'd feel the acute loss when she wasn't standing in the kitchen next to Daphne baking cookies.

With every mile I traveled in the rental car, I felt my nerves pick up. How would my family greet me? Would they be irritated that I'd stayed away for so long?

I wasn't ready to talk about what happened or why I was here. But it was too much to hope that my brothers would stay out of my business.

The only way to shut them out was to move hundreds of miles away and rarely come home. I parked the car in front of the main house.

The house looked like it could use a fresh coat of paint. I knew Dad resisted Teddy's efforts to do any major repairs or make changes to the property.

Dad sat in the rocking chair on the front porch waiting for me.

"Daddy." Warmth flooded through my chest as I leaned down to hug him.

He held me tight. "It's good to have you back."

"It's good to be back," I said as I straightened, catching the unshed tears in his eyes.

Dad stood. "It's chilly. Come inside. I'll make you some coffee."

"That would be great." I followed him inside, bracing myself for the familiar smells and the memories.

The house was exactly the same as when I was a kid. The same framed photographs hung on the wall, ending with my high school graduation picture. After that, no one bothered to print pictures and hang them. The kitchen sported the dated cabinets and cracked countertops. "Have you thought about renovating?"

Dad shook his head. "The farm barely earns enough to pay for itself. The boys deserve to earn money for their efforts too."

My lips twitched. "Those boys are in their twenties and thirties now."

"I'll always think of you as my little girl."

I rolled my eyes. "I haven't been little in a long time."

Dad sighed as he moved around the kitchen. "You haven't needed me for longer than that."

"I know it feels like that at times, but I'll always need you."

Dad raised a brow. "What about your brothers?"

I chuckled. "I could do without them."

The door opened, and Jameson walked in. "Who can you do without?"

"You," I teased, the mood lightening with him entering the room.

"You know you love me," Jameson said as he hugged me. When he pulled back, he asked, "What's for breakfast, old man?"

"You come for breakfast and expect Dad to cook for you?" I was interested in their dynamic now that Jameson was an adult but still living in the apartment above the garage.

Jameson winked. "You can cook for me too."

"Fat chance of that."

Jameson raised a brow. "You still can't cook, can you?"

I waved a hand at him. "I'm too busy working."

He frowned. "Everyone needs to eat."

"Can you cook?" I asked him.

"I can do the basics. After..." He cleared his throat. "We all pitched in to help. Although Daphne ended up being the best cook of any of us."

"You can say it. After Mom died." The familiar guilt and shame washed over me. I was nineteen when Mom died. I missed her illness because I'd selfishly stayed in school. I left my younger siblings to handle that and the aftermath. Even after she'd died, I hadn't moved closer to help. I'd stayed away.

I'd justified it to myself because Teddy had switched to a college closer to home. But Daphne was the youngest; she shouldn't have been the one cooking for a large family.

Jameson winced slightly at my comment but didn't say anything. He was generally easygoing and happy. Not much got him down.

I knew they avoided saying Mom's name because no one wanted to bring up memories or trigger my dad. But I was tired of tiptoeing around the past. Still, the guilt was never far away. "I'm sorry, Dad. I shouldn't have said anything."

Dad shook his head. "It's fine. You can say her name. I won't break down."

I reached over to squeeze his hand.

"It's good to have you back," Dad said gruffly.

"It would be even better if Axel and Ryder could make it home," Jameson grumbled.

"Axel doesn't have leave?" I asked them as Dad poured coffee grounds into the machine.

Dad shrugged. "He almost never has it over Christmas."

"Axel's life is controlled by the military," Jameson added.

I remembered Aiden telling me the same thing when he'd broken off our relationship. He hadn't wanted my life to be dictated the same way his would be.

"And you know Ryder; his wife wants to spend every holiday with her family," Jameson said dryly.

"That doesn't seem fair."

"Some men get married, and they are absorbed into their wife's family. It's not his fault," Dad continued, referencing Ryder and his situation. We'd talked at length about Ryder and his wife, Stacy, how we never saw his daughter even though she was eight.

Jameson braced his hands on the counter. "How is it not his fault? He should tell her it's our turn. Besides, I want to see my niece every once in a while."

I loved that Jameson seemed to be a family man. I hadn't been around for his teen years, so I'd missed his maturing. All I knew about him was that he lived in the apartment above the garage, worked as a firefighter, and was perpetually a kid at heart.

"I feel like we barely know her," Jameson added.

"Ryder said they're close to the grandparents on that side. It's nothing personal. You guys are going to grow up and move on. Not everyone is going to stick close to home," Dad said reasonably.

I certainly hadn't.

Jameson's jaw tightened. "It would be nice if they visited. Izzy should have a relationship with her cousin."

"I agree with you, but we can't control what other people do. All we can hope for is that Ryder comes around at some point. That he sees what he's missing out on."

25

Jameson grabbed a glass and filled it with water. "By the time Ryder comes to his senses, Faith will be eighteen. It'll be too late."

"Whenever he comes back, we'll welcome him. Faith will always be a member of this family. This year, we have Fiona at home, and we see Izzy often. We have a lot to be thankful for."

"Have you seen Izzy since you've been back?" Jameson asked me.

"I haven't. But I saw Daphne at the party at the inn last night."

"She's the only one in the family that went. That's more of a Monroe event," Jameson said.

"Even though it's held at the Matthews Inn?"

Dad scooped coffee beans into the machine. "Marley is dating a Monroe. It's a Monroe event."

"I hope to see Izzy later today."

Dad filled the machine with water, then pushed the button to brew the coffee. "She'll love that. She talks about you nonstop whenever you video call her."

"I hadn't realized that."

Jameson winked at me. "You're her favorite aunt."

I gave him a look. "I'm her only aunt."

Jameson grinned, touching his hand to his chest. "I'm her favorite uncle, and there's five of us."

"Is it because you live the closest?" I asked.

He pouted. "That's not the reason. It's my charming personality."

I didn't argue with him because he was charming, even if it drove my other brothers crazy. "What's your schedule like this week?"

"I work one day on, two days off at the firehouse. Then I substitute at the middle school one day and drive a bus one day."

"You teach and drive buses?" I asked him, surprised by his answer.

"The middle school is hard up for teachers. No one wants to substitute for that age group. I don't blame them. Those kids can be little—" Jameson broke off, looking apologetically at Dad.

"Thanks for not finishing that sentence," Dad said dryly.

"They're okay with me. I can handle them."

"I didn't realize you wanted to teach." I hadn't been around long enough to know who my siblings were now.

Jameson flashed me a smile. "I'm just filling in."

"What about the bus driver thing?" I wanted to get to know him now.

He shrugged. "I do it for extra cash. It's fun. I dress up for the little kids, and they love it. One day I was a ketchup bottle, and the other day, I was Dr. Seuss. It's fun."

"Do you need to work all those jobs if you're a firefighter? Shouldn't you be resting?" Working twenty-four-hour shifts couldn't be easy.

"It's something I enjoy doing, and I like to be busy."

My impression of Jameson was that he was go go go all the time, but he was so easygoing and happy-go-lucky, we never worried about him. Now I wondered if his personality was a direct result of Mom dying. He felt the need to lift everyone else up. I'd never know for sure because I wasn't here.

Dad poured coffee for us and passed us the mugs.

I blew on the hot liquid. It felt weird to be home, to get to know all the people I'd abandoned over the years, but at the same time it felt oddly right that I was here. I hoped it wasn't too late for me to make amends to my family and even to Aiden. Then maybe I could move forward with my life.

Jameson held up his mug. "Cheers to my big sister being home."

Dad smiled. "Cheers."

I clinked mugs with them, then said, "To a good holiday season."

Now that I was home, I could get to know my siblings again, see what I'd missed out on.

❧

After I'd drank coffee with Dad and Jameson, I headed over to Daphne's cottage. It was perfect for just Daphne and Izzy.

Izzy opened the door. "Aunt Fiona!"

I held my arms open as she jumped into them. "Umph. You're huge."

"Mommy said I've grown a lot this year."

"I believe it," I said as I set her down.

Daphne hugged me next. "It's good to have you home."

"What did you and Cole do last night?" I asked as I came inside, hanging my coat on the hook by the door.

"He showed me the building he constructed at his new house. It's for my pies. You should see it. Here, let me show you the pictures."

I waited while Daphne sifted through the pictures on her phone and tilted the screen toward me. There was a picture of the front porch and the interior. "It looks bigger than what you have here."

Daphne beamed. "Cole wanted me to have space to grow. I think he was afraid I wouldn't want to move in."

"Are you sure you want to move in without being engaged, though?" I'd taken marriage off the table ever since I'd offered to marry Aiden and he'd turned me down flat.

Daphne held out her hand, her smile telling me before I saw the sparkling diamond. "He proposed last night."

"It's beautiful. Congratulations." I hugged her tightly, surprised by the intensity of my feelings.

"Thank you. I'm so happy."

"I'm happy for you."

"Come into the kitchen. I'll get you something to drink."

I followed her. Izzy stayed in the living room.

Daphne grabbed a glass and filled it with ice, then water. "Cole and I kept our relationship a secret for a long time, worried that our families wouldn't accept it. I was worried Cole would choose them over me, but in the end, he realized that we were his family."

That was sweet and unexpected. I'd pushed so far away from my family, I wasn't close to them anymore.

Daphne handed me the glass of iced water. "How are you? Why did you decide to visit?"

"You know I was up for that promotion."

"Did you get it?" Then Daphne saw my face. "They gave it to that guy. Was it Don?"

"He wasn't there as long as me. But he went to some Ivy League school, and his dad owns a competing hotel chain." I didn't think it was necessary to tell Daphne I'd dated Don because I wasn't even upset that I'd broken things off.

Daphne's forehead wrinkled. "Isn't he just going to leave and work for his dad?"

"I would think so. He's biding his time here until he can work for Daddy."

"Then why would they pick him?"

"I think it has something to do with keeping the competition close. I don't know, honestly. I feel like I worked hard, and I deserved that promotion. I put so much time and effort into that job, and now what?"

Daphne shrugged. "You could look for another job."

I shook my head. "When my boss told me that I was passed over for the promotion, I couldn't think about anything else other than getting away from there. I said I was taking all the vacation I'd accumulated over the years."

"Do you think he's concerned you'd leave?"

"If so, he didn't say anything. He didn't offer another position or even a raise. It's like he just assumes I'll keep doing what I'm doing. Working my ass off without any acknowledgment."

"I'm so glad I don't have to worry about that stuff."

"You work for yourself. That has its own challenges."

"I don't have to share my profits with anyone else, and I don't have to prove anything to anyone but myself."

"I love that. It's badass."

Daphne laughed. "I don't know about that."

"I'm sure Cole would agree with me." I didn't know him, but he was obviously smitten with my sister. He had to be to show up at Thanksgiving dinner and apologize in front of my family.

"What do you think you'll do when you go back to work?"

"I don't want to even think about it. I just want to spend time with my family."

Daphne smiled. "It's wonderful to have you back. Izzy adores you."

I frowned. "I haven't been here. Not really."

"You're her cool aunt that she gets to talk to on video."

"I want to be more than that. I'd like to be the aunt that's in her life. Physically."

"I'd like that too," Daphne said. "We're all so happy to have you. Now we just need Axel and Ryder home at the same time."

I didn't think we'd all been home at the same time since Mom's funeral.

"You'll figure it out."

I'd assumed I'd go back to work like I always had, but I'd keep my options open. If a position opened somewhere else, I'd apply for it. I should take this time to consider all my options. Maybe things would be clearer after a few weeks away from work.

Just the thought of going back to work and being Don's subordinate didn't sit right with me. He'd started a few years after me and wasn't as good at the job as I was. Everything was numbers to him. I tried to think about the customer's experience when I made my recommendations. But maybe the higher-ups only cared about the bottom line.

Izzy appeared in the doorway. "Will you play with me, Aunt Fiona?"

"I'd love to." I was so lucky to have this time with her, to get to know my niece. It was time I might not get again. Who knows when I'd accumulate this kind of leave again?

I followed her upstairs where we played tea party at her little table and chairs, and then with the dolls in her dollhouse.

When I went home later that night, Daphne held me tightly and whispered. "I'm so happy you're home."

"It's good to be home." For once, it felt like the truth. I wasn't itching to get back to my apartment in a city where I had few friends and filled my time with work.

CHAPTER 4

FIONA

When I parked at the inn, I wasn't ready to go up to my room. I never had any issues going home to my apartment. Probably because it was an extension of work. Now that I'd taken leave, I didn't have anything to fill my time. Visiting home raised issues I hadn't given myself space and time to consider.

I wanted to see the fountain that Aiden showed me the night before, so I entered the gardens, breathing in the cool night air, as I followed the path to the center and the bench I'd shared with Aiden.

I closed my eyes, listening to the comforting sound of the water trickling into the fountain.

"What are you doing?" Aiden asked.

I startled, my eyes flying open.

Aiden stood a few feet away with his palms up. "Sorry, I didn't mean to scare you."

I forced myself to relax. "It's okay. I just came here to think."

"You spent the day with your family?" Aiden asked as he sat next to me, his knees spread wide.

I nodded. "My dad, Jameson, Daphne, and Izzy. It's nice to

have time with them. I haven't seen Teddy or Weston yet. I'm sure they're busy with work."

Aiden shifted, the length of his thigh resting against mine. "When I came home, my grandmother had died and my parents were already gone."

"Does it take some time to get used to the changes?" I asked, trying to ignore the heat I felt through his jeans.

Aiden gave me a look. "I kept expecting my parents to show up."

I covered his hand with mine. "I know how much you hated them."

His jaw tightened. "I wouldn't let them affect me like they used to. I'm a different person."

My heart ached for him. He'd always acted like he was strong, like his mother's words hadn't gotten to him. But on some level, they had, or he wouldn't have felt the need to prove himself in the military. "I feel like everyone has changed, and I have no idea who anyone is."

"I guess that's to be expected. You were gone a long time." Aiden's voice rumbled through my chest.

"I feel guilty for not being here when Mom died. I missed everything that came after. I wasn't there for them, and my siblings grew into people I don't know much about. I didn't stick around like Teddy did." The guilt clawed at my throat.

"You didn't do anything wrong. You did what you had to do."

"I saved myself." I lifted my feet to the bench and wrapped my arms around my bent knees, dropping my forehead onto my arms.

Aiden shifted on the bench, his hand coming to rest on my shin. His touch was comforting and grounding. "I don't know what to say to make you feel better."

Tears stung the back of my eyes. "I just have to feel it, I guess. Maybe have a conversation with the siblings I left behind. Apologize for being selfish. For thinking that I could bury myself in classes and work so that I didn't feel the loss."

"You didn't do anything wrong," Aiden said again. "You coped the only way you knew how."

"But Teddy changed schools to be closer to home. He was there, and I wasn't."

"What did Teddy give up to be there for his family? Did he give up on his dreams? Did he shove them down deep so that he never saw them again? Or was it something he wanted to do? We can't speculate."

Lifting my head, I blinked my eyes, wondering if he was right. Our actions had consequences, and I didn't know what Teddy was going through. "While I'm here, I want to get to know them."

"When I enlisted, I told my best friend, Heath, to look after Marley, and he ended up falling in love with her. He broke things off when they were younger and only just now reconnected."

"Marley turned out just fine. She went to college, runs a successful business."

"You're right. She can support herself. She doesn't need me. That's a tough pill to swallow sometimes. It makes me feel—"

"Useless?" That's how I felt since I was home. That I wasn't doing anything right, work or relationships.

Aiden sighed. "Something like that."

I knew some men liked to be needed. Maybe it was hard for him to know that his little sister didn't need him in the same way she did when they were growing up.

I set my feet on the ground. "We're both a mess from our childhoods." Although mine had been nice. It was just Mom's illness and death that had thrown me for a loop.

"We'll have to stick together," Aiden said as he looked up at the sky where a million stars shone.

We were quiet for a few minutes, both lost in our thoughts.

Finally, I asked, "How are things going with the inn?"

"I feel like I'm barely holding my head above water some days. The tasks are endless, and then I'm constantly being interrupted by the phone or a guest that needs to check in, or there's a problem with the room."

I could tell him to hire someone, but he'd already said that wasn't possible. "You want me to take a look at things? I used to oversee the running of the hotels. I'd fly to the location, evaluate how everything was run, and make recommendations for improvements. My boss loved to cut costs, so that was a big part of the equation. I'm used to being cautious with my advice."

"You would do that? Aren't you supposed to be on a break?"

I sighed. "I need to keep busy, or I'm going to go crazy."

"I can show you around tomorrow. We're heading into the busiest part of the holiday season, and Marley has all these ideas. Maybe you can help me sort through them, figure out which ones could work and which ones won't."

"I'd love to."

"She wants to show old holiday movies in the great room."

I smiled. "I kind of love that idea. The black-and-white versions?"

"I guess so."

"That seems like an easy offering. You play the movie and serve popcorn and drinks?"

"Do we have enough seating to accommodate everyone? Will anyone be interested in attending? I'm also wondering if we should renovate the old movie theater in the basement."

I shifted on the bench, remembering how we'd sneak into the back and make out while the movie ran in the background. "I have so many good memories of that place."

"Gram used it at some point, but when the projector broke, she never replaced it."

"How neat would it be to open it up again?" I asked, excitement shooting through me.

"No one's been in that room in years. It would need a lot of work. I'm not even sure it's possible to make it what you're envisioning."

I closed my eyes. "I'm thinking of red velvet chairs, a large movie screen, and black-and-white holiday movies. I can practically smell the popcorn."

"I'll show it to you tomorrow. Then we can go from there. But in the meantime, I'd like to see if it's possible to show the movies in the great room."

"I'd love to help." For the first time since I realized I wasn't getting the promotion, I felt excitement. I hadn't felt that with my job. For so long, I was held back by red tape, money concerns, and others who didn't have the same vision that I did. Not that Aiden would necessarily be different. But there were less people involved. It was just Aiden and Marley. I had a feeling they'd be motivated by what their guests would enjoy. I'd be limited by whatever their budget was, but I hoped we could reopen the theater.

"I appreciate you taking your time to look at it. I know you're here to reconnect with your family. I feel bad putting you to work."

I rested my hand on his thigh. "Don't be. I haven't been this excited about something in a long time. But I need to get to bed. I'm exhausted."

Aiden stood and held his hand out to me. "I'll walk you back."

I placed my hand in his, feeling the warmth of his palm. My heart contracted as he closed his hand over mine. It felt like old times when we'd walk holding hands. I hadn't cared where we were, only that we were together. I'd felt his love even if we couldn't show it in public. "I love the holiday decorations. They make the place warm and inviting."

"We advertise that we're next to a Christmas tree farm, so

Marley insists on trees on every floor. I think she'd prefer trees in every room."

"You could offer that as an additional service. For extra money, you get a decorated room."

Aiden chuckled. "That's not a bad idea."

"I'm used to working with a large hotel chain. We were constrained by bureaucracy and a modern decor. But here?" I nodded toward the grand porch. "We have so many possibilities."

We headed inside, and he stopped when we reached my door.

He dropped my hand and shoved his in his pockets. "Do you put a tree up in your place in the city?"

"I never have the time. I wasn't home long enough to enjoy it, and I had no one to share it with."

"Now that you're here, and helping me with this place, I'd like to show you some of the holiday events. The Monroes have a light display."

My breath caught. That sounded like a date. But he'd said it was payback for me helping him. I could have told him I was busy or that I had a million other things to do while I was home, but I wanted to see the lights with him. "That sounds nice."

Aiden grinned, and I was struck by how handsome he was. No longer the boy I dated, he was all man. For a second, I almost wished for more. But this was two old friends reconnecting. It wasn't our second chance at love. I couldn't forget how he ended things. He'd turned down my proposal of marriage. There was no getting over the humiliation of that. "Good night, Aiden."

"Night, Fiona," he murmured as I shut the door firmly.

Our relationship had been over for years. There was no reason to think of starting things up again. My life was in Chicago, and his was here.

The next morning, I got up early, showered, and drank my coffee in front of the window facing the front of the property. I'd seen Aiden go for his morning run. But I hadn't seen him come back. Not that I was stalking him or anything. I was just bored.

I'd checked my emails, disappointed not to see any from work. I'd hoped they'd say they reconsidered and thought I deserved a promotion or even a raise. Or at least an email saying to cut my vacation short, that they needed me back. But there was nothing. I'd never felt more expendable than I did now. I always thought my work was valued, but now I wasn't so sure.

A red truck with lettering on the passenger side door rumbled down the lane. There was a tree in the bed. I wondered if Marley had ordered another tree for the inn.

At some point, I'd need to meet Aiden to check out the theater, but I didn't have any set time for that, and there was nothing else on my to-do list.

A few minutes later, there was a soft knock on the door. I looked through the peephole and saw Aiden. I opened the door. "Aiden, what are you—"

He was carrying a tree along with another man.

"That's for me?" I asked as I moved out of the way.

Aiden strode inside. "I thought you could use a tree while you're staying here."

They set it against the dresser, and the second man placed a tree stand on the floor.

"You remember Heath."

"How could I forget your best friend?" I said, wondering if Heath knew about us.

Heath threw a thumb over his shoulder. "This guy thought you needed a little holiday cheer."

I smiled. "This should do it, but I don't have any decorations."

"Let me get the tree up first. I have some extra decorations downstairs," Aiden said.

I sat on the edge of the bed. "You thought of everything."

Heath grinned. "We take our holiday cheer seriously around here."

Aiden looked up at him from where he knelt on the floor. "Are you going to help get this tree up, or you just going to talk?"

Heath chuckled. "I'm helping. Don't get your panties in a wad."

Aiden grumbled something too low for me to hear.

I liked their banter. "You and Marley are engaged?"

"He used to be my best friend. But now he's Marley's," Aiden said when he stood and backed up to see if the tree was straight. "A little to the right."

Heath adjusted the tree in the stand. "I'm still your best friend. Although you've been a grumpy ass lately."

"Everyone seems like a grump to you now that you're in a relationship," Aiden said.

"Mmm. How's that?" Heath gestured at the tree.

I went to stand next to Aiden. "I think that's good."

"Me too," Aiden agreed before bending to pick up the needles that had fallen when they brought the tree inside. "I can clean up the rest. Let me grab the decorations and the vacuum. I'll be right back."

Then Aiden was gone, leaving me with Heath.

He leaned against the dresser, resting one leg over the other. "So you're a Calloway?"

I chuckled. "Is that going to be a problem?"

Heath raised a brow. "Not for me. But my brothers might not like me giving a Calloway a tree."

I couldn't help but smile. "I can get my own. Is that right?"

"Something like that. But you're Aiden's, so—"

I shook my head. "Oh, I'm not Aiden's."

Heath sobered. "He said you had a thing back in high school. I didn't know, and I was his best friend."

"We wanted to avoid the gossip. You know how mean the kids were back then." They made comments about Aiden, saying he was trailer trash. If we'd been vocal about our relationship, it would only have gotten worse. And I didn't want my dad to tell me I couldn't date him. It was better to keep it hidden.

"I can't judge. I had a secret fling of my own with Marley. I've always regretted how I handled things back then."

"What did Aiden say about us?" I asked, but Aiden came into the room with a vacuum and a box he placed on the bed. I hoped Aiden hadn't told him how I'd proposed and he'd said no.

"I'll let you get back to whatever you had going on today," Aiden said to Heath.

I wondered if he wanted to be alone with me.

Heath straightened. "Selling Christmas trees?"

"Yeah, that," Aiden said with a nod.

"It was nice to see you again," I said to Heath.

"Come see our light display. It will get you in the holiday mood for sure."

"You aren't worried I'll take all your secrets and share them with my brothers?" I couldn't help but tease.

"There aren't many secrets to a holiday light display, and Talon made it by hand. So I doubt you could replicate it. I think it's about time we move past some of that stuff."

"What would Emmett have to say about that?" Aiden asked.

Heath frowned. "Emmett will come around, eventually."

"I appreciate you accepting my sister."

"She's good for Cole. I wouldn't stand in their way." Heath exchanged a look with Aiden. Then he said, "I'll see you around."

After Heath closed the door with a soft click, I said, "He said he knows about us."

Aiden sighed. "We've talked since I've been back. I told Cole too. When he was having trouble with Daphne."

"It's weird that people know about us. It's been a secret for so long."

He plugged in the vacuum. "You don't mind that I talked to him, do you?"

I let out a breath. "I guess not."

"I'll vacuum. Why don't you see if you like any of the decorations in there." He nodded toward the box.

I opened the lid, pulling out lights, then ornaments. I set each one on the bed.

When the vacuum turned off, Aiden moved to stand next to me. "These are old ornaments. The ones my grandma put on her tree."

"Are you sure you want me to use them? Shouldn't they be in your apartment?"

"I don't put up a tree."

I raised a brow. "Yet you thought I needed one?"

"You can help me put one in my apartment too if it bothers you," Aiden said lightly.

I bumped shoulders with him. "I think that's a great idea. If I have to have holiday cheer, then so do you."

Aiden moved, and I thought for one brief second that he was going to kiss me, but he merely snagged the lights. "These need to go on first."

How was I going to be around Aiden when every time he came near, I thought he was going to kiss me? I needed to stuff those feelings down deep, because Aiden didn't feel the same way about me. He'd been abundantly clear about that when we were nineteen.

CHAPTER 5

AIDEN

When I went for my run this morning on the Monroe property, I had the nudge to give Daphne a tree. She was so down last night. I wanted to do something for her, to lift her mood, to remind her why the holidays can be magical.

I can't say I'd felt that way in a long time. Not when I was living with my parents or later when I was enlisted in the military. But I saw how the guests reacted to the inn's ambiance. It made people feel better, and I wanted to lift Fiona's spirits.

Fiona was so hard on herself, feeling responsible for how her siblings felt after their mother's death. But she was just a teenager herself.

Now I was alone with her in her room, and there was nowhere else I wanted to be. It was a nice respite from the day-to-day of the inn.

"Do you need to be at the front desk? If so, I can handle this."

I grinned. "Marley's down there for now, and I wouldn't give you a tree and leave you to decorate it yourself."

"Always a man of responsibility," Fiona said, and I wasn't sure if it was meant as a compliment.

"I suppose that's true." I had a strong sense of right and wrong. My parents were impossible to please. But the military was cut and dry. I knew exactly what was expected. While others struggled in that environment, I thrived. For the first time, I belonged. I learned skills and contributed to something bigger than myself.

The downside was that I wasn't around for Marley and Gram. And I'd let Fiona go, but I was here now. I had a lot to make up for. I wanted to ease the guilt, but I also wanted Fiona to be happy.

I arranged the lights on the tree, then plugged them in. "How does it look?"

Fiona adjusted one row of lights, then stepped back. "That's better."

This entire scene was domestic. If I'd said yes to Fiona's proposal, would we have stayed together? Would we be decorating our own house for the holidays? Would we have kids? Or would Fiona have regretted her decision? I cleared my throat. "Are we ready for ornaments?"

Fiona smiled softly. "I think so."

We worked together for several minutes. I hung the ornaments on the higher branches, and she covered the lower ones.

"We should play some holiday music to get us in the mood." Fiona grabbed her phone from the nightstand and hit Play. "Is this okay?"

"It's more than okay." I hadn't anticipated that decorating a tree together would spark so many hopes and desires. So many what-ifs. There was no way to know what the future might have been. We made our decisions—right or wrong—and we had to live with them.

Fiona had moved on, and I had too.

We worked in silence, Fiona occasionally asking me for my opinion about the placement of one of the ornaments. I never cared about decorating before, but I wanted this to be perfect for her. I wanted her to lie in her bed at night and stare at the twinkling lights, knowing I'd given them to her. I wanted to make her life beautiful.

I couldn't reconcile my feelings for her. My desire to make her life better with the idea that our relationship was in the past.

When Fiona placed the last ornament on the tree, we stepped back to consider our work.

Fiona pointed toward the top of the tree. "We're missing a tree topper."

"I'll have to look for one. I'm sure we have extras somewhere."

Fiona shook her head. "Don't worry about it. This is fine."

But I wanted her to have everything.

Then Fiona's stomach rumbled, and she covered it with her hand.

I raised a brow. "Did you eat breakfast?"

"Just coffee," Fiona said sheepishly.

"Come down and grab a muffin. Then we can take a look at that old theater."

Fiona clapped her hands together. "We can do that this morning?"

"I have to take advantage of Marley working the front desk."

I waited for Fiona to put on her shoes. Then we went downstairs to the kitchen. There weren't many guests milling about. By this time of the morning, most were already exploring the area, visiting historic Annapolis, shopping, or even taking the drive to Washington D.C.

In the kitchen, I pulled the cover off the pastries, waiting for Fiona to choose a croissant before I covered it again. Then I poured her more coffee.

Fiona sat on the stool at the counter. "I could get used to the service here."

I winked at her. "Especially when your server is so handsome."

She chuckled. "If you say so."

"You never complained before." She'd always said how good looking I was when we were dating.

Fiona frowned as she pretended to consider me. "You're okay."

I shook my head. "I should come over there and kiss you. Remind you how things were between us."

Her lips parted. "We can't."

I shook my head. "Sorry. I don't know where that came from."

"Our relationship is in the past. We can't be anything more than friends." Fiona's tone was unyielding.

"I can handle that." I wasn't so sure I could be friends with her and not follow through on my promises. Spending time together in her room decorating that tree brought out all the dreams and hopes we'd had for our future. I was supposed to wait for her to graduate. Then we'd move in together, get married, and start our life.

The one thing we always missed in those plans was what I would do. That was one of the reasons I'd looked into the military. I couldn't afford college, and my parents wouldn't fill out any of the paperwork so I could apply for scholarships. I wasn't sure I was college material, but I'd wanted to be with Fiona.

Fiona blew air over her coffee. "Good. Because that's all I can handle. I'm on break from my job and my last relationship."

"What do you mean?"

"The guy who got the promotion was my boyfriend."

I sucked in a breath. "He broke up with you?"

She shook her head. "I did the honors. I was upset that he didn't stand up for me, ask why he'd gotten the job over someone who'd been there longer and had more experience. He was happy to take the promotion, no questions asked. Maybe that was unfair."

I chuckled without any humor. "I don't think so. It doesn't

sound like he deserved the job. He should've stepped back. A better man would have."

"You always see things so black-and-white, right or wrong."

"It was easy to see those lines when you grew up the way I did." Dodging insults, hunting for food in my grandmother's house to feed my little sister. I'd crossed many lines back then by necessity. I tried to be better about that now.

"We didn't have a good relationship. We were together because we worked together and it was convenient. I wasn't even upset after I broke up with him. I wasn't invested in him."

A guilty expression crossed her face. I wondered what that was about.

I cleaned the counters, and when she was done eating, I said, "Let's check out the theater. Then I need to take a shower."

I'd completed my run, then detoured to Heath's to ask him about a tree for Fiona. I hadn't had time to take a shower, and I didn't want to put this off for later. I was worried Fiona would come up with some reason why it wasn't a good idea.

Fiona placed her dish in the dishwasher.

I moved closer to her. "You don't need to clean. You're a guest."

"You're not treating me like a regular guest. Unless you provide freshly cut Christmas trees for everyone else? Then stick around and decorate it?"

I chuckled. "You're right. I'm not."

"Then I can clean up after myself while I'm here."

Time seemed to stand still. I wanted to reach out and brush the strand of hair on her forehead away. I wanted to see if kissing her would be any different than when we'd kissed as teens. But now wasn't the time.

Fiona took a step back, breaking the spell. "Should we check out the theater now?"

I cleared my throat, trying to erase the desire for her out of my head. "Let's go."

I led her down the hallway to the door for the basement. "When Marley renovated, she focused on the guest rooms and the common area. But we didn't touch anything down here."

At the bottom of the stairs, I turned on the lights. The hallway was wide and the ceilings tall, so it didn't feel like a basement. Although it was musty from disuse. When we were kids, this area was open for hotel guests.

"What else is down here? I can't remember anything but the movie theater and maybe a room with pool tables."

As we passed each doorway, I opened the door and let her get a glimpse before we moved onto the next. "A bowling alley, a game room, a bar, and the theater."

"This could be amazing," Fiona said, her voice filled with awe.

"You think we should open it up again?"

Fiona reached for my hand. "I got tingles when I came down here. I can see the guests getting a drink at the bar, bowling, or playing pool. It sets your inn apart from regular hotels. This place has so much history, so many possibilities." She turned so we were facing each other.

Her energy was contagious.

I flicked on the lights for the theater. The seats were covered in white cloths. "We'd need to do a lot of work. The carpet needs to be replaced, the curtains, maybe even the seats."

Fiona walked down the aisle and came to a stop before the stage, then turned to face me. "I'd want to preserve everything we could. You said you work with Heath in his contracting business?"

I nodded as I stuffed my hands into my pockets. "When I have time."

"Would you be willing to put in a little sweat equity here?" Fiona gestured around the room.

Her entire body radiated excitement in a way I hadn't seen since she'd been back. I wanted to see more of her passion for this project. "I don't think we have money for something like this. But we could look into fixing the carpet in the hall and the theater. Then we can add on as we go."

"I wish we could do it all. I'd love to bring this place back to life."

I wanted that too. I wanted to keep Fiona in this heightened state of passion. I had to curl my hands into fists so I wouldn't cross the room and kiss her.

"What are you doing down here?" Marley's voice came from the doorway.

I felt like we'd been caught doing something we shouldn't when all I'd been doing was showing Fiona the space.

Fiona crossed the room toward Marley. "I hope you don't mind. Aiden mentioned the theater, and I had to see it again. This place is more gorgeous than I remembered."

Marley grimaced as she looked around. "It's something all right. It's dusty and worn. No one's been down here in years."

"What do you think about restoring it, keeping as much of the original architecture as possible?" Fiona asked.

"I told her we didn't have the money for a full renovation now. But maybe we could look into what it would take to have a working theater again," I said to Marley.

Marley looked at Fiona. "Tell me what you're thinking."

I didn't want to get Fiona's hopes up, but Marley had an instinct for this kind of thing. She knew when something was valuable and when it wasn't. So I backed away while Fiona took her through the theater, telling her everything she wanted to keep: the chairs, the curtain, and even the wood on the floor of the stage.

"We'd have to get a contractor's opinion. Maybe have Heath take a look at it and give us an estimate," Marley said.

"I can help with the work," I offered.

Marley raised a brow. "How are you going to do that and

run the front desk, fix whatever needs to be repaired, and handle breakfast for the guests?"

I let out a breath. "If you're on board with renovating the theater, I'd consider hiring someone to handle the front desk."

Marley nodded. "I think Cole's sister, Charlotte, is looking for a job. She's been helping around the shop and the farm. We could talk to her about it, but are you sure you're ready to give up the day-to-day running of the inn?"

"I'll still be around. I'll fix things as issues arise, but it would be nice to have more freedom and not be tied to the front desk." Marley and Heath used to live at the inn to assist with the daily operations. When I got more comfortable with it, Marley and Heath moved back to his cabin. It wouldn't be easy handing that duty over to someone who wasn't family but I wanted to free up time to work on the theater.

Marley grinned at Fiona. "I've been trying to get him to hire someone for ages. I guess we have you to thank."

Fiona's eyes widened. "I don't know about that."

I waved Marley off. "Let's not make a big deal out of it. You wanted to show movies to the guests, and we can play them in the great room on a projector, but a theater would be even better."

It was small, nothing like a regular movie theater, but it could hold a decent amount of people.

"If you want to keep the original seats, we'd be able to get more people in here for showings. Most theaters have those recliner-style seats, and they take up more room."

Fiona peeked under one of the cloths, sending dust into the air. "I think we should keep them. They add to the ambiance."

"I agree."

"Do we sell tickets, or is it something we offer for free?" Marley asked Fiona, and I could tell she was testing Fiona's knowledge of marketing and business.

"I think people expect to pay for a movie, especially in a setting like this. Hotels host movie nights, but guests usually sit on the floor, and they're directed toward kids." Fiona leaned a hip against the arm rest. "This will be a full-service theater. There's even a concession stand."

I was positive it was the tone Fiona used when she consulted with various hotel managers on site.

Marley nodded. "Let me think about it. I'll get Heath over here to inspect the space. I suspect we'll need to add larger bathrooms to comply with building regulations."

From what I remembered, there was only one individual bathroom down here, but there was plenty of space to expand.

Fiona considered Marley. "What do you think about renovating the entire space?"

"Fiona worked for a large hotel chain in management."

"I dealt with a lot of red tape and bureaucracy that doesn't exist here. We have the freedom to do whatever you want. There's a lot of exciting potential here. If you renovated this space, it will place Matthews Inn above the rest, and you have a lot of competition in Annapolis with all the historic inns."

"I think so too. But this time, I don't want to do this on my own. Hotel management and renovations are not in my wheelhouse. If we decide to go forward with this project, will you partner with me on it?"

Fiona's mouth opened then closed. Finally, she said, "I'll have to think about it. I can get you started, and maybe even consult long-distance. But I suspect you want someone on site."

"If we do the entire project, yes." Marley waved a hand in her direction. "But we have time to think about it. We don't know what Heath is going to say or what the estimate will be."

I was positive Heath would give her a good deal, but he'd need labor which I was happy to provide. I wanted to see Gram's inn restored to its original glory. Some part of me wanted to prove that I was no longer that kid who lived in a trailer. I was better than that. And if it meant Fiona would be working beside me, I was all for it.

CHAPTER 6

❄

FIONA

I promised myself I would take a break and spend my free time getting to know my family. But I was excited about the movie-theater project. It was the kind of thing I wanted to do in my regular job, but the hotels were too big and modern and lacked the historic details that Matthews Inn possessed.

When I called Daphne to see if she had time to hang out, she said she was spending the afternoon moving her things into their new house and could use the company.

When I arrived at her cottage, I joined her in Izzy's room. "I thought you were going to take things slow? See if Izzy was okay with moving in with Cole over time."

Daphne looked up from the box she was packing. "Izzy wants to live with Cole. She adores him. And he built that amazing kitchen for my business. It doesn't make sense to stay here anymore. Especially during the holiday season. I need the additional space."

"That makes sense." It felt like Daphne was moving on with her life in big ways, getting engaged to Cole, moving in together, and expanding her business while I was stuck. I was unhappy with my current job. I felt undervalued. Yet I didn't know what I should do.

"How are you feeling taking so much time off?" Daphne asked as we resumed packing Izzy's toys and books.

"It's an adjustment, but I've been busy."

"What have you been up to?"

I carefully stacked Izzy's books in a box. "This morning, Aiden brought me a tree and helped me decorate it."

Daphne stopped folding Izzy's clothes. "You know, when you didn't visit over the years, Teddy thought it had something to do with Aiden. That you'd dated in high school, and it ended badly. But you've never talked to me about it."

I shrugged. "There wasn't anything to talk about. We broke up when he enlisted. Then he was gone."

"You don't have any feelings about that?"

I chuckled without any humor. "I have lots of feelings about how we ended. None of them good."

Daphne resumed folding clothes and placing them in a suitcase. "You must be getting along if he decorated a tree with you."

"That's because I was the one who wanted more. We'd agreed that we'd move in together once I graduated. But he didn't wait. He enlisted. He said something about needing to prove himself, be a man. I don't know." I couldn't see past the pain.

Daphne's forehead wrinkled. "He was the one who broke things off?"

"It's worse than that. I was so young and immature. I proposed."

Daphne gasped, setting down the pants she'd been folding.

"I said I could move with him once he knew where he'd be stationed. But he didn't want a future with me. It was better to end things now."

Daphne touched my hand. "I'm sorry."

I shook my head. "It's okay. It was a long time ago."

"Still, that kind of rejection sticks with you."

I smiled to cover my pain. "It was a good learning experience. I didn't let myself get close to anyone else. It wasn't worth it. Not when I was so set to succeed in school and then my career."

"That's kind of sad. You let one moment dictate your future relationships."

I frowned, wondering if she was right. "I'm not ready to settle down, so there's no point in pursuing a relationship." I dated and had fun, but I never got serious. Work always came first. I made that clear to anyone I spent time with. Aiden's rejection was never far from my memory. Maybe that's why breaking up with Don wasn't even a blip on my radar. I wasn't emotionally invested in the relationship.

"Are you sure you're okay with spending time with him now?"

I flashed her a smile. "He was being nice bringing me a tree."

"Is that a service he provides to all his guests?" Daphne hadn't resumed packing, but I kept my gaze on the stack of books, rearranging them in the box.

"It's something Marley wants to do, but it's a lot of trees. I suggested making it a paid service. An add-on to the room."

"That's not a bad idea. But I don't understand why Aiden went out of his way to get *you* a tree. Especially if he didn't have any residual feelings for you."

"I think he feels guilty. That's the kind of guy he is. He feels badly he left Marley with their parents, and he feels regret over hurting me. But it's not necessary. I'm fine. I'm not that same girl." I wasn't that naive kid who thought I'd marry the love of my life, and that guy was Aiden. I wasn't sure I even believed in it anymore.

"I don't know."

"It doesn't mean anything." It couldn't. I wouldn't let it mean anything more than a nice gesture from an old friend. One who wanted to relieve his guilt over his part in the breakup.

"If you say so." Daphne resumed folding Izzy's clothes.

I wasn't used to sharing my feelings with anyone. I usually felt the need to put up walls, to keep people out. Mainly because I worked in a male-dominated field where emotion was frowned upon. Besides, I'd been vulnerable once, and it had bitten me in the ass. I wouldn't make the same mistake again.

"You have any boxes that can be taken to the truck?" Cole asked from the doorway.

"You're here," Daphne said as she stood and wrapped her arms around his neck.

He leaned down to give her a soft kiss.

I couldn't look away. The movement was so natural for them. As if they always greeted each other this way.

That was something I'd done when I was with Aiden. But we were teens and each other's first love. We felt things so deeply back then. I thought adult relationships were more practical, forged out of a friendship and a desire to be with one person the rest of your life. I hadn't expected the display of intimacy that Cole and Daphne were sharing.

Daphne stepped back and gestured at the few bags and boxes we'd managed to pack. "We have a few things ready, but we've been talking."

Cole crossed his arms over his chest. "About what?"

Daphne looked at me. "Fiona was telling me how she's spending some time with Aiden."

In an effort to stop her from telling the story about the tree, I interjected, "He wants to renovate the old movie theater in the basement of the inn. He asked if I'd help with the project."

Daphne dropped to her knees to put the last of the clothes in the suitcase. "Are you going to?"

"It's the kind of project I'd love to be involved with. But he's thinking about renovating the entire basement, and I won't be around long enough for that." It was probably best that I go back to my job in Chicago and look for a new one. I couldn't stay even if I wanted to see my family more often. Not with Aiden living here full time.

He may have moved on, but it was clear I had unresolved feelings when it came to him.

"Aiden mentioned that you'd dated when you were younger," Cole said.

I knew he'd talked to Aiden, and I wasn't sure what he'd told him. "We were young, and we went in two different directions. I was at college, and he enlisted. We wouldn't have worked."

Daphne's brow furrowed. "It sounded like you wanted a future with him. That you were willing to—"

"I don't want to talk about it. It's over. There's no point in rehashing what happened. We were young and stupid." I was an idiot to think that Aiden would want to stay with me. I was going through so much back then. My mom had died; I'd decided to stay in school. I wasn't willing to give it all up to go home and be another mother to my siblings, even though Teddy had done something similar.

Selfishly, I thought Aiden would join me, and we could rent an apartment together. That he could get a job doing something. I wasn't sure what.

"Sometimes, you only get that one chance at love," Cole said.

I waved a hand at the two of them. "You think that everyone can have what you share, but that's not realistic."

Cole took the filled bag of stuffed animals from Daphne. "Why not?"

"Because it doesn't always work out. People want different things, or they're in different stages of their lives. Or one person likes one more than the other."

Daphne frowned. "Is that what you think happened? You liked him more than he liked you."

"I was willing to follow him anywhere, and he obviously

wasn't." He'd been very clear that day. There was no convincing him to do something different. He was determined to enlist and go it alone. He didn't want me following him.

"I don't want to break anyone's trust, but there're two sides to every story," Cole finally said.

I huffed a sigh of frustration. "If he doesn't tell me his side, how will I ever know? I'll just assume that we weren't right for each other." That he didn't want me. That was the truth that was the hardest to deal with.

My mother died, and he'd enlisted. I'd never felt so alone. I'd intentionally separated myself from my family so I didn't have them for comfort, and they were all dealing with their own issues.

"I was over him a long time ago. We can work together without any of that coming up." We'd already spent time together, and there wasn't any awkwardness. There was that one moment in the kitchen when I thought he was going to move closer and touch me, but he hadn't. I needed to stop looking for things that weren't there.

There was some saying about believing people when they told you who they were. Aiden hadn't wanted me, and nothing he said now would change that reality. He couldn't go back and change the past.

"I think we need to pick up the pace if we want Izzy to sleep in her new bedroom tonight," Cole said.

Daphne smiled softly at Cole. "I love that you allowed her to decorate it any way she wanted."

"Why wouldn't I? It's her home now."

I felt like I was intruding on a private moment. It was clear that Daphne was excited to move in with Cole. That this was a big step for their relationship, and she couldn't wait to live with him.

"I for one, can't wait to see how she decorated it. Let's get a move on." I moved quicker now that we weren't talking about my love life.

I focused on packing and vowed to be a better big sister. I'd be there for my siblings. I'd just have to find a way to keep in touch with them when I was back at work.

I helped Cole carry out the boxes and bags to his truck, and Daphne went to her room to pack her clothes and toiletries.

I carried a box outside.

Cole took it from me and threw it in the bed of his truck. "We'll need to make a few more trips. But this should be enough to have them settled for tonight."

I leaned against the side of the truck. "I'm happy you're in Daphne's and Izzy's lives. They obviously love you."

He threw the last of the bags into the back. "I love them too."

He'd defied his family's wishes when he dated Daphne, since their families had an ongoing rivalry. But he'd stood by his love for Daphne and Izzy. I admired that.

He cleared his throat. "I don't want you to think that love isn't available for you. That you can't have it if you want it."

"You don't have to worry about me. I'm not looking for love." And most likely never would be. I'd bury myself in work. That had always been effective in keeping my mind off my personal life.

Cole opened his mouth as if to say something, but Daphne came outside with a suitcase and a duffle bag.

He pushed off the truck and took the bags from her. "Did you get everything you need?"

Daphne's shoulders lowered. "We can come back and get the rest another day."

Cole carried her bags to the truck, and Daphne stopped in front of me. "We're having dinner tonight at Cole's. I want to show everyone the house and my new kitchen. I'd like for you to come."

"I'll be there." I didn't expect that Aiden would need me to work on the movie theater today. It might take a few days for Heath to check out the space and write up an estimate.

Daphne exchanged a concerned look with Cole. "It's just that Cole invited Aiden. They're friends."

"I can hang out with Aiden. I told you we're working together on the movie-theater project."

"Yeah, but this is different. It's more of a relaxed setting. I just wanted to be careful of your feelings."

I flashed her a smile. "I told you; Aiden and I were over a long time ago. Looking back, we were never anything. Everyone has that first love. It doesn't mean you're supposed to be together forever. We can hang out together as friends."

Daphne placed her arm around me as she walked me to my rental car. "I'm starting to think you're protesting too much."

Her arm fell away when we reached my driver's side door. "We hung out this morning, and there was zero awkwardness."

Daphne scrutinized my face. "I'm just worried about you."

If my heart held out hope that we could reconnect while I was in town, my brain would overrule it. There was no way I'd let Aiden hurt me again. But I was safe because he was unaffected by my presence. "You don't need to worry about me. I've always been the strong one."

Daphne narrowed her eyes on me. "Dad said you're strong on the outside but soft on the inside."

I laughed. "I'm going to have a conversation with him, because I'm tough. We had to be growing up with five brothers."

Daphne hugged me. "I'm so glad you're home. I wish you could stay."

"Me too." I swallowed over the lump in my throat. It wouldn't be a good idea to stick around. I needed to cut ties and to go back where I was safe. Where my heart was protected.

I followed Cole's truck to his new house. I'd only seen pictures of it before. The house itself was hidden from the road by tall trees. A tire swing hung from one in the front yard, and there was a swing on the porch.

Inside, we immediately got to work setting up Izzy's things so it would be ready for her when she got home. Her bedroom had white furniture, a pink canopy, and a full-length mirror with flowers on the edges.

Fiona touched the details on the frame of the mirror. "She's still a little girl, but she's going to want big girl things soon too."

"I think she's going to love the cozy chairs." There was a round one and one that hung from the ceiling.

"I wanted her to be comfortable here. I know it's a transition moving. We lived with Dad for the first few years. Although I don't know if she remembers it," Daphne said.

Cole poked his head in. "The bus is dropping her off here?"

Fiona nodded. "I double-checked with the school this morning."

"Is Dad going to be upset that you're moving off the farm?" I asked her.

"He understands, and I think he wants Izzy to have a father figure. He wants her to have everything, and he knows this is what's best for us." Then she smiled wide. "If you're so worried about him, you could stay in my cottage."

"I might do that. Although I'm kind of enjoying the service at the hotel." I had a decorated tree and breakfast downstairs waiting for me. And Aiden. As much as my brain knew it wasn't a good idea to be around him, my body and heart felt differently.

Daphne winked at me. "I bet you are."

"Ugh. I didn't mean that." I couldn't help but think about what it would be like if Aiden snuck into my room at night and serviced me. Now I was hot and bothered in front of my sister and future brother-in-law.

"You think she'll like the lights?" Cole turned on the string of lights he'd hung on the ceiling.

"She's going to love it." What little girl wouldn't? I was so happy for Daphne and Izzy. They were getting everything they'd ever wanted. If I felt a pang of loneliness, that was to be expected. It wouldn't be the first time I felt these emotions if I was going to continue to dedicate myself to my career.

Daphne glanced at her phone. "Speaking of the bus. It's due any minute."

Both of them hurried out of the room as if they couldn't wait to see Izzy and show her to her new space. It was heartwarming to see Cole want to meet Izzy at the bus stop. I couldn't have asked for a better man for my sister.

I took a few pictures of the room. Then sent one to Aiden. I wasn't sure why I did it. We'd spent a good portion of the morning together, and I wanted to share this with him too. He was friends with Cole, so hopefully he wouldn't think it meant anything more than it was—a friend sharing her day with him.

> Her room looks great. Make sure you get a good picture of her reaction when she sees it.

I heard the front door open and close and voices getting closer.

I typed out a quick response so I could get in position to take Izzy's picture.

> On it.

I was very aware that this was a private moment with a new family, and I should have left them alone, but at the same time, I wanted to document the moment. I started the video when Izzy ran into the room and skidded to a stop.

"There're lights."

Cole moved close to her. "You picked out the furniture, and we chose a few other things you might like. I hung the lights, and your mom picked out the mirror."

"You might not need it now, but when you're a teenager—"

Izzy stood in front of the mirror with her hands on her hips. "Is it a magical mirror? Can I step through it and into another land?"

We all chuckled at her question, and Daphne said, "I'm sorry to disappoint you, but it's just a regular mirror."

"I think it's magical," Izzy said as she turned and jumped into Cole's arms. He seemed to anticipate her movement and crouched at the exact moment so he easily caught her. The video was still rolling, and I didn't want to stop. Daphne hugged both of them.

Sensing it was time for me to leave. I turned off the video and quietly snuck out. I was happy for them, but the sensation of loneliness persisted.

CHAPTER 7

❄

AIDEN

I was surprised when Fiona sent me the picture of Izzy's new room. Then I didn't hear from her after I asked her to take video of the big reveal. Maybe Fiona realized her mistake in reaching out to me. I wasn't sure why she felt the need to send me the picture, but I took it as a good sign.

Fiona was starting to remember what it was like when we were together. We were friends as well as lovers. We shared our hopes and dreams. I tried not to weigh her down with the extent of my parents' toxicity, but she always knew when it was bad. She had this way of coaxing it out of me.

I'd kept myself busy over the years, so I wouldn't think of Fiona and the moment I broke her heart. But now that I was home and she was too, I couldn't help but wonder if this was our time. I hadn't found anyone else that I loved as much as her.

I wasn't sure she felt the same way, especially after I hurt her. She'd proposed, and I'd callously turned her down. The truth was, I'd panicked. The last thing I wanted was for her to quit school and follow me around the world. I didn't want to get in the way of her living her dreams.

Unfortunately, she didn't see what I was doing. She shut me out, and I wasn't sure I'd ever get close to her again.

There were a lot of trucks in the driveway when I arrived. Mostly red ones with Monroe Christmas Tree Farm logos on the doors, but there was one Calloway truck. I hoped everyone was able to keep things civil tonight.

I was grateful I wasn't part of that drama.

I knocked on the door, and Fiona answered. She immediately joined me on the porch, closing the door behind her. Then she pulled me to the side of the porch where a swing hung. "I've been wanting to show you the video."

I sat next to her. "I wasn't sure if you'd gotten it since I didn't hear back from you."

"The video was too long to go through over text." She kept her attention on her phone.

"Let's see it," I said to cover the tightness in my throat.

She moved closer, her head almost touching mine while she hit Play. It started the moment Izzy ran into the room and turned in a circle in the middle of the room. "There're lights."

Fiona touched my thigh and squeezed. "She loved the lights."

I sucked in a breath. The warmth of her palm seeped through my jeans, and electricity shot through me. I shifted on the seat, wondering if she noticed what she was doing. If she moved her hand any further, she'd be dangerously close to my dick.

Fiona glanced up at me. "Did you see that? It's so cute how kids believe in magic."

I forced myself to focus on the video and not her hand that rested on my thigh. "Have you thought about having kids?"

Her face screwed up. "I don't have time for kids with my job. I'll be the best auntie. I know I haven't been in the past, and I rarely see Ryder's daughter—"

"We can always make changes to our lives. You should do what makes you happy."

Her gaze met mine. "I am happy."

I grunted instead of saying what I was really thinking. From what I'd gleaned the last few days, she worked long hours and didn't have time for relationships. That didn't sound great to me. "I retired from the military because I wanted more."

Fiona frowned. "I thought you felt guilty over leaving Marley, and then your grandmother died."

"That was part of it. But I was starting to feel like I was missing out on something. I wanted something I could get excited about."

Fiona kept her gaze on my face. "And the military wasn't doing that for you anymore?"

"I enlisted so that they'd turn me into a man."

Her hand moved up my thigh, and I tensed. "Surely, you must know that your job doesn't make you worthy. It's who you are."

Her words wrapped around my heart.

Then she squeezed my thigh one more time before releasing it. "We should get inside. The others are going to wonder where we are."

I wanted to stay on the porch all night talking to her about our dreams, wants, and desires. But she was retreating. I didn't want to let her go. She was supposed to be home for a few more weeks. I just hoped I wouldn't waste the time I had.

Inside, it was loud. Most of the guests were part of the Monroe family, but Fiona's father was here too. I'd never officially met him, but I'd seen him around the Calloway farm when I snuck around to visit Fiona.

"Do you want me to introduce you to my father?" Fiona asked.

"You probably should." I was done sneaking around. If her father asked about our relationship, I'd be honest with him.

Fiona raised a brow. "Are you sure? I promise he doesn't

know anything about us. My brothers do, but we keep that kind of thing from him."

We approached him where he was talking to Lori. "Dad, this is Aiden Matthews, he co-owns the inn with his sister, Marley."

"You can call me Al. Thank you for your service."

"Nice to meet you, sir." I was surprised he knew anything about me, much less that I was retired from the military. But then again, it was a small town.

"I'm not going to bother telling you not to address me as *sir*. It would be wasting my breath." Al chuckled before he asked Fiona, "How are things at the inn? He treating you right?"

Fiona stiffened. "He's been a good host. He showed me the gardens and even some rooms in the basement he's thinking of having renovated."

Al turned his attention to me. "I remember there was a movie theater on site years ago."

"What do you remember about the inn when it was fully functional?" I asked him, genuinely curious.

"I heard there was a theater, and maybe even a bowling alley. I can't say I was ever a guest," Al said thoughtfully.

I nodded. "There's also a game room, but it's mainly billiards, and a bar. It's quite the set up."

"You going to restore her to her former glory?" Al asked me.

I tipped my head toward his daughter. "Fiona seems determined that we do."

Al touched Fiona's shoulder. "She's good at what she does. Her bosses don't listen to her ideas though. Make sure you do."

Fiona flushed with pleasure. "How do you know what my bosses listen to?"

"Daphne tells me what you two talk about. At least when it comes to work."

Fiona chewed her lip. "I didn't realize she shared."

"I want to hear how you're doing," her father said.

He struck me as someone who loved his children and just wanted to be part of their lives.

Fiona smiled softly. "I'll be better about keeping in touch."

"I know you're busy," her father said gruffly.

Lori pulled him away to get a drink, and Fiona leaned in close. "That wasn't so bad, was it?"

I lowered my voice. "I mean, if he knew I'd taken his daughter's virginity when she was eighteen, it would have gone differently—"

Fiona clapped a hand over my mouth. "Shh. That's the last thing I need my father knowing. He seems to like you. Let's keep it that way."

When she slowly removed her hand, I asked, "You think he'd care after all these years?"

Fiona nodded. "I think he'd feel guilty that he didn't know what was going on. That he wasn't more involved in my life. But he had seven kids. He was doing the best he could."

If anything happened between us, I needed to have that conversation with her dad. I didn't want there to be any secrets. I wouldn't go into details, but he should know we dated and that we were in love.

Heath and Marley appeared at our side. I was so engrossed in talking to Fiona, I hadn't even thought to greet them.

"How are you doing?" Heath asked me.

"Good. Marley talk to you about the inn?"

"She said you wanted to do some renovations. I can probably look at it tomorrow. We didn't check it out before we did the first round."

"The priority was getting the inn functional again. Now we're looking to increase our services, and that basement is set up perfectly for it. I wouldn't have even thought about doing it now if Fiona hadn't mentioned it," Marley said.

Heath nodded. "I'll take a look and let you know if it's feasible."

"Hopefully, Fiona is going to help us. She has amazing ideas," Marley gushed.

Fiona's face flushed from the praise.

"You in town for a while?" Heath asked Fiona.

Fiona nodded. "A few weeks. I'm due to head back after the New Year."

"That's not long if we're going to do a renovation together," Heath said to her, and I knew he was trying to figure out what was going on and if he needed to protect me from Fiona. Which he didn't.

Fiona's expression turned thoughtful. "I have a lot to think about. I could extend my vacation, but I don't think my boss would like that."

"Why don't you meet me in the theater tomorrow before I head to work? You can tell me what you were thinking," Heath offered.

"That would be great. Thank you."

Then talk turned to the upcoming holiday.

Shortly after, Daphne urged everyone to sit at the dining-room table. "We want to thank everyone for coming tonight, and Emmett for constructing this gorgeous table where all our family can eat together."

"Where are the rest of the Calloways?" Emmett asked.

Daphne's uneasy gaze met Cole's.

Cole stood next to Daphne. "The Calloways needed to be at the farm, and I wasn't sure if I was ready to have everyone in the same room."

"They'll come around. Just give them time," Al said.

Fiona leaned closer and said, "I thought it was too much to have all the Calloways and the Monroes in one place."

Before I could respond, Cole continued, "One day, both of our families will be together in one place. I just hope it's before our wedding."

"I'll drink to that," Al said, and we raised our glasses. "To the Monroes and the Calloways."

Fiona's hand rested on my thigh as she leaned close, her hair brushing the scruff on my chin. "Can you imagine all that testosterone in one room? There would definitely be an explosion."

"Yeah, maybe," I said because her proximity never failed to get to me. It was difficult to breathe in deeply, and her father raised his brow from across the table.

"Your dad is watching," I said quietly.

Fiona returned to her seat but flashed me a smile. "Everyone knows we're working together. It makes sense that we're friends."

"Sure," I said, but I wasn't ready to talk to her father yet. Not until I knew if there was anything between me and Fiona.

Fiona was familiar with me. It made sense because we dated previously, but I wondered if she noticed how her touch affected me. Was she doing it on purpose or was she oblivious? It was hard to imagine that she was unaware.

For the rest of dinner, I fielded questions about the inn and the proposed renovations, but no one talked about Christmas tree farms. Both families were in the middle of their busiest season, and since the businesses were the source of tension it was best to avoid talk of it.

After dinner, everyone helped clean up. Then the male Monroes congregated on the back patio. Apparently, it was a Monroe tradition.

Somehow, I was herded out along with them.

"I never thought we'd be here, celebrating Cole moving in with a Calloway," Emmett said.

"Don't cause any trouble," Cole said tightly.

Knox nodded. "Daphne won't be a Calloway much longer. They're getting married."

Cole looked around the crowd. "I'd be honored if you'd stand up for me. I'd like all my cousins by my side."

"I'd be honored too," Knox said.

Heath clasped his shoulder. "Happy to."

Sebastian nodded. "Wouldn't have it any other way."

"We'll be there," Talon said.

Then everyone's gaze moved to Emmett. "I can do that."

"I don't want any issues at our wedding. You'll need to get along with Daphne's brothers," Cole said.

I had a feeling I'd need to keep an eye on things, make sure there weren't any arguments.

"We're not Neanderthals. We can behave for a few hours at a wedding," Knox teased.

"You're not the one I'm worried about," Cole said.

"I know you're all worried about me, and how I'll react. But don't you think you should be worried about the Calloways? They aren't here tonight."

Cole cradled his beer. "The Calloways run the farm themselves. They don't have any help. I assure you; that's the main reason they're not able to be here tonight."

"That's no way to run a business. You need to hire people," Emmett said.

"You were the same way. You were reluctant to hire anyone who wasn't family," Cole admonished him. "We're not here to criticize how the Calloways run their business. Their main jobs come first."

"That just means their business suffers because of their practices, not anything we're doing on our farm," Emmett continued.

Cole held up his hand. "No talk about Christmas tree farms or business. Not when we're together. Surely, we can talk about something besides that."

Knox wrapped an arm around Cole's neck. "We can talk about my favorite cousin finally getting married."

Cole easily flipped out of his hold. "Don't let Charlotte hear you say that. We're also not going to resort to being fifteen again. No wrestling."

Knox frowned. "You're no fun now that you're tied down."

"Everyone's tied down," Talon said.

"Except Charlotte," Emmett pointed out.

Cole scowled. "She's in no place for a relationship. She's trying to get back on her feet."

"Have you talked to her about working at the inn? If we're going to renovate the theater, I'll need more help," I asked Cole.

"I'm sure she'd love to do that. She's good with people."

"It'll take a lot off my list. I want to be able to focus solely on the theater," I said.

"When you get it up and running, you should have a private family showing," Sebastian said.

I swirled the beer in my bottle while I considered it. "That's not a bad idea. We can do a test run of sorts to see if everything operates smoothly."

The slider opened, and Marley walked out, followed by the rest of the women.

"We haven't even looked to see if renovating that old theater is feasible yet," Heath said.

Marley slipped her arm through his. "We all want a movie theater. You need to make it happen."

Heath looked down at her with so much love on his face. It reminded me of how I used to feel when I was dating Fiona. We had to keep things a secret, but when we were together, we never held back. We loved freely and easily. I wished things were that uncomplicated now. I wasn't sure I'd ever be able to unravel the hurt I'd caused.

"We decided to crash your party," Fiona said to me.

"I don't think the Monroes will be able to carry on the tradition of the men hanging out after dinner for much longer. They're outnumbered," Marley said.

Fiona curled her hand around my arm. "You got that right."

Someone mentioned starting a fire, so everyone moved to the firepit in the yard. Chairs were brought out. There weren't enough, so people were sitting on the ground, in camping chairs, and even a few kitchen chairs.

For once, I was content to just be. Fiona sat next to me, her arms resting over her bent knees. "You're not worried that someone will think something's going on between us?"

She flashed me a smile. "Nope."

I wanted to be so much more. I wanted to go back to the moment I broke her heart, and I wanted to handle it differently. The only thing was, if I'd let her move with me, would we still be together? Would getting married young have ruined us or made us a stronger couple?

There was no way of knowing.

Izzy crawled into Cole's lap, her head resting on his shoulder. What would it be like to have a little girl with Fiona's dirty blond hair and brown eyes? Would she be just as strong as her mother?

"Aren't they sweet together? I can't get over how Cole interacts with Izzy. It's like they were always meant to be together."

"It's something, all right." Were Fiona and I meant to be together? Was this reunion supposed to happen? If so, I should relax and trust the journey. But it was impossible.

CHAPTER 8

FIONA

*E*arly the next morning, I met Heath, Aiden, and Marley in the basement of the inn. When I arrived, Marley handed me a to-go cup of coffee.

I immediately accepted it. "I love you."

Marley laughed. "That was easy."

Aiden waved off the coffee. "You're interrupting my morning run. Let's get started."

"Someone's cranky this morning," Heath teased as he led the way around the theater. Occasionally, Marley or I would mention what we loved about the space, what we wanted to keep, and what we could do without.

It was exhilarating to be working on a project like this. It's what I'd always dreamed of doing, creating a unique space that guests could enjoy.

Instead, I was stuck working with a large hotel chain that was cookie-cutter in its design and its management style. They weren't open to new ideas. In fact, the consensus seemed to be that we should look like every other hotel. It was frowned upon to be distinct. But it went against every one of my marketing instincts.

Treasures like this theater kept people talking about your business for years to come, and I had a feeling the local papers would do an article on the renovation.

"I'll write up an estimate but think about what you're willing to spend on something like this. It's a nice add-on, but we're not talking about more rooms to rent. You're not going to make a lot of money from the theater even if you charge for tickets."

Marley frowned. "This will draw people in and keep guests talking. They'll always remember that inn that had a bowling alley or a theater in the basement."

I nodded. "It's unique things that make the best impression. Not looking like everyone else."

"We have the original paintings upstairs, the gardens outside, and the historic feel of this place. But I can't help but think we need to bring this back to life," Aiden said.

My gaze moved from Marley to Aiden. There was emotion under Aiden's stoic expression. This theater meant something to him and their family. They wanted to bring their grandmother's legacy back, and I wanted to help them with it. I'd love to see the project through in its entirety, but it wasn't possible.

"We appreciate you taking the time to look at it and write up an estimate," Aiden said to Heath.

Marley wrapped a hand around Heath's arm. "I think Gram would love that we're doing this. She'd want to see people enjoying the theater again. Closing this space and eventually the inn was her greatest regret."

"I have to agree," Aiden said.

It was the perfect project for me to see if this was something I wanted to do going forward. Would I enjoy it, or would it be too personal? It felt like we were uncovering a treasure, making it shiny and new again. It gave me hope that there was a possibility for me and Aiden. But he'd never said he was interested in rekindling the past.

"Let me walk you out," Aiden offered.

Heath paused to kiss Marley. Then he and Aiden left the room.

Marley moved closer to me. "When Aiden lets me help, money isn't an issue."

I smiled. "I love when there's no cap on spending."

Marley held up her hand. "I think it would be a travesty to put the dust covers back on and close the doors. This place was meant to be enjoyed."

"It would be an experience for sure."

"You really think people will appreciate the history of this place, sit in these smaller velvet chairs versus the recliners at the new theaters?"

"I think so. Especially if you're a guest at the inn. You came here for this experience. A historic inn outside of town next to a Christmas tree farm. You can capitalize on all those aspects when you're marketing. I have a feeling this theater will be spoken about and pictured in reviews."

"I think you're right. I got tingles when you talked about it. Everything in my body is telling me to go for it," Marley gushed, and her energy was inspiring.

"You don't think we should wait to decide until Heath provides the estimate?"

Marley shook her head. "Aiden won't like it, but I want to personally finance the renovation of the basement."

"What won't I like?" Aiden asked, returning to the room.

Marley rolled her eyes. "This is something I want to do."

"We have to look at the estimate and see if it's possible. You know we're tight right now. We only just reopened, and we aren't booked solid yet."

Marley moved toward the stage where she lifted herself on it to sit. "This will bring people in. It will create a buzz. It's the perfect marketing tool."

Aiden's jaw tightened. "I don't want you to fund it. I think the business should run itself."

Marley placed her hands on her hips. "I co-own the property. I want to invest in it."

"You may have inherited it, but you added me to the deed when I retired from the military and moved home."

"I did, and I'll listen to your opinion on the matter. But I think this is something we have to do."

"You follow your gut. But we need to look at the reality of a situation. It's not feasible to do everything you want."

Marley cocked her head. "I'm successful because I listened to my intuition. You'd do well to remember that."

Aiden held up his hands as if to ward her off. "I'm proud of you. But I don't know how you make decisions that way."

Marley thought about it for a few seconds, then said, "You're used to people telling you what to do." Then she touched her chest. "You have to get in touch with yourself, listen to the feelings in your body. The more you do it, the better you'll get. You'll know when something is right for you."

I couldn't help but compare the situation to me and Aiden's relationship. He wouldn't have known what was right back then because he was so consumed with this idea that he wasn't good enough. That he had to prove himself to someone. He wasn't in touch with his true feelings. He had no idea what he wanted. That helped ease the pain because if I thought he broke things off because he truly didn't want me, that was the worst.

"What do you think, Fiona?" Marley asked, pulling me out of my thoughts.

I leaned against a chair. I couldn't wait until we could sit in the theater and get the full effect. "I want to see Heath's plans for the space. I don't think we can move forward without that. I'm just used to working with numbers." I also didn't want to get between the siblings in an argument over money. They'd have to make the hard decisions themselves. "I'm happy to help with the movie theater renovation and consult on the rest of it."

"I appreciate that. I'm excited to work together," Marley said to me, and then to Aiden, "I guess we're stuck until Heath gets back to us. Good thing I know the contractor. I'll make sure he puts us on the top of the list."

Aiden sighed. "I'm sure he already did."

Marley checked her phone. "I have to record my podcast. But I'll let you know as soon as I hear something."

She hugged Aiden and waved at me before she left.

"We can't move forward with all the renovations, but if you're sure we're renovating the theater, we can at least clean it."

I rubbed my hands together. "I can't wait to get started. But I thought you had to stay close to the front desk?"

"I installed a video." He showed me the feed. "And the phone is forwarded to my cell. Charlotte's coming in later today to discuss the job."

"That's exciting. I bet you can't wait for her to start."

"I like to be in control, so it might be hard for me to let her handle the front desk and the incoming reservations."

"Do you really want to handle the customers? You don't seem like a people person." I asked as we worked together to remove the sheets hung over the chairs.

"I can handle the basics: reserving a room, checking someone in, and showing them to their room. But what I don't like is telling them about the paintings of the inn for sale or Holly's ornaments."

"You don't like to sell to people." I sneezed from the dust.

He gestured wide with his hands. "But this? I won't have any issues telling the guests about it. It's going to be perfect."

"It's this little gem that's been hidden down here for too long. When we reopen it, there will be people who remember coming here when they were younger, and others who can't wait to see a piece of history."

"It's like the ballroom upstairs. It's unique for a small inn. I'll run and get a couple of vacuums so we can clear out some of this dust."

"What do you want me to do with these cloths?" I gestured at the pile we'd made on the ground.

"Throw them out. We won't be needing them anymore." I loved that Aiden was so into the renovation of the theater. I thought it would be good for him to do something for his grandmother. He was still deployed when Marley performed the other renovations. I wondered if being down here would bring up other memories for him.

I carried the cloths to the dumpster. It took several trips, and when I was done, Aiden was running one of the vacuums down the aisle. I took the second one and ran it over the red carpet. The aisles had tiny lights that lit the way for guests. When we finished with the floors, we moved onto the chairs that were red velvet with gold detailing.

Aiden stopped the vacuum and wiped the sweat from his brow. "Should we keep the wallpaper?"

I ran a hand over its silver swirls. "It's worn in several spots."

Aiden walked down the aisle and hopped onto the stage in one smooth motion. "Heath might need to fix a few weak spots on the stage. Hopefully we can salvage it though."

I loved that he was strong and built from his time in the military. He obviously took care of his body.

I joined him using the stairs on the side of the stage.

Aiden gestured at the seats. "What do you think?"

"It's amazing. I love that it's here. I love the history. What movies were shown here? Did people dress up to go to them?" I tapped my chin. "That gives me an idea. When we do the private showing, we should make it old Hollywood glam."

Aiden chuckled. "I'll let you handle those details."

"What's the first movie we should show?"

Aiden pursed his lips. "I*t's a Wonderful Life? Miracle on Thirty-Fourth Street?*"

"Something black-and-white for sure."

Aiden reached for my hand. "When I retired from the military, I thought I'd come home and help Marley. I'd reconnect with the sister I'd left behind. But she's a woman who can take care of herself."

"That's for sure."

"She has this crazy successful business where she keeps making more and more money. She has Heath. The inn."

I tilted my head to the side. "Are you worried that you don't have everything figured out yet? You should be proud of your military career. You did something amazing and completely selfless."

"There's some collateral damage to that decision. You. Marley. Gram."

I swallowed over the lump in my throat. "Your grandmother knew why you did it. She only wanted the best for you." I may not have spent any time with Aiden's parents, but I drank tea with his grandmother and talked to her. She was a special person.

My biggest regret was that when Aiden broke things off, I never came back to see her. She wrote me in school, and I'd written back, talking about my courses and the friends I was making. She never asked about Aiden, and I never said anything.

"She wanted me to get out of here. When I told her about enlisting, she told me to go. That I should do whatever I needed to do. She'd take care of Marley."

I rested a hand over my heart. "I love that woman. Did she say anything about us?"

"She just said, *I hope you know what you're doing.* That was it. Cryptic and not much guidance for a stupid nineteen-year-old."

"You weren't stupid. You were running on a deep desire to get away from your parents. No one blames you for leaving." It was more about him not taking me with him. Or we could have dated long distance. But he'd shut down every possibility. He'd made me think he didn't want me.

Aiden hooked an arm around my neck and pulled me forward so that I rested against his chest. "I wish Gram were here to see this. She would have loved it."

"I think so too." The warmth of his body seeped through the thin material of his shirt, and he smelled of man, that cedar scent that I'd come to love. My fingers curled in his shirt. If I kept my body rigid, I wouldn't melt into him. I wouldn't feel every hard plane of his body against my curves.

Aiden's mouth was on my hair. "Relax. I remember how much you loved hugs when we dated."

I sighed at the memory, allowing my body to relax inch by inch until my eyes closed and my palms pressed flat against his chest. I felt the steady thud of his heart beneath my cheek.

"You ever think we'd be working together like this?"

"Never." I never thought I'd see him again. In fact, I'd hoped to avoid him.

Aiden eased back slightly. "I wouldn't want to do this with anyone but you."

Warmth spread through my chest. It was dangerous because he was standing so close to me; all he had to do was dip his head slightly and our lips would meet.

I let out a shaky breath and stepped back. I couldn't get involved with him again. He'd been clear about his feelings when he was nineteen, and I wouldn't let him hurt me twice. "We should get back to ridding this place of dust. I keep sneezing."

Aiden ran a hand through his hair. "There's no windows down here, so we can't open it up."

"Maybe we should use air cleaner or dehumidifiers."

Aiden pulled out his phone. "I'll order some online. We don't want it to be musty down here."

For the rest of the morning, we worked together, sucking up as much of the dust as we could.

When we paused to stretch our backs, Aiden said, "I have no idea how we're going to salvage these curtains."

They had holes in them and were heavy with dust and mildew.

"I'll look online to see if there's someone who restores things like this."

"In the meantime, I'm going to grab us some food from the kitchen."

I tucked my phone into my back pocket. "A sandwich would be great right now."

"I make a mean sandwich."

I laughed. "I bet you do. You're not cocky at all, are you?"

"I'm afraid that's something I picked up in the military, but I prefer confident."

I assessed him. He usually held his body rigid as if he was worried about a commanding officer showing up at any second, but he'd slowly relaxed during our time in the theater. I think it was the same reason he'd pulled me into a hug.

He felt closer to his younger self here. Spending time together was conjuring up old memories and feelings of nostalgia. That's all this was. I'd be foolish to think it was anything else.

In the kitchen, Aiden poured me blueberry lemonade from a pitcher in the fridge. "We usually keep water in the lobby during the summer season."

"This is lovely. Especially after being around so much dust. I need a long shower."

Aiden winked at me. "I could join you."

Then he got to work making cold meat subs for us. He put both on plates, cut up an apple, and threw a few chips on the side.

"This is great, Aiden. Thank you for feeding me."

He sat next to me. "You're helping me."

My lips twitched. "I keep saying this, but I'm not going to want to leave."

His brow furrowed. "Would you? I thought you wanted to stay here versus your family's home."

"I'd prefer to avoid the memories. But Daphne's living with Cole now. I could move into her cottage." But if I did that, I might want to stay. I'd get too settled. I'd fall in love with the quiet, the slower way of life, and seeing my family all the time.

"Is that what you want?" Aiden said, waiting for my answer.

"I don't know what I want anymore. I have to go back to my job in a few weeks. I was hoping to find some clarity. That the right thing to do would just hit me. But so far there's been nothing."

"I don't think you can rush these things. I've been home for almost a year, and I don't know what I want. I enjoy working at the inn, but I also like to work with my hands."

"You want to do more jobs for Heath," I said as I drank the cool lemonade.

"I just can't fit it in."

"Here's hoping we both get some answers soon." Because I wasn't any closer to that than when I came home.

CHAPTER 9

AIDEN

A few days later, I met with Heath, Marley, and Fiona in the inn's dining room to discuss the estimate and the scope of the work. Heath stood at one end of the table, his diagrams spread over the surface. "It's nothing fancy. But you get the idea."

"This looks like what I envisioned," Fiona said, pulling one of the illustrations closer to her.

"I've asked around, trying to find various people who've done this kind of restoration before so I could get some insight. We can salvage as much of the stage as we can, restoring the wood to its original luster and replacing any rotted planks. We'll have to get someone to look at the curtains. I think we'll need to strip the wallpaper and get new. We could paint too. I'd suggest a soft gray to keep with the original look."

"I like that," Marley said.

Fiona considered the one drawing he'd done in color. "There's enough going on in that room that we don't need wallpaper."

Heath let out a breath. "I was hoping you'd say that."

"I talked to an expert, and I think we can restore most of the seats. We might need to reupholster a bunch of them, but it's doable. New carpet on the floor and lighting. The projector room needs a complete overhaul with updated equipment."

Heath slid the estimate in front of Marley. She didn't flinch or give any outward sign of her reaction. "I can do this."

"This is assuming we have free manual labor from Aiden, Cole, and Fiona," Heath added.

"I said I'd help with this." I held my hand out to Marley for the estimate, but she held tight to it.

Her gaze met mine. "I want to cover this."

I kept my hand where it was. "Let me see it."

"I anticipated this." Heath handed me a second estimate.

The number had my eyes widening, and I whistled. "This is the cost after the family discount?"

Heath chuckled. "I'm charging you for costs and my crew. The restoration experts don't come cheap, and I can't control that expense."

"If we want to do this right, we need their advice and assistance. If we need to replace a chair, they know where to look for something similar. It sounds like it's important to everyone that we maintain the original charm."

"I agree with that," Fiona said.

"Are you sure you can afford this?" I asked Marley. She'd said she was financially secure, and I'd heard net worth numbers floating around, but I wasn't sure if they were true. I'd saved money while I was in the military, but it was tiny compared to the estimate. I always struggled with the belief that I didn't have enough to go around.

"I consider the inn an investment. I'll make the money back tenfold. Besides, this place means something to me. It's more than just a business."

Marley had a good head for investments, so I chose to take her at her word. "If you want to bankroll the project, I won't stand in your way."

Marley's eyes widened as she let out a soft laugh. "I was expecting an argument."

"I want this as much as you do. I see the potential, and nothing has gotten me this intrigued since I came home." I was searching for a purpose, and right now it was restoring my grandmother's inn to its former glory. If Marley could afford the repairs, then I was okay with that.

Marley's eyes were suspiciously shiny. "I want this so much. Thank you, Aiden."

"Of course." My voice was gruff.

"Let's talk timelines," Heath continued, not missing a beat. There was a sense of anticipation in the room. The financial piece was out of the way, and we could get to work. "We're able to get started tomorrow since Fiona and Aiden got a head start on cleaning."

"We have air cleaners and dehumidifiers running to clear out the mustiness," I said.

"Whatever we need to do, let's do it. I want it done right." Marley's tone was confident. She was used to making decisions quickly and assertively.

I was proud of her. She wasn't the same sister I'd left behind. The one that was ashamed by her upbringing and kept to herself in school. She was a confident woman who was sure of her moves.

I was a little envious of that confidence because when it came to Fiona, I wasn't sure what approach to take. So far, I'd taken the slow one. I was waiting for her to feel the connection between us, remember the good times we had. But she seemed to pull away whenever there was a moment, like the one on the stage. I couldn't blame her, but I wanted to reach her on a deeper level. I couldn't do that if she was resistant.

"I'm going to record content for my business today so I can focus on the theater for the rest of the week. But I was wondering if you would agree to me filming it for my social media accounts?" Marley asked me.

I frowned. "What does the restoration have to do with your work? I thought you talked about business and coached budding entrepreneurs."

Marley smiled. "This is my personal life. My followers love when I share it with them. And they're absolutely fascinated by the inn and the Christmas tree farm."

"I'm okay with it if you are. I can't imagine it would cause any harm. In fact, it might drum up interest in the inn itself," Fiona said thoughtfully.

I let out a breath, knowing that whatever Marley wanted, I'd give in to. "If you're okay with it, I am. Just don't want cameras interrupting the work."

Marley held up a hand. "I'll do the filming, and I'll stay out of the way. I promise."

I nodded my assent.

Marley grinned. "I have some work to do at home, but I'll see you bright and early tomorrow."

"You two have plans for the rest of the day?" Heath asked me and Fiona.

"I should probably start looking for a new job. But I'm much more interested in this project." Fiona lifted the diagram of the theater for emphasis.

I felt a pang of unease that her visit would be drawing to an end soon. A sense of urgency flew through my blood.

"The family will host a walk-through of the holiday light display at the farm soon. We'll have drinks and hang out around the fire. You should come and see it."

Fiona raised a brow. "Are your brothers okay with a Calloway on site?"

"I'm sure Cole is planning to bring Daphne and Izzy."

"Safety in numbers," Fiona mumbled.

"Emmett's all bluster," Heath said as he gathered his things.

Fiona gestured at the illustrations. "Can you leave these? I'd like to take another look at them."

"I can do that," Heath said.

"Did you have a chance to check out the rest of the basement?" I asked Heath.

"I'm heading down there now. Marley's excited about this project." He gave me a pointed look.

"You want me to let her bankroll it." That irritated me, because it should have been a matter between me and my business partner. But Heath was her significant other and the contractor. He had a say too.

Heath's gaze was serious. "Marley wants to restore the inn. It's not about money for her."

I leaned back in my chair. "Don't you think we should look at whether it's a good investment? You don't want to sink money into something that's never going to generate a return."

"Marley's considered all the angles. Don't forget it's a tax write-off, and she thinks it will pay for itself over time. She's looking to the future. If one of your kids wants to continue to run the place, it will be done. They won't have the burden of renovating it themselves."

I could appreciate that. "Kids is a long way off, isn't it?"

He merely raised a brow. "That's between me and your sister."

I winced because at some point, Heath had moved from the role as my best friend to my sister's fiancé. I should have been accustomed to the change, but I wasn't.

"Look, I'm not trying to be an asshole—" Heath broke off.

"I get it. I'm just not ready for that myself."

Heath shook his head, his lips curling into a smile. "You'd have to find a woman who could put up with you first."

If we were alone, I would have teased about wishing Heath had a sister. But Fiona was here, and it wasn't worth alienating her for a joke. "Women can't resist a man in uniform."

Fiona raised a brow but didn't say anything.

I didn't want her to think that I was a player since I'd been home. In fact, it was the exact opposite, but I couldn't resist teasing Heath. I missed our easy-going camaraderie.

"I'll leave you to it. I'm going to head downstairs," Heath said.

"I'll be down in a minute," I said to him, knowing I wanted to clear things up with Fiona.

When he was gone, I said, "I was just giving Heath a hard time. It didn't mean anything."

Fiona plastered a smile on her face. "It's none of my business who you date."

"I haven't been with anyone since I've been home. I've been too busy with this place, and frankly, I haven't been interested in anyone." Not until now.

"Like I said, you don't owe me an explanation." She stood and rested the strap of her purse on her shoulder. "Do you mind if I leave the drawings here?"

"It's a good spot for them. We don't use the dining room."

I rounded the table, stopping near Fiona.

"Did you have something else you wanted to discuss before I leave?" Fiona asked.

I opened my mouth intending to tell her I hadn't been interested in anyone but her, but I couldn't get the words out. I was afraid she wasn't ready to hear them. That I'd scare her away. At any moment, she could leave, go back to her apartment and her job. "Thanks for helping us out with this."

Her face softened. "Of course. I'm excited to get started."

"I'd better join Heath in case he has any questions."

Fiona nodded and moved to leave. When she was almost to the doorway, I asked, "Would you come with me to the light display? I feel weird going alone. I'm not a Monroe, and Marley's with Heath."

"I don't know—"

"You should experience some of the holiday things while you're here."

"That's not a bad idea."

And I want to be the one who experienced them with her. "I'll knock on your door at seven. Maybe we can have dinner in your room."

"That would be nice."

"I'll see you then." I walked out before she had a chance to back out and tell me the reasons why it was a bad idea.

In the basement, I found Heath in the bar. "This craftsmanship is top-notch. And the wood is mahogany."

"You think you can keep the bar itself?"

"Most of it's good. It's solid construction. Someone took their time with this." His fingers ran over the details on the side of the bar. "We want to keep as much of the original wood as possible." Then he stepped back and considered me. "I'm surprised you caved to Marley paying for this."

"She wants to restore Gram's pride and joy. We both want to see it come back to life. If she can afford to do that, then why should I stop her?"

Heath squeezed my shoulder. "You're growing up."

I shrugged him off. "I'm already a man."

Heath raised his brows. "In some ways."

My shoulders stiffened. "What are you trying to say?"

"Have you talked to Fiona? Have you tried to make things right with her?" Heath asked softly.

"I'm not sure I can."

He leaned against the bar. "Not talking about it isn't going to do anything. Then she's going to leave thinking you didn't want her."

My jaw ached from the tension. "She's moved on from me."

"Are you sure about that?"

I blew out a breath. "Honestly? I'm not sure of anything. I

certainly haven't moved on. I haven't been interested in anyone until her."

Heath nodded. "Now we're getting somewhere."

"I just don't know what to do about it."

Heath shrugged. "Talk to her. Clear the air. Then start from there."

"You make it sound so easy."

"From where I'm standing, it is."

"Talking about feelings isn't easy."

"I guess not how you were raised. I'm sure your parents would've told you that you were a crybaby for having feelings. I remember some of what your mom used to spew at you."

"Thankfully, they're gone now."

"But those memories stay with us. They form the core of who we are."

"That's why I went into the military. I'm not that same guy." I'd hardened myself against my parents. I'd like to think if I ever ran into them again, I'd be immune to their barbs.

Heath shook his head. "It's who you are, and you need to heal from it to move on with someone."

"Fiona and I have a history. Don't you think it would be easier to move on with someone else."

Heath chuckled. "If only you were interested in someone else."

"Sometimes I hate you." He never failed to tell me how it was.

Heath sobered. "You need to talk to her about it. Tell her why you did what you did and that it had nothing to do with her as a person. That you never stopped having feelings for her."

"How do you know all of that?" I couldn't help but ask.

"It's obvious to anyone who's spent time around you two."

I thought I'd been professional when we were around Heath and Marley, but I guess I was wrong.

Heath grinned. "You should make sure she comes to the

walk-through light display. When I was trying to win over Marley, I took her to all the holiday events. I wanted to show her the magic of the farm and the season."

"You wooed her." The fact was that Heath was more emotionally mature than me. He'd won over Marley despite the fact that he'd broken things off when they were teenagers. He'd been worried about his promise to protect her. The promise he made to me.

The difference was I'd promised Fiona that I'd wait for her to finish college. But I hadn't. I'd broken that promise, and I wasn't sure she'd ever forgive me for it.

"You'll never know if you don't try. The worst thing that will happen is that you'll talk it out, and you both move on from there."

The words got stuck in my throat. I wasn't prepared to move on from Fiona. Just the thought of it weighed on my chest, making it hurt to breathe.

"You don't like to talk about your feelings, do you?"

"And you do?" I asked him as we walked behind the bar. The glassware was still hanging on the hooks, covered in dust. It would need to be washed.

"When you're in a relationship, you have to dig deep and be honest about what you're thinking and feeling. It's hard but worth it." When I gave him a dubious look, he continued. "What's the alternative? Not talking about it? Her believing that you didn't want her?"

I shook my head. "I don't want that."

"Then you know what you have to do."

He let the topic drop, and we walked through the space, making notes of what was salvageable and what wasn't. The good thing was the basic setup was fine. We just needed to restore what was there.

When we stepped inside the bowling alley, Heath said, "I

don't know anything about bowling alleys. There's got to be someone who fixes these kinds of things."

"I'll make some calls."

Heath stepped onto the lane. "We can polish the wood floors."

I touched the leather of the chairs. "Marley and Fiona might want some new seating."

There was a small bar in the back of the room and a space for bowling shoes. "Can you and Fiona get rid of these and see what it would cost to order new ones?"

"You got it."

"This place is small. You planning to make it available to the public? Or is it just for guests?"

"I can't speak for Marley, but I would think we'll keep it for guests. More of an incentive to book a room here. Even for locals."

Heath nodded. "You're creating an experience for them."

"That's how I like to think about it. That seems to be Fiona's specialty."

I helped him measure the seating areas. "I think we could add a table here, and guests could place their shoes and bags underneath. You want to build that?"

"I'd love to work with my hands again."

"Get this place up and running smoothly. Hire good people to run it for you, and I'll give you a team."

I chuckled. "I think I'll have my hands full with this place for now."

"Let this be your first project."

Despite my fear that I'd screw something up, I said, "That would be a good start."

"Fiona mentioned looking for a job. Is that why she's home?"

"She was passed over for a promotion and coming off a recent breakup. I think she's licking her wounds, trying to decide if she wants to go back to that job or look for another."

"Mmm." Heath jotted something down in his notebook.

"What's that supposed to mean?" I leaned a hip on the bar.

"It means this is the perfect time for you to convince her that something else is available. Something closer to well—"Heath touched the bar top—"here."

"She doesn't want to stick around here." And maybe that was the reason I'd been slow to do anything about this building attraction.

Heath raised a brow. "When are you going to learn that you can't have what you don't go after?"

My stomach rumbled. "Are you done giving me shit? Because I'm starving."

He gestured toward the exit. "Lead the way to the kitchen."

"You know, just because you're working at the inn doesn't mean I'll be making you lunch every day."

"That's exactly what it means," Heath said as he followed me up the stairs. "We should probably widen these and make them sturdier. Building codes have changed since these were built."

I let him draw me into his plans for the basement as I made us sandwiches. Fiona joined us, listening and commenting from time to time. It was good having all my favorite people in one place. If only Fiona was sticking around. Then everything would be perfect.

CHAPTER 10

FIONA

We spent the week clearing out the rest of the basement. In the evenings, I visited Daphne and Izzy in their new place. As much as the project excited me and fueled me in a way my regular job didn't, I couldn't lose sight of the fact that I was home to see my family.

Today, we were focused on the bowling alley, throwing out the shoes and measuring for new shelves. Apparently, Aiden was taking on that project himself.

As we washed the dust off our hands, Aiden asked, "What are your plans for tonight?"

"We're having a family dinner at my dad's. Everyone in the same place. Or at least everyone who lives here: Jameson, Teddy, Weston, Daphne, Cole, and Izzy."

"That'll be nice."

"I'm going to take a shower first because it looks like I was in a dust storm."

He wiped a hand over my cheek where I was sure I was covered in a fine coating of more dust, sending tingles down my spine. "Have a good time with your family."

His voice was low and husky, and I wanted to ask him if he'd join me in the shower. But that was a bad idea. We'd always had chemistry, but that didn't mean anything.

The problem was that the more time we spent together, the more I remembered how good of a guy he was, how much I enjoyed spending time with him. He was interested in what I had to say. I couldn't remember the last time someone listened to me that intently.

But I couldn't forget that I wasn't who he wanted in the end. I wasn't enough for him.

I stepped away from him. "You look like you could use a shower too."

"I'm heading to my apartment just as soon as I put out a snack for the kids. We have a few families in town for the holidays. I like to put out cookies."

"That's sweet."

"It's totally worth it when the kids come down here looking for a treat and find it. They get really excited." He grabbed the cookies from the cabinet. "These are store-bought, but I'd love to find a local baker who could supply us with treats."

"Hmm. I'll have to ask Daphne if she'd be willing to do that. She can bake, but she prefers pies."

"Maybe if not, she knows someone who would."

"I'd be happy to talk to her."

We headed to the lobby where the stairs would take me to my room. He opened the tray of cookies and arranged them on a plate. I'd made it up a few steps before I heard the pounding of little feet on the stairs.

"Slow down. There's plenty for everyone." Aiden smiled at them and then looked up, catching me watching. He winked, and my face flushed.

I continued ascending the stairs because watching Aiden with kids was dangerous to more than just my heart. I could see him with a child following him around the inn while he did repairs. He'd carefully instruct the child how to fix things. He'd be patient and loving.

I shook my head. Just because he was good with the guests didn't mean he'd make a good father. Except I remembered when we would talk about his parents, he'd been adamant he wouldn't be anything like them.

Since I'd come home, I was confronted with my past. It was nice to reconnect with people. But Aiden was different. I didn't feel like we were moving forward as friends. I felt like we were building a foundation for something more, which was ridiculous. A foundation for what?

He'd been the one to say that he didn't want a relationship with me. There was no future for us. He'd made that clear. When he touched my cheek in the kitchen, I'd wanted him to kiss me, despite the warning signs and our history.

Logic didn't come into play. It was all sensations. The tingles from his touch, the unsteadiness of my breath. The ache in my core.

I needed to keep Aiden securely in my past. Maybe I should consider moving into Daphne's place. At least I wouldn't be around Aiden as much. We'd still need to work together, but surely, I could compartmentalize that part of my life. We were coworkers.

I took a shower, relieved to wash off the layer of dust on my skin. I worked a corporate job, and I visited different sites, but I never got dirty like this. It felt good to be hands-on with this project when I didn't get the opportunity.

As I got ready to go to my dad's, I found myself slowing my movements, dreading that moment when I'd walk inside the kitchen and my mom wouldn't be there. I'd been okay the last time I visited, but I couldn't help the nerves from kicking in.

I told myself I could do it. It was no different than last time. I'd be fine.

I grabbed my purse and my jacket and walked with purpose down the hall and the stairs. Marley was at the door. "Off for a hot date?"

I laughed. "I'm eating with my family tonight."

Her face fell. "Not as fun as a hot date."

"Definitely not."

Marley came around the counter and hugged me. "Thank you so much for helping Aiden with the theater project. You've been a godsend."

"You're welcome. I'm enjoying it."

"If you're thinking about a career change, I have an entire basement that needs your touch, and I have a feeling you have more ideas for programs we can enact."

"It's tempting. I love this inn. It brings back so many memories, tea with your grandmother—" I broke off before I could say anything about her brother.

"Were you going to say something about Aiden? It's okay. I can handle it." Then she chuckled. "Maybe not the more intimate details."

"There's nothing to talk about. We were kids back then, and things didn't work out."

Marley shook her head. "I'm speaking from experience when I tell you this—it's hard to forget your first love."

Between visiting my family's home this evening and Marley referring to Aiden as my first love, I felt a little off keel. "I need to get going."

"Of course. I wouldn't want to keep you. Have a good evening." Marley moved behind the counter, and I pushed the heavy front door open. I hesitated on the steps, and seeing a rocking chair on the porch, I sank into it. There was a beautiful tree next to me, and I pulled my knees up to my chest and dropped my head.

A few minutes later, the door opened, and someone stepped outside. "I thought you were going to your dad's for dinner."

I looked up just as Aiden sat in the second rocking chair. "You don't want to go, do you?"

"I want to spend time with my family."

"Is it being in the house, knowing your mother isn't ever going to be there again?"

"How do you see me that well?" Tears pricked my eyes. He didn't have that kind of relationship with his parents, yet he saw the relationship I'd had with my mother.

"You were gone when she was sick. I bet it's different for you than your siblings who were there for it." He held up his hands as if to ward me off. "Not that I think you should have done anything else, but it is more challenging for you."

I let my head fall back. "It shouldn't still feel like this, right? It's been years, and it's not like I haven't been at the house several times."

"Not if you've been avoiding the feelings that arise when you're there."

I wondered if he'd avoided his feelings when he broke things off with me. If that's what made it so easy for him. "You know I have. I've buried myself in school, then work."

"Now you're slowing down; you're home. Everything is coming to the surface. Things you haven't dealt with yet."

I picked at the material of my sweater. "So what should I do?"

"Feel your feelings. Whatever they are."

"I can't cry in front of my brothers. They hated when me and Daphne cried. Although I hear they're better with Izzy."

Aiden sighed. "I think they want to fix things for you, and they feel helpless when you're upset."

I smiled. "I'll get through it."

"I'll be here tonight if you want to talk about it."

"Thank you. It's nice because you know what I went through."

"You were protecting yourself, and your mom would have

wanted you to finish school. She'd be proud of the person you've become."

"I hope so." I wasn't sure what I wanted to do next, but I was proud of my career, everything I'd built. Even if my boss couldn't see it.

I unfolded my legs and stood. "I'd better get going before my brothers send out a search party."

"We wouldn't want that to happen," Aiden said, his voice low.

There was no one nearby. We were alone on the porch, partially blocked by the tree, and I wanted nothing more than to feel the comfort of being in his arms.

Aiden raised a brow as if he'd read my thoughts. "Come here."

I practically fell into him. I was so desperate to feel his strength and breathe in his scent. He'd recently showered, and he smelled like soap. I sighed as I melted further into his body. His muscles felt hard, and his heart beat steadily under my cheek. I wished we could fall right back where we were, but we couldn't. Too soon, I forced myself to step away. "Thanks for the hug."

Aiden shoved his hands into his pockets.

I wanted to think that he did it so he wouldn't reach for me again. That he felt the familiar pull and had to check himself.

He dipped his chin. "The offer stands. I'll be here when you get back."

"Thanks, Aiden." I turned and walked toward my rental car. Aiden was offering to be there for me as a friend. What if I couldn't be around him without wanting more?

I was interested in Marley's offer of working on the inn's renovation. It sounded amazing, but I wasn't sure I could do it and work next to Aiden. I wasn't sure I wouldn't do something I'd regret, like kiss him.

When I arrived at the farm, I bypassed the line of cars

entering to get trees, noting it was shorter than I remembered when I was growing up. Back then, the line would stretch down the road, and occasionally we'd need a police officer to direct traffic. Now, Teddy hired local high school students who needed volunteer hours to graduate.

Now there were just a few cars at the gate house, where they could get a map of the fields and a saw. I always loved this time of the year: the smell of the trees being cut, and the holiday music playing over the speakers. It felt good to be back except not everything was the same.

I parked next to Teddy's blue cruiser and Weston's black-and-gold Department of Natural Resources truck. I was proud of my brothers for their chosen professions, even if I never had any urge to go into law enforcement.

Before I could turn the knob, the door opened, and Jameson engulfed me in a hug. He squeezed me tight, and when he let me go, he said, "It's good to have you home for a long visit."

"Thanks, Jamey."

He winced. "I don't go by that anymore."

I grinned. "Why not? I think it's cute."

He just gave me a look. "Women do not want to go out with a man named Jamey."

"So Jameson is more manly?" I asked, enjoying the banter. He'd always been the more relaxed brother, the one who loved to joke around. The rest of my brothers were a little more uptight, and his easygoing ways sometimes drove them crazy. My dad was worried for a long time he wouldn't graduate from school or choose a profession. That he'd be living at home forever. He still lived in the apartment above the garage, but at least he'd settled into his role as a firefighter.

It was so easy to be around Jameson, I almost forgot about my anxiety. Teddy and Wes stood in the kitchen where Dad was getting things ready for the grill.

When Dad saw me, he pulled me in for a hug and kissed the top of my head, making me feel like I was a kid again. "We're just waiting on Daphne and Cole."

"Let's be honest; everyone's waiting on Izzy," Wes said.

I couldn't help the smile that spread over my face as he held his arm out for me. Every time I was home, I marveled at how large my brothers had gotten. They'd filled out in the years since I left, growing into men who commanded respect at their jobs.

"It's good to have you home, sis," Wes said.

I looked around the kitchen, at my brothers who seemed to take up all the space and my father who'd aged a bit but was still a large man. "It's good to be home."

"You sound surprised," Teddy said as I hugged him next.

"I don't know what I expected. Maybe that things would feel different without Mom—" Then I broke off, remembering that my brothers didn't like to talk about her after she'd passed.

Jameson leaned a hip against the counter, an amused expression on his face. He was always smiling. Even when Dad would get frustrated with his grades or his laid-back attitude. "I guess it's different for you. You didn't live here after—"

I swallowed over the lump, not expecting to broach this subject with my family. "It's different."

"We're just happy you're home for the holidays," Dad said as he poured olive oil over the cut-up veggies.

"I am too," I said, surprising myself. I never had time to take off. There was always a new project to work on, another hotel that needed my help. But now that I'd made the time, I wanted to do it more often. If my boss couldn't see my worth, was it necessary to work through holidays, never taking any vacation days?

"I'm going to fire up the grill." Dad handed Teddy the veggie platter and they went outside.

Wes grabbed a box of crackers from the pantry and dumped them onto a plate. "I heard you're spending a lot of time with Aiden at the inn."

"I'm staying there, and his sister, Marley, wants to renovate the basement. Hotels are kind of my specialty, so she asked for my advice."

"You could stay here. Daphne moved out of the cottage," Jameson said, sounding like he would prefer that.

"I was worried that staying here would be hard for me," I admitted softly.

Wes nodded. "I can understand that."

"I didn't handle things the best back then. I didn't come home. I didn't help out. Not like Teddy did."

Weston frowned. "Dad wanted you to stay in school. He would have been pissed if you quit."

"Teddy moved closer."

Teddy had taken on a larger role when Mom died, He'd moved closer to home to keep the rest of the kids in line, making sure they went to school and their grades hadn't fallen.

"He knew he wanted to be a police officer near home. It made sense for him to move back. Mom always thought you should go away to school, experience all that life had to offer. When she got sick, she made Dad promise that nothing would change. That everything would go on as it had before."

"You can't lose someone like that and expect everything to be the same." I'd felt bereft after she died, and then when I lost Aiden too, I thought I'd never recover. That I'd always have this hole in my chest.

"Between Dad and Teddy, they tried to keep things the same, but they weren't," Wes said.

I shook my head, guilt seeping into my tone. "I'm sorry I wasn't there."

"You did what you were supposed to do, lived your life. Dad was proud of you," Weston said.

"Everyone's all grown up, and I feel like I missed it," I said fondly.

"Not everyone's grown up." Wes glanced at Jameson, who said, "Hey," and threw a cracker at him.

"You're right. Nothing has changed around here," I said with a smile, and my brothers' shoulders relaxed.

I enjoyed my brothers' teasing.

"When are you going to grow up and get a real job?" Wes asked Jameson.

"I have a real job. Besides, I wasn't cut out for police work. I don't want to arrest people. I like helping them."

My heart warmed at Jameson's comments. He'd always had the biggest heart. "I think it's great that you're a firefighter."

"I suppose it's better than living in the basement, playing video games," Wes said light heartedly.

I remembered there was a time when Dad was worried about Jameson, when he couldn't' seem to make a decision about what he wanted to do with his life. But not everyone had their life planned out in high school. "The important thing is that he's happy now."

An emotion passed over Jameson's face, one I couldn't place.

Then the front door opened, and Izzy came running through. "Aunt Fiona," she cried right before she launched herself into my body.

"Umph," I said as my arms came around her, and I bent to breathe in her scent. "You smell like graham crackers and strawberries."

"That's about right," Daphne said as she joined us in the kitchen.

"You look right here, sis," Daphne said as she hugged me with one arm, then made the rounds with our brothers.

"Dad and Teddy are outside," Wes offered.

Cole inclined his head. "I'll go see if they need help."

The exchange with Cole was more reserved than how my

brothers usually were with each other. I hoped that eventually Cole would be considered one of us, and he'd be teased mercilessly.

"Did you see my dollhouse?" Izzy asked as she took my hand and dragged me into the living room.

"It's surprising, isn't it?" Daphne asked as she followed us. "He never let us have a dollhouse."

"There were so many of us. I'm sure it was expensive for them to buy us toys."

"And it was easier to tell us to play with the boys' toys."

I never cared about dolls, but Daphne had. She was more girl, loving to bake with our mom and play dress-up. I'd always been more serious, reading a book, or riding my bike over the farm.

"I love having you here," Daphne said as she sat on the floor in front of the dollhouse.

I lowered myself onto the couch. "It's good to be back."

"I wish you could stay longer."

I surprised myself by saying, "Me too."

Izzy handed Daphne a doll. "You be the mom."

Daphne smiled. "I can handle that," and then she asked me, "Have you decided what you want to do?"

I thought about Marley's offer and Aiden's promise to be there for me. "I don't know."

"You have time to figure things out. My life has changed so much this year, and it wasn't always easy, but I wouldn't have wanted it to happen any other way."

If I'd stayed at work, I'd be too busy to think about the bigger picture, like what I wanted. I was starting to think that working in an office and flying from one hotel to the other wasn't living my best life. Being here helped me see that my life could be fuller.

Here, I could enjoy the time with my family and think about

what was important. Work wasn't at the top of the list anymore. Especially when it didn't give me the same passion as working on the inn did.

CHAPTER 11

AIDEN

I fixed a sink in one of the guest rooms. When I was satisfied that it wasn't leaking anymore, I changed the designation for the room in the system to available. After that, I fielded a few requests for extra towels and toiletries. Then the night slowed down.

I wanted to stay occupied. I wasn't ready to go to my apartment yet. I was hoping to see how Fiona felt after dinner with her family. She'd been so nervous about the visit home, even though she'd been once before. I almost offered to go with her, but her brothers would immediately think something was up. There'd be no reason for me to be there. I wasn't friends with any of the Calloways. Not like I was with the Monroes.

Finally, I sat on the front porch, admiring the tree and wondering how this became my life. I'd gone from living in a trailer on the back of the property to owning this place. Even though Marley had inherited the inn because Gram didn't think I could run it while deployed, Marley had added me to the deed when I moved home.

I hadn't paid for the inn, but it felt good to own something. The inn was my legacy even if I felt like an outsider in it growing up. That had nothing to do with my grandmother but my parents who never failed to remind me that the inn wasn't ours. Grandma would never give it to us. That I shouldn't expect a handout, even though that's exactly what they'd been getting their whole lives.

They asked Gram for the trailer and money. She'd given it to them because she wanted me and my sister to be taken care of.

I must have nodded off in the chair because the next thing I knew, lights were shining in my eyes. I straightened. Was it Fiona coming home?

Fiona closed her car door and made her way up the porch steps.

"How was it?" I asked her, regretting my decision as soon as her hand went to her chest.

"You startled me."

I stood and moved toward her. "Sorry. I just wanted to see how you were doing."

She smiled, and I could see that she was more relaxed than before. "Can we sit on the swing?"

"Of course." It was our favorite place to sit when we hung out here as teens. My parents rarely came to the inn itself, saying Gram didn't want our family lurking around. My mom's favorite thing to taunt us with was that everyone thought we were trash.

We settled on the swing, and I pushed off with my foot to move it.

"I forgot how my brothers teased each other. And it's nice to see Jameson more settled."

"Is he the one that's a firefighter?" I'd heard a little about her brothers over the years, mainly how most of them were in law enforcement.

"And he substitute teaches at the middle school. He said that they are in desperate need of teachers, and apparently the kids love him."

"Middle school kids love him?"

Daphne smiled. "That's what he says, and I believe it. He's the brother that's charming. The rest of them didn't get that same trait. Apparently, Jameson fills in for bus drivers too."

"How does he have time for all of that?"

Fiona frowned. "I probably should be worried about him doing too much, but I'm just so happy he figured out what he wanted to do with his life; I can't give him a hard time."

"Your brothers aren't your responsibility."

Fiona sighed. "I know, but I've always worried about them. Especially since Mom died. I had her for nineteen years, but they didn't. I know Teddy and Wes kept an eye on our younger siblings."

"You don't have to worry."

"I don't think you ever stop worrying about your family."

"You're probably right." I thought about Marley and how I worried about her when I was deployed. I relied on her and Gram's letters to feel like I was on the right path. Occasionally, Gram would tell me how Fiona was doing. It hurt to read that Fiona had moved on, but at the same time, she'd graduated from college and had a successful career. That's what I wanted for her.

"It was nice. I'm glad I went."

I felt better knowing that she was okay. "Good."

"I'm no closer to knowing what I want to do with my life, but I like spending time with my family. There's something about being able to swing by for family dinner night, or to watch Izzy for Cole and Daphne so they can go out."

I was almost afraid to ask, "Do you want to move closer to home?"

"My job takes me all over the place. I have to travel to whatever hotel needs my help but my home base is in Chicago."

"You like traveling?" I continued to use my foot to push the swing.

"At first, I did. I thought I'd be able to see all these cities, but you end up just working all the time. Then I'm exhausted from the travel."

I wished she was ready for a more relaxed lifestyle. But I couldn't push her. It had to be her decision.

Fiona stood. "Thanks for listening to me, but I should get to bed. We have another full day tomorrow."

I stood and followed her inside. "

There was something intimate about walking Fiona to her room. It wasn't something I'd been able to do when we dated. I didn't get an opportunity to knock on her door, talk to her dad, and be grilled by her brothers. Then kiss her on her porch at the end of the night. I never thought I'd missed out on anything until now.

Back then, I didn't think I was good enough to meet a girl's parents. That no one would want me to show up on their doorstep to take out their daughter. But things were different now.

When we reached her door, Fiona paused and turned to face me. "Thank you for being there for me tonight. You didn't have to."

My heart squeezed at the grateful look on her face. I reached out to cup her jaw, wishing I could lean in and touch my lips to hers. Instead, I let my hand drop away. "Anytime you need me, I'll be there."

I expected her to argue with me, to say I was the one who'd already walked away. I wasn't there when she needed me. But instead, she merely nodded, then turned to open her door. "Good night, Aiden."

"Night, Fiona." I fisted my hands so that I wouldn't knock on her door and kiss her like I wanted to. We were slowly easing into a friendship, but there was no way she was ready for anything more.

A few days later, they were calling for a big snowstorm to come in earlier than expected. Most of the guests were checking out early, cancelling their stay, or pushing back their check-in date. It sucked, but I couldn't control the weather.

There was a lot of excitement in the air about the impending storm.

I'd kept busy with Fiona in the bowling area, building the new shelves. She was my assistant, and every so often I lost her when she consulted with Marley or Heath. Heath had brought in a crew to start work on the theater.

We hoped to open the theater sometime in the New Year. I would have loved to schedule a private showing around Christmas for us and maybe the Monroes. For now I kept those plans to myself.

"Do you want to go to your dad's for a few days?"

"Why would I do that?" Fiona asked as she continued to measure and mark the wood. She measured, and I cut; it was a good routine we'd established. It had the added benefit of me getting to work closely with her.

"The storms coming in. You might get stuck here for a day or two."

Fiona paused what she was doing and looked up at me. "You want me to stay in my dad's house."

"You said Daphne's cottage was available."

"Yeah, but I'd be by myself."

I checked my phone when I got an email notification. "The last guest just checked out early, and all the incoming ones have delayed or cancelled their reservations."

"Are you saying we'll be here by ourselves?" Fiona asked.

I nodded. "If you stay here, we can continue working."

Fiona smiled. "Let's do that. Not that I don't love my family, but it doesn't make sense to stay at the cottage by myself when I can help you here."

"This project isn't interfering with your ability to spend time with your family, is it?"

Fiona shook her head. "You know, I see them most evenings."

When another notification buzzed on my phone, I pulled it out again.

> The family is going through the light display tonight. It will be a private event. We're closing the farm because of the storm. You want to come and invite Fiona?

Heath had already left for the day, and we were working late. "Heath wants to know if we want to see the light display tonight. It will just be the Monroes."

"Are you sure they want me to come?"

"Heath specifically invited you." I showed her the text exchange.

"Will Daphne be there?"

"I can ask."

> Are Cole and Daphne going?

> They don't want to venture out if the storm comes earlier than expected. They don't want to get stuck.

"It will just be the Monroes who live on the farm."

> If Fiona is worried, tell her not to be. Everyone knows I invited her.

I tilted the screen toward Fiona, and she leaned in to read it.

Fiona blew out a breath. "Maybe this will ease some of the tension between the families. Daphne said there's been a sense of competition. Then when Emmett found out about Cole's relationship with her, he was upset."

"I don't get it. From what it sounds like, the Monroes set out to make their business more profitable. The Calloway farm is closer to town, so it's more convenient for customers. The Monroes were trying to draw people to their farm with the promise of an experience. Marley came up with a lot of new ideas for marketing, and I think it's working. They opened the shop, and they have various events, like movie night and an Easter egg hunt."

"My brothers were grumbling about the low turnout this year. I think we're going to have to do something different going forward."

"Maybe you can help them with that?"

"I consult on hotel management. I don't know anything about running a tree farm. Plus, I don't want to take any of the ideas the Monroes are using."

"It's just business. I think you might be able to help."

"I've been listening to Marley's podcast. She's so inspiring. I love how she empowers women to be better with money. I can see how it gives them more confidence and a sense of power."

"I listened to every one."

Fiona's eyes widened. "You did?"

"Marley's my sister. I wanted to see what she was doing, and I enjoyed her message. It helped me go through some of my baggage from my parents and release some of those old beliefs. I realized that family isn't just blood. It's who you chose to surround yourself with."

"I love my family. I had a good upbringing. But Marley is making me think about what I really want out of life. Do I want to work somewhere I'm not appreciated?"

I grunted in agreement.

Fiona tipped her head to the side. "Do I want to have a boss at all?

"It doesn't feel good not to be appreciated, and I have to say, I'm enjoying being my own boss. I partner with Marley, but we work together well."

Fiona looked down at the board she'd been measuring. "She's giving me something to think about."

"You could talk to her about it. I'm sure she'd give you advice."

Fiona carefully marked the board with a pencil where I should cut it. "Marley's a coach. That's her job. I wouldn't want to take advantage and ask for free advice."

"She's my sister. Feel free to take advantage."

Fiona handed me the board, and I stacked it on my to-be-cut pile. "Besides, she's the one who offered me a position here. I'd be working for her."

"She offered you a position in a consultant capacity. Independent contractor kind of thing."

"She wants me to work here. Her opinion might be biased."

I took off my goggles and put away the saw. "I think she could advise you even though she wants you here. She's good at seeing those things."

Fiona chewed on her lower lip. "It's easier for us to give someone else advice. It's harder for us to see what to do in our own lives."

"True. You ready to grab some dinner and head to the light display? It's late."

"We should go before the snow starts. Is it crazy to say I'm excited? I've seen snow in Chicago and when I've traveled, but it's not the same when you live in a city."

"Not at all."

We put away our tools and materials and headed up the stairs. I turned off the lights when we got to the top. "Are you saying you want to play in the snow?"

A smile curved over her face. "I think I do."

"I can make that happen. We have sleds and even a snowmobile."

Fiona raised a brow. "Just one?"

"You can ride with me."

Fiona settled on the stool. It had become our routine to cook a few times a week and heat up leftovers the other days. I'd offer to order something, but I liked the time we spent together. Each day, she opened up a little more.

Fiona grinned as she rested her elbows on the counter. "I feel like a little girl again, excited for a day off of school."

"You promised we'd get some work done. It will be nice not to have any guests to attend to."

"How's Charlotte working out?"

I set the container of pork chops and potatoes on the counter. "I have to admit, she's amazing. She's so good with the guests. They love her."

Fiona gave me a look. "You should have hired someone a long time ago."

"Yeah, but I think it's Charlotte I like. We could have gotten someone who wasn't good with people or didn't show up on time. But she's amazing. She comes in early, works late, puts out coffee and that flavored water pitcher. Then she even arranged for a baker to provide afternoon snacks. And like I said, she's so good with the customers. She has an upbeat, positive personality. Always quick with a compliment and a suggestion for a restaurant or a tour in town. We've sold more ornaments and paintings with her manning the front counter."

"I love that for you. You deserve to have good help."

"I just hope the hotel continues to turn a profit, or we won't be able to keep her employed."

"You're doing all the right things. The customers will come. I looked at the reviews online last night."

I plated the food and put one into the microwave, hitting Cook, then turned to face her. "There aren't that many."

Daphne scrolled through something on her phone. "They're all positive though. *Quaint inn just outside of Annapolis!* Here's another: *We enjoyed our stay. Top-notch service. My kids loved the cookies served in the afternoons. Unique touches like this make me want to come back.*" And then there are few who specifically mention the holiday decor and proximity to a Christmas tree farm. *Perfect for a holiday visit with the family. Will be back!*"

I cleared my throat. "I try not to look at those. I'm afraid of what they might say."

Fiona put her phone down. "Everyone who posted had a positive experience."

"That's good to know."

The first plate heated, I removed it, put the second inside the microwave, and hit the button to cook it.

"You're building something amazing here. You're going to get tourists and locals who want a romantic evening away. You're family friendly too. I saw the reviews initially because Marley posted them on social media."

"What did she do?" I asked as I placed a plate in front of her.

"She posted videos on social media. Each slide has a different review. These are perfect for social proof." Fiona showed me the video, and I was surprised by how well done it was.

"Thank God for Marley. I wouldn't be able to do that kind of thing without her."

"Maybe not. But you could hire someone who's good with marketing and social media."

I tipped my head to the side. "Someone like you?"

"I consult on marketing for hotels too. I don't usually create the posts and videos myself. But these are great. Marley's doing an amazing job showcasing the inn."

"It wasn't my dream to run the inn, but when Marley said she was going to stay here and make a go of it, I wanted to do it with her. It felt like I needed to do it."

"You wanted to do this for your grandmother and your sister?"

"I think so." I ate slowly, savoring the taste of the food and the feeling of being with someone who understood me so well. Maybe this was why no one else fit for me. Fiona knew me better than anyone. We'd only dated a couple of years, but it was enough to know each other inside and out. That's why I should've known she'd take my rejection hard.

I just hadn't anticipated her asking me to marry her.

CHAPTER 12

FIONA

I'd spent more time with Aiden these last few days than I had when we were dating. Back then, we had stolen moments when we'd sneak out and talk in the bed of his truck or make out for a few minutes before I had to go inside.

But now, we'd been working together, sharing meals, and I was in the cab of his truck on our way to the Monroes. It smelled overwhelmingly of him: cedar and all man. I wanted to reach over and hold his hand like we had when we were kids.

But we weren't dating. We weren't anything. Coworkers. Maybe friends. What if we reconnected just for my trip? Could I handle a physical relationship without losing my heart to him? I'd started to suspect I'd never truly gotten over him because I got all tingly when he got too close. It was getting harder to hide my reaction to him.

Thankfully, he hadn't hugged me again. I wouldn't survive another encounter where our bodies were touching. I'd grab his neck and bring his mouth to mine. I let out a shaky breath.

Aiden glanced over at me, his hand resting on the top of the wheel. "Are you nervous to hang out with the Monroes?"

If I thought him driving a truck was sexy, I was in trouble.

"Not really. I'm not involved in whatever's going on with the farm."

"You've always been confident in yourself." His tone was full of admiration.

"That's a good thing, right?" I watched his face for his reaction.

His lips quirked. "I always found it sexy as hell."

"Are you talking about when we dated before?" I shifted on the seat so that my knee was on the cushion and I was facing him.

Aiden glanced over at me quickly before he turned his attention to the road. "You knew I was attracted to you."

"Yeah, because of my looks maybe, but not—"

Aiden interrupted me and said, "You think I was that shallow? That I wasn't attracted to you as a person? You stood up for me in third grade when one of the kids called me trailer trash. You said, and I quote, *You think you're better than him?* And when he just laughed, you yelled, and I quote, *Shut the fuck up.*"

I shook my head, embarrassed at that outburst. "I got into trouble for that one. Dad hated when any of us swore. But Teddy said I should have punched him."

Aiden's lips twitched. "I bet you could have."

I smiled softly at the memory. "My brothers taught me to defend myself."

Aiden shook his head. "Like I said. Sexy as hell."

Warmth flushed through my body, and tingles ran up and down my spine. I don't know why, but his admission was a huge turn-on for me. Some guys were intimidated by me, but Aiden liked it. "Well, that's good to know."

He reached over and touched my thigh, squeezing it before retreating to his side of the cab. "You know you're attractive."

"That wasn't exactly what you said though. You tied it to my strength instead of just my beauty." I had this primal urge to straddle his lap and grind myself over his cock. Because I had a feeling he was hard just talking about his attraction to me. We'd always burned hot as teens, but now that we were adults, I was interested to see if it was even better.

He probably learned a few new things on the way. Goosebumps erupted over my skin at the possibility.

"I thought you were pretty. I still do. But I'm attracted to you because of your personality, how you hold yourself, and how good of a person you are."

I winced. "You still think I'm good when I left my family after my mother died?"

Aiden shook his head. "You didn't leave. You were away at college."

I huffed out a breath. "I didn't come home."

"You were there for the funeral. Besides, no one wanted you to quit school." Aiden reached over and touched my hand. "You didn't do anything wrong. You were grieving, and there's no wrong way to do that."

"If you say so," I conceded knowing my family had said same something similar.

Aiden raised a brow as he turned onto the farm's lane, drove past the white farmhouse.

"I love these lights," I said as I admired the poles on the side of the road where strings of lights hung.

"Heath said they put them up after their father's death because their mom was walking the grounds late at night."

"Wow. That's just—"

"Beautiful?" Aiden asked as he parked behind a line of trucks all pulled off to the side of the road.

I looked at the lights, then at him. "Yeah."

"You ready to see the lights?"

"Let's do it," I said as we opened the doors and got out. Aiden met me at the hood and held his hand out to me. "I don't want you to fall. The terrain is uneven."

"Are you sure?" I asked him, wondering what the Monroes would think to see us holding hands.

"Heath and Marley know about our history, and who cares about the rest?"

The Monroes weren't our family. It was just Marley and mine I was concerned about. "True."

For one night, I could enjoy the feel of his hand in mine. I could pretend that we were more than we were. That we were dating each other and didn't need to keep it a secret.

When I rested my hand in his, he squeezed it briefly before we started walking. It was dark out so we could see the glow of lights up ahead.

"Talon built the lights. He designs light fixtures, and he's been featured in various magazines. We've been in talks with him to design something for the basement."

"Marley said not to worry about the lights. That he would make something that would fit the space."

"His work is impressive and unique. I'm excited to see what he comes up with."

"Me too." The renovation would go on when I moved back to the city. The thought made my heart jump. I didn't like the idea of not knowing what was going on here, not being involved in the final decisions, the decor, and eventually the grand opening. The project had become important to me. It felt like I was a part of something bigger than anything I'd ever done before.

When we reached the crowd of people, Marley and Heath broke away from the group and moved toward us. Aiden dropped my hand, and I tried not to let that hurt.

"You came," Marley said as she pulled me into a hug.

Marley was great at making me feel like I belonged. "I can't wait to see the lights. I don't get much time to do holiday things in the city."

"Well, you can't avoid them here. You're surrounded by Christmas."

Heath clapped Aiden on the back. "Thanks for coming."

Aiden nodded, and we moved forward with the rest of the group. If anyone thought it was weird I was here, they didn't mention it. But then again, I was staying at the inn. It made sense for Aiden to invite me. Especially since we worked together.

I had the whole explanation in my head in case anyone asked about me, but it wasn't necessary. Heath introduced me to his brothers—who I knew vaguely from school—their significant others, and their nieces, Addy and Ember. Lori rode in a golf cart with Talon and Holly.

Occasionally, Talon would pause and tell us a story about why he came up with the design or what he was thinking when he made one thing or the other. The display was separated into different categories, like holiday scenes and nursery rhymes. It was interesting to hear how his mind worked as an artist.

It felt similar to what we'd done with the renovation. We were inspired by something or the other. For me, it was nostalgia. I could remember going to the movie theater with Aiden and cuddling in the back to watch whatever was playing. There, we didn't have to hide. Even though that's exactly what we were doing.

Aiden didn't hold my hand again, but he stayed close, occasionally touching my elbow or my lower back. His proximity had all my nerves on edge. I wanted him to touch me, to kiss me. Being this close to him wasn't a good idea, and I was about to be snowed in with him at the inn with no other guests.

"Are you okay?" Aiden leaned in close to ask.

I sucked in a breath. "Yeah, I was just thinking about the storm."

Aiden looked up at the sky, and I admired the scruff on his jaw. "You can feel it in the air."

We'd reached the end of the display, where a Santa popped out of a present. The movement was neat and captured my attention for a few seconds. The girls had already seen the display and were chasing each other around.

"Can you imagine yourself settling down one day, maybe even having kids of your own?"

"You already asked me that," I said, my back stiff.

"Maybe it's too soon, but I wanted to see if being here changed your perspective on life." Aiden's voice was soft.

He wasn't pushing me; he was genuinely curious.

I shrugged. "I'm not sure." I knew what I was supposed to do. Go back to my apartment and job in the city and work hard. Look for a job where my boss appreciated me, but what if I never found that? What if I felt lonelier than ever when I returned? What if I wasn't fulfilled by my job anymore? Now that I'd seen how people lived here, living on Christmas tree farms, at the inn…

Aiden's hand ghosted down my arm, and his fingers tangled with mine. "You feel it, don't you?"

"How magical it is here?"

A smile spread over Aiden's face.

"You two coming to the bonfire at the main house?" Heath asked us.

Aiden didn't drop my hand, and my heart pitter-pattered when he said we could come for a bit.

Heath grinned. "I heard all the guests checked out. It's just you two in that big inn. You want to stay with us?"

"Nah. We're good where we are," Aiden said.

Heath and Marley used to live at the inn too, but when Cole bought his own place, they moved back into their cabin here. Charlotte stayed in their guest room.

Heath gestured around the property. "Each one of us built a cabin."

"I'm surprised you can all live here without fighting."

"Oh, we do that too. But we like being close. We want our kids to grow up together, to be raised the way we were. We loved running these fields." Heath watched Ember and Addy as they giggled and chased each other.

"See you there," Aiden said as we walked toward his truck.

We had to go through the whole light display a second time to get to our vehicles.

This time, everyone talked among themselves, the couples holding hands, or with one arm flung over a shoulder. It was nice. I wished my family got together like this. It seemed like we were never in the same place at the same time.

It couldn't necessarily be helped, but I didn't have to be the one not making an effort to come home. I could still visit even when I went back to work. But I knew that was unrealistic. I traveled most weekends to hotels. Now I'd need to report to my ex who was hired after me and didn't have the vision I had. It would be awkward at best.

My chest tightened.

"What are you thinking about?" Aiden asked when we were inside the cab of his truck.

"Work."

Aiden patted my hand. "No thoughts about work tonight. We have a bonfire to get to, s'mores to eat, and a snowstorm to experience."

"That sounds nice." I relaxed into the cushions of the seat, watching Aiden as he put the truck in gear and drove behind the line of other trucks down the hill toward the main house.

"By the time you have to go back, you won't want to leave."

"Is that your plan?" I teased him.

He glanced over at me, and his expression was more serious than I expected. "Would you be upset if it was? I just want you to be happy."

I let out a breath. "No."

"Good," Aiden said as he parked and we got out, meeting

everyone behind the house by the fire pit. Knox and Emmett threw wood on the fire, and Lori went inside with Sarah and Ireland to grab the fixings for s'mores.

When Aiden returned to my side, I asked, "Are you sure that Emmett doesn't mind that I'm here?"

"He might, but he won't say anything. From what Heath has said to me, they've talked to him about accepting Daphne and her family."

I tipped my head to the side. "He's still not okay with it?"

"Probably not. But he'll get over it, and if he says anything to you, I have your back." Aiden threw his arm over my shoulder and pulled me into his chest. It could have been construed as a friendly gesture, but it felt like a claiming. My hand touched his chest to steady myself, and I felt his heart beating under my palm.

"You see what you do to me? What you still do to me?" Aiden's voice was low and husky. I wanted to suggest that we get out of here, but we'd only just arrived, and maybe I'd misconstrued his statement.

"What are you two doing over here by yourselves?" Heath held out beers for us.

"Thank you," I murmured as I accepted the bottle.

"Fiona's worried that Emmett is having an issue with her being here, seeing that she's a Calloway." Aiden tipped his head in Emmett's direction.

Heath frowned, then looked across the fire at Emmett, who'd picked up Ember and was tickling her. When Heath turned back to us, he said, "Honestly? He has more of an issue with your brothers. We'll handle him if he gets out of line. Marley works with you, so you're here as our friends."

Interesting that he hadn't said I was here as Aiden's date or guest. He had to be wondering if working together was changing things between us. I spent more time thinking about it than I wanted to.

Heath dipped his chin. "The offer stands if you want to chill here instead of at the inn."

Aiden cleared his throat. "I need to clear the snow and make sure things are running smoothly. There aren't any power outages, that kind of thing."

"We can keep working on the shelves in the bowling alley too," I added.

Heath raised his bottle slightly. "I have the bowling alley mechanic coming out at the end of the week. Hopefully, the snow's cleared out by then."

"Should be."

Heath looked around the group. "Let me know if you need help."

"You have enough to keep up with here," Aiden gestured around at the farm.

Heath turned his attention to Aiden. "Yeah, but I have four brothers. You just have yourself."

"That's what I'm used to. I'll get it done."

I wondered if Aiden was used to relying solely on himself. Surely, he relied on his fellow soldiers in the military. But at home, he went back to his old ways, doing everything himself.

"We'll let you know if we need anything."

"Enjoy your evening." Heath winked. "And the storm."

"Does he think something's going on between us?" I asked Aiden.

"I think he wants everyone to be paired off. He fixed things with Marley. He thinks we can do the same."

"Things are different with us. I live in Chicago, and you live here. Neither one of us wants to move." Except I wasn't so sure about that anymore.

"Marley lived in California. But she had an online business that could be run from anywhere, and she fell in love with the farm, Heath, and his family. I don't have that kind of pull. I just own an inn and have a sister. No parents I'd want to introduce you to, and my grandmother already passed away."

"I had a great relationship with your grandmother. Did you know she wrote me when I was in school?"

"She gave me updates on your progress but she never said how she knew."

"Maybe she didn't know if you'd want to know she kept in touch with me. But I loved your grandmother, and she's still here." I touched his chest over his heart. "And in the inn. She's in everything you do there."

Aiden cleared his throat. "I like that."

We considered each other for a few seconds and then a flurry fell between us.

"It's snowing," I said as I lifted my face to the sky.

The flurries quickly turned into big, fat flakes.

"The weather app says it's going to come down at a rate of an inch an hour when it starts," Emmett read from his phone.

"You two better head back to the inn before it gets worse," Heath called over to us.

Aiden stepped forward, touching Heath's shoulder, promising to see him soon. Then he hugged Marley. I did the same, and we were inside his truck with the heat cranking in no time.

I turned on the radio, searching for holiday music. "I'm looking forward to being snowed in."

Aiden smiled over at me. "I am too."

CHAPTER 13

FIONA

"The new projector arrived. Want to see if it works?" Aiden glanced over at me as we headed home.

Home. To the inn. Where I was staying temporarily for the holidays. "Can we watch it in the theater?"

Aiden's lips twitched. "Of course. Where else would we test it out?"

"That would be amazing." And remind me of all the times that we snuck into the theater, making out in the back row. I'd had such hope for a future with Aiden.

"I knew you'd be up for it," Aiden said as he turned onto the lane for the inn. He parked next to my rental car. The rest of the lot was empty.

"I can't believe we have an entire inn to ourselves," I said as we sat in the cabin admiring the lights.

"It hasn't been empty since Marley renovated."

"Let's enjoy it before the guests come back." I opened the door and slid out.

We met on the porch. Aiden unlocked the door and pushed it open for me. "You first, my lady." Then he did a little bow, and I couldn't help but giggle.

This was the Aiden I remembered from high school. He was fun when he let go of the mask he wore in front of others. I understood that he hadn't trusted the other kids not to say something mean about his living situation or his family, and he always defended Marley. He had to be tough. But with me, he could just be himself. I stepped inside, looking forward to more time to ourselves.

"Let's grab some snacks." Aiden led the way into the kitchen, and opened a cupboard, revealing a jar of popcorn kernels, Junior Mints, and bags of M&M's and Skittles."

"Did you plan this?" I asked lightly.

"When I heard that it was going to snow, I might have considered reenacting our movie nights."

"This time, we don't have to sneak around."

"Or make out in the back row," Aiden said as he filled my arms with the candy, then grabbed the container of kernels for himself.

I felt almost giddy as we headed downstairs. "Hopefully, we'll have power."

"There's a generator."

"We can enjoy the movie and have heat."

"There's a hot tub in my apartment we can check out later."

"That would be nice." I dumped the candy on a table we'd been using in the back of the room for our things. "I'm going to grab some sodas."

Aiden nodded. "The projector equipment isn't in, so I brought down the portable one we use in the great room. I'll get the movie running. Any requests?"

I thought about it for a few seconds. "Something holiday related. I could go for a Christmas movie."

"One Christmas movie coming up." Aiden flashed me a grin, and I wondered if I'd be able to keep my hands to myself while the movie played.

I went upstairs and stuck my head in the fridge for a few seconds, trying to cool my overheated body.

There was a handsome man waiting for me downstairs. He hurt me, but I didn't see any traces of that guy now. He was steady and true, and it made me wonder if I could let go and enjoy myself with him for one night.

I knew I was being foolish, thinking I could do anything with Aiden and keep my heart separate, but I wanted him too much to stay away from him.

I grabbed a couple of sodas. In the theater, the opening credits for *Miracle on 34th Street* were paused on the screen. There was a small popcorn maker on the table now.

"Did you buy this recently?" I asked him, not remembering having seen it before.

"I thought it would be good for nights when we don't want to use the concession stand."

Except it wasn't big enough for the Monroe family much less a packed theater. What was he thinking when he purchased it? That he'd be using this for a date night with someone else, or was he thinking about me? "Who did you intend to use it with?"

"I'm not seeing anyone if that's what you're thinking about," Aiden said as he scooped kernels and dropped them into the machine.

My shoulders tensed. "I wasn't."

Aiden assessed me for a second before pouring the butter. "I thought we could use it when we tested the projector."

He'd bought the candy and the popcorn machine for us to spend this time together. It was like reenacting our dates as kids. Except this time, we were the only two people in the theater. "Are you ready to watch? I have a remote for the projector."

"Well, that's handy." I grabbed the sodas and candy and followed him down the aisle to the middle of the theater.

"Does this work?" Aiden asked.

"This is perfect." We sat next to each other, arranging our food on our laps. "Should we add cup holders? Or will that not look right with the old chairs?"

"People expect it. No matter the age of the theater."

He hit Play on the movie, and we settled back, eating popcorn out of one bowl. Each time our fingers brushed, I couldn't help but sneak a peek at his face. Usually, he was focused on the screen, but every once in a while, he winked at me.

When we'd eaten our fill of popcorn, we moved onto the Junior Mints. "This tastes like our teen years, if that makes sense."

Aiden chuckled. "You know what it reminds me of?"

"No. What?" I asked despite my better judgment.

He set the box of candy and my soda on the ground, and he cupped my face. "It reminds me of how you used to taste like popcorn, butter, and mint when we kissed."

I sucked in a breath. Was he going to kiss me?

His eyes heated. "If you don't want me to kiss you, tell me now."

I closed my eyes briefly, and when I opened them again, I said, "Do it."

He lowered his lips to mine, and his tongue swept into my mouth. His hand moved from my chin to my hair, where his fingers tangled in the strands.

There was a hand rest between us, so I moved, careful to avoid the soda cans and bowl of popcorn, placing one knee on either side of his thighs. "I remember there being more room when we were kids."

Aiden looked down at his spread thighs. "I think we were smaller."

He was smaller back then. He'd filled out in a way that made my heart race. This time, I touched his chin, tipping it up, and kissed him, slowly, sensually as if I was saying hello again. It was a coming together, a meeting of our bodies after so many years apart.

We kissed, his hands on my ass, pulling me down to grind against his hardening cock. When he tugged on my hair, I whimpered against his lips. I angled my neck so that he could kiss and suck on the skin. "I want you."

"I want you too. Do you want to finish this movie?" Aiden breathed across my skin, and I didn't care about the movie. But the sides of the chairs were biting into my knee, and I knew we couldn't comfortably do anything in these chairs.

I sighed, need swirling in my core, but I moved my leg off his and settled in my chair. I looked at the movie that still played. Santa was on trial.

Aiden adjusted himself in his jeans, then reached across the armrest to interlace his fingers with mine. I rested my free hand over our joined ones. Warmth settled in my chest. I wanted to stay here all night. When the characters found their dream house, and the credits rolled, I didn't feel tired.

Aiden turned off the movie and stood. "Let's clean up, and we can check out my hot tub."

"That sounds nice." My muscles had been sore lately because of the physical labor we'd been doing in the bowling alley.

We gathered up the trash and carried it to the kitchen, throwing it away. Aiden turned on the light to the back porch, and we watched the snow fall.

"It's beautiful. But I have a better view in my apartment." His voice was lower, almost hushed as if he were afraid of waking someone, but no one else was here.

"I bet you do," I teased.

Aiden chuckled. "I was talking about the snow."

My lips curled up. "I might have been talking about something else."

Aiden paused in front of his door on the third floor. The

ballroom double doors were firmly closed. "Are you sure you want to do this?"

He wasn't asking if I wanted to come inside; he was telling me he wouldn't be able to keep his hands off me. It was written in his tight muscles and in the heat in his eyes.

"I want this. I want you."

Aiden groaned as he pulled me against him. My arms went around his neck as I pressed my breasts against his hard chest. I wanted him. There was no point in denying myself anymore. We were both adults. We could handle the consequences, the resulting fallout.

His hard cock pressed against my belly.

I pulled back slightly, needing a few seconds to regroup. "Let's check out that hot tub."

His hand slid from my hip, turned the knob, and he pushed the door open. "I don't have a bathing suit for you."

I leaned up on tiptoes and tugged on his earlobe with my teeth. "That sounds perfect."

He growled as he lifted me into his arms, kicking the door shut behind us. My legs went around his hips as he carried me deeper into his apartment. I didn't get a good look at the scenery passing by. I was too focused on the saltiness of his skin as I ran my tongue over it.

He finally set me on the ground. "I can't think straight with your mouth on me."

"That was the idea." I pulled my sweater over my head and unbuttoned my jeans. I pushed them down over my hips, leaving me in a bra and panties.

Aiden quickly followed suit, shucking off his shoes, shoving his jeans down with his black boxer briefs. I pushed his shirt up and over his head.

Aiden Matthews was gloriously naked. I couldn't help but run my hands over the hard planes of his chest, the ridges of his abs, and finally lower. His muscles jumped at my light touch. I licked my lips when my gaze fell to his cock. It was hard, precum beading at the top. I wanted to lick it off.

I lifted my gaze to Aiden, who tapped the lace at my hip. "These have to go."

I hooked my fingers into the sides of my panties. "Do you mean these?"

He cupped my breasts through the lace, flicking his fingers over the hard nubs. "And this."

My breath caught in my throat, and I couldn't remember what I was supposed to be doing. Aiden leaned close and sucked on my earlobe. "Fi, your panties. As much as I love them, I want to see *you*."

The familiar nickname and the emphasis on the word *you* had heat zinging to my core. With trembling fingers, I slipped my panties down my legs and off. I kicked them to the side as Aiden unhooked my bra, and the straps fell.

I expected Aiden to touch my breasts, to maybe suck a nipple into his mouth. I was anxious to feel his tongue on my body. But instead, he reached down to turn on the hot tub. Then the jets. The water was illuminated with green lights.

Aiden held his hand out to me, and I took it, trusting him with my body. I wasn't sure about my heart. But I knew I wanted him. That I wanted him to make me feel good.

I sighed as I slipped into the steaming water.

Before I could find a bench to sit on, Aiden tugged me into his lap. "I'm not done with you."

I felt the tension easing from my body as the water heated me from the outside in. I bit my lip as my pussy bumped against Aiden's cock. He gripped my hips, guiding me to slide over him. Then his head lowered as he sucked a nipple into his mouth.

I held him to me with a hand on his neck. His cock slid through my folds, the tip of it teasing my entrance. He wasn't wearing a condom, and I felt naughty. I wanted to let go and just feel.

Aiden lightly bit my nipple. The resulting electric shock flowed through my body, straight to my core. "I need you."

"I've waited years to be with you again. I'm not going to rush it."

My breath flew out of me in a rush. "I wish you would." I wanted him hard and fast. I wanted to feel him filling me up, making me his.

"I want to play," Aiden said before he sucked the other nipple into his mouth.

I nearly groaned with frustration. This Aiden was different from the one I'd been with when we were teens. He was always game to rush through the foreplay and get to the part where we were joined as one. I loved it. We never took things slow because we didn't have the time, and it was usually uncomfortable in the bed or cab of his truck.

Then Aiden stilled. "Look at the snow coming down."

I hadn't realized it before, but the hot tub was surrounded by floor-to-ceiling windows. Huge flakes came down sideways. "We're going to get a lot of snow if it keeps coming down at this rate."

"I hope so," Aiden said as he ducked his head and sucked on my nipple again.

A thrill shot through me. The storm gave us this time alone, and it felt right to be with Aiden. I wasn't positive he wouldn't hurt me, that this wasn't a one-night thing. But I was determined to not think about the what-ifs.

This time when I moved over him, his tip slipped inside, and we both stilled.

Aiden groaned, the sound reverberating through my body. "I want to slide inside you. But I'm not wearing a condom."

I chewed my lip. "I'm on birth control, and I've been tested."

Aiden's face softened. "I'm clean too."

Did I trust him enough to go without a condom?

"I can get one." Aiden shifted to move me off his lap, but I stopped him with a hand on his chest.

"We don't need one."

"Are you sure?" Aiden asked, his muscles tense with the effort to hold back.

"I trust you."

With a growl, Aiden positioned his cock at my entrance, and I slowly sank down while looking into his eyes. They were filled with awe as if he couldn't believe I was here.

This entire moment felt surreal: the hot tub, the snow, and his bare cock inside me. I slowly lowered myself until I was filled.

"You feel incredible, but I need you to move." Aiden's words were clipped.

With my hands on his shoulders and his on my hips, I moved up. He thrust from beneath me. We moved in an orchestrated rhythm, enjoying the feeling of coming together. My entire body felt flushed; whether it was from the heat of the water or the sex, I wasn't sure.

Aiden kissed me, and I was lost in the moment, his tongue sliding against mine, his cock filling me like only he could. Each time I lowered myself, my clit rubbed against his body, creating delicious friction.

I moved faster, chasing that feeling as the orgasm built inside me.

When Aiden pulled his lips from mine and bit down lightly on my nipple, it was like I detonated. I cried out as he continued to move through the waves of pleasure coursing through me.

His movements sent a second ripple through me. I'd never felt anything like this before. Finally, he drove deep and stilled as he emptied himself into me.

It was primal. It was intimate. This didn't feel like a one-time thing. It felt bigger and more expansive than anything we'd shared before. Was it because we were adults?

His forehead rested against mine as we came down from the high. I tightened my arms around his neck and held on.

Finally, he pulled back slightly to see my face. "I never thought we'd be together like this again."

"I didn't either."

He kissed me softly, erasing any thoughts about this being a one-time thing. "Stay the night. We have the inn to ourselves."

I nodded shakily. "I can do that."

I wanted to do that. I wanted as much as he was willing to give me.

We stayed wrapped up in each other for a while, until our skin wrinkled and the air around us chilled. Eventually, Aiden turned me so we could watch the snow fall. It was the closest I'd ever felt with anyone.

CHAPTER 14

AIDEN

We finally got out of the water. I handed Fiona a heated towel to dry off. I quickly dried off, then pulled on sweats. I went into the living room to throw a few logs onto the fireplace, and then padded into my kitchen to make hot chocolate. We were both quiet, reflective.

I hadn't planned for anything to happen. I couldn't wrap my mind around it, and I suspect she couldn't either.

I heated the milk on the stove, and when it was boiling, I poured it into two mugs, and stirred in the hot chocolate mix we bought for the guests. I dropped a few mini marshmallows on top, then handed her the mug.

"Thank you," Fiona said, blowing air across the top of the liquid.

"Let's sit on the couch." I guided her off the stool and to the couch by the windows where I wrapped us in a cozy throw.

I was enraptured by the snow. It was quiet except for the occasional crackle of the fire and the slap of the flakes against the windowpane.

"I have a feeling if we went outside, it would feel like the snow was covering the earth like a blanket."

"We'll go out tomorrow." I had no desire to leave the warmth of the room, especially since I wasn't sure the backup generator would work if the power went out and how long we'd be snowed in. I had plenty of food and wood because I'd stocked up for the week.

Fiona rested against my chest, her head tucked under my chin.

I never thought we'd be together like this. Our relationship as teens was different. There was no cuddling on couches or baths to be shared. This felt better in a lot of ways. We could spend more time together.

"You don't think we screwed up, do you?" Fiona asked so softly I wasn't sure I heard her right.

I tensed. "Does it feel like we did?"

She was quiet for a few seconds, and then she lifted her head to see my face. "It felt right."

"How could something that felt right be wrong?" Even though it felt good, I couldn't help but worry about what it meant. Fiona was leaving soon to go back to her life, and I couldn't forget that.

"I don't think it's wrong. I'm just not sure there will ever be a right time for us."

I didn't contradict her because it was the same feeling I was having. Our timing sucked. And that might be the reason why we weren't meant to be together. But we could enjoy this time we had now.

When Fiona got sleepy, I carried her into my bedroom, watching the snow fall as she slept with her head resting on my shoulder. I didn't want to close my eyes because I didn't want to miss any minute of being with her.

I'd dreamed of nights like these, holding her close. I wasn't sure I'd ever stopped loving her. But it was too soon, and I wasn't sure she'd ever be ready to hear that.

Eventually, I couldn't keep my eyes open anymore.

I woke a few hours later to a dark room and Fiona placing light kisses on my abdomen. Her other hand pushed my sweats down. I helped her shove them off so my cock sprang free.

Even though I wasn't entirely awake, my dick was on board with Fiona's plans. She encircled the base with her hand and pumped.

My hips shot off the bed, and I fisted the sheets to stop myself from touching her.

"Please touch me."

Hesitantly, I stroked her hair with my hand, loving the feel of the silky strands.

"I want to know you're touching me," Fiona said as she licked the head.

I gripped her hair more firmly, a steady weight on her head without pushing her.

Her eyes fluttered closed in pure pleasure as she sucked me inside her mouth.

"I love your mouth on me," I said, my voice tight.

She hummed around my dick as she continued to lick and suck and jerk me with her hands. The sensations were too much. I was on sensory overload, and when she sucked me deep, swallowing around the head, I couldn't hold back. I shot my load into the back of her mouth. When she pulled off, I sighed. "I'm sorry. I should have warned you."

"It was perfect," Fiona said, and I had a feeling she was talking about more than a blow job.

"I want to taste you." We hadn't had a chance to do this earlier, and I wanted it. I wanted to show her how good I could make her feel. We experimented as teens, but I was more experienced in pleasuring a woman now.

I flipped her so that she was on her back, her legs spread wide. I held her ass in my hands as I lifted her to my mouth. I breathed her in, wanting to feast on her.

Fiona raised up on her elbows. "I want to watch you."

I growled deep in my throat as I licked, keeping my gaze on hers. Fiona bit her lip, and her arms trembled as she struggled to stay upright.

"You taste better than I remembered."

Fiona made a choking sound, and I sucked her clit, using a finger to enter her. Her head dropped back, and I alternated circling her clit with my tongue and sucking on it.

She finally fell back, her hips lifting, and when I used two fingers, she let go, her muscles spasming around me. I wanted to always give her pleasure. To worship her. To make her mine.

It was dangerous to think like that because she wasn't mine anymore. I wiped my mouth on the sheet, then moved up her body, dropping kisses as I went. Then I gathered her into my arms, her ass nestled against my dick. I was semihard but wasn't pressed to fuck her again. This had always been about more than the physical. It felt amazing to be with her like this again. But it was so much more.

I enjoyed spending my days with her, working and talking about the future of the inn. But this wasn't her home, she didn't work for me, and we sure as hell weren't together. She had her own life, far away from mine, and she was happy there.

She hadn't said anything other than she didn't feel comfortable in her parents' home, but I suspected she didn't want to move back because of the memories. One steamy night wasn't going to change anything, even if I wanted it to.

Her head rested on my bicep, and I felt her breath evening out a few minutes later. The next time I woke, the bed was empty, and the room was lighter. I turned to see the gray sky and the flakes coming down, smaller and slower than last night but still at a steady pace.

Just when I thought that I should go in search of Fiona, wondering if she'd retreated to her own room, the bed dipped.

"You're awake," Fiona said.

I turned to find her holding two mugs. She set them on the

side table, then kissed me. Warmth flooded my body. I wanted to wake up every morning just like this. "Morning."

Her lips quirked. "Good morning. I can't believe the snow is still coming down."

"I think they said there would be two bands of heavy snow."

"This must be the second. But it's smaller flakes."

"You want to play outside?" I pulled to a seated position.

A smile spread over her face. "I'd love to."

She handed me the mug of coffee. "But first, caffeine. Then I thought we could have breakfast, and then go outside. I'm starving."

"I can cook for you." I wanted to feed her. It was something I'd never been able to do when we were together. The only kitchen I had was the one in my trailer, and her family didn't know we were dating.

"You know when we were teens, I wasn't embarrassed to be dating you. That's not why I kept us a secret."

Fiona was strong-willed even back then. She knew what she wanted, and she didn't want her family in her business. I'd respected that. "I never once thought you were embarrassed."

Relief filtered over her face. "Oh, good. I was worried about that."

"If I thought you were, I wouldn't have continued dating you." I'd felt her love, as young and naive as we'd been. We thought it could stand the test of time, growing together.

Fiona sipped her coffee. "I never thought we'd end up here."

I chuckled. "You thought we could work together and keep things platonic."

"Didn't you?" Fiona asked, genuinely curious.

"I wasn't sure that this was a good idea. With you living somewhere else and me invested here at the inn."

She reached over and curled her fingers around mine. "Let's not talk about the future. I want to enjoy this and however many days we have together."

I let out the breath I'd been holding. "I want that too."

Fiona grinned, looking so much younger, more like the girl she'd been in high school. Then her stomach rumbled.

"Let me feed you." I gave her a smacking kiss on her lips, reveling in my freedom to touch and kiss her whenever I wanted. Then I lifted off the bed, searching for the sweats we'd removed last night. I pulled them on, and Fiona smirked.

"It's going to be hard to cook without getting distracted. You can see everything in those," Fiona pointed at my crotch where sure enough my semihard dick was visible.

I caught her wrist, encircling it with my hand. "Behave."

Fiona threw back her head and laughed.

I let go of her, walking out of the bedroom and into the kitchen. I loved seeing her so carefree.

She followed a few seconds later, holding both of our mugs, and set them on the counter. "What are you making?"

"Pancakes. We're going to need the energy."

Fiona rounded the counter and ducked under my arm, her hand on the bare skin of my chest. "Oh, we will. Will we?"

Then she kissed me.

I sucked in a breath. "I can't make breakfast with you doing that."

"I want to taste you." She placed kisses down my chest, then my stomach, pulling the waistband of my sweats over my hips until they pooled at my feet. I stepped out of them and kicked them to the side. She sank to her knees, gripping the base of my cock while she looked up at me.

I braced my hands on the counter, every muscle in my body bunched with the effort of my restraint. I wanted to bend her over and fuck her from behind. I wanted her with an intensity that overwhelmed me. Why did I want her again? Why was it more intense each time we came together?

Emotions swirled around me even as my blood heated with desire.

Fiona gripped the base tight and sucked hard. When she reached into her panties to touch herself, my skin tingled.

I let my head fall back slightly as she took me into her mouth. When I couldn't take it anymore, I hauled her up by her arms. She ripped my T-shirt off over my head, and I tugged her panties down. Then I turned her around to bend over the counter like I'd imagined. I ran a hand down her spine, enjoying the sight of her milky-white skin on display.

I nudged her feet farther apart, her pussy already glistening.

"Are you wet from sucking me?" I asked her, my voice controlled.

She nodded jerkily.

She wanted me with the same intensity as I wanted her. I eased my fingers between her folds, gathering the wetness I found to enter her with one finger, then two. Fiona pushed back on them, and when I couldn't take it any longer, I lined up my cock with her entrance and slowly slid inside. I closed my eyes, enjoying the feel of her walls surrounding me.

Then I opened them because I didn't want to miss a second of a naked Fiona in my kitchen on display for me.

Fiona looked over her shoulder at me. "I need you to move."

I pulled back and snapped my hips so that my cock filled her. "Yes."

I gripped her hips tightly, spreading her ass cheeks so I could see the spot where my dick entered her. It was visceral. The orgasm starting at the base of my spine quickly threatened to overwhelm me.

I reached around and pressed on her clit, needing her to come with me. As soon as she spasmed around me, I let go. I rested my weight over her back, placing a light kiss there.

Finally, I eased out and grabbed a washcloth, warming it under the water before moving back to clean her.

I helped her pull on her panties. I couldn't believe Fiona Calloway stood in my kitchen in only a tiny pink lace thong. I grabbed her ass, pulling her against me. "I'll never get enough of you."

Her tits pressed against my chest, revving me up again. With a groan, I pulled back, running a hand through my hair. I gave her my shirt. "Put that on, or we'll never get breakfast cooked."

Fiona giggled, and I relished the sound.

I pulled on my sweats, washed my hands, and got to work mixing the batter and pouring it into the pan. When the pancakes were cooking, I pulled her into my arms and kissed the top of her head.

When we'd dated, I held her every opportunity I got. I didn't get much attention at home. I didn't want to be near my parents, and my grandmother was nice to us, but she wasn't overtly affectionate.

It felt good to touch and be touched again.

"I missed this," Fiona said as she nestled into my chest.

"I did too." With one arm around her, I checked the pancakes as they cooked. I wasn't ready to let her go. When she walked out of my apartment, I wasn't sure if she'd throw up her walls again and remember the day I broke her heart by turning down her proposal. I couldn't blame her for being cautious, but I was going to enjoy every minute of this.

When we had a stack of pancakes, I grabbed the syrup and whipped cream while Fiona cut up strawberries.

When our plates were piled high and the pancakes smothered in whipped cream and strawberries, Fiona said, "This looks so good. I never have time for a breakfast like this."

I gestured at my plate. "This is the reason why I usually run every day. I love to eat."

Fiona laughed.

We dug in, and I couldn't take my gaze off her. She moaned with the first bite, whipped cream on her nose.

"You've got some there." I swiped the dollop with my thumb and sucked it into my mouth.

"We might need to use whipped cream later—"

"Much later. I have plans for you and the snow."

"I can't wait," Fiona said, and I felt that connection. The one that had felt so unbreakable.

Not only was I attracted to her, but I had fun with her. And I couldn't wait to spend the day together, and one more night.

"Tonight, I want to cook for you. Let's get dressed up and eat in the dining room. I can find a good wine, light some candles."

"That sounds amazing."

I leaned over and kissed her softly. "Then that's what we'll do."

"It's very romantic—" Fi began, then broke off.

"I can be romantic."

Fi smiled softly. "You used to leave flowers where I'd find them."

"That was harder than you think. I had to avoid your brothers and put them in a place you'd find them and they wouldn't."

"I found them in the basket of my bike with a new book you thought I'd like," she said slowly as if she was conjuring the images in her memory.

"You know, I picked the flowers from the gardens here and borrowed the books from the library. The librarian was so happy I was checking out books. I didn't have the heart to tell her they were for someone else."

Fiona covered my hand with hers, then pulled away. "It was the thought that counted. Not how much money you spent. But how did you know which books I'd like?"

I cut another bite of pancakes. "I paid attention to what girls your age were looking at. Sometimes I asked my sister. She assumed it was for a girl."

"So you've always been romantic." Fiona popped a strawberry slice into her mouth.

"I'm only like this with you." I racked my brain trying to

remember a relationship that lasted longer than a few months and whether I did more than cook them dinner. I never bought anyone else flowers.

"I feel special."

"You are special." She was everything. But I didn't want to scare her away with words. I'd draw her in make her melt with my romantic gestures. She didn't stand a chance.

CHAPTER 15

FIONA

Something had changed overnight. If I thought this was a one-night stand, a chance to see if we still had the same chemistry we did when we were younger, I was wrong. The energy coming off Aiden was that of a man who was in deep.

If he liked me, if he always had, why had he turned down my proposal? Why had he walked away from me, knowing I might never give him a second chance? I still wasn't sure I wanted to. I was scared of what happened last time. But not fearful enough to go back to my room.

I wanted to spend the day with him.

When we finished eating, we drank our coffee slowly, watching the snow fall. Then we got up to clean the plates, placing them in the dishwasher.

"What do you want to do first? We can go for a hike, build a snowman, or I can take you for a ride on the snowmobile. Although I might want to do that when it's dark. There's something I want to show you."

"What's that?"

"Talon built lights under the water of the pond on the Monroes' farm. We could take a ride over there."

"I'd love to see it. Are you sure they won't mind?"

"I'll give Heath a heads-up. Did you bring your snow gear?"

"I did only because I was hoping to go skiing one weekend. But I figured I'd need to travel farther north for good snow."

"You're in luck then. Want to get dressed, then meet in the lobby?"

I sensed a hesitation in him, as if he wasn't ready to let me go or he thought I might change my mind. I stepped close, wrapping my arms around his neck. "Sounds like a plan." Then I kissed him before grabbing my clothes from the night before.

When I walked by Aiden, he smacked my ass. I gave him a disgruntled look, and he winked.

"You're impossible."

He opened his mouth, then closed it.

I wondered if he was going to say, *That's why I love you*, and then thought better of it. We might have loved each other at one time, but that's not what this was. There was too much hurt, too much pain to get back to that innocent place we were in when we were teens.

"I'll see you in the lobby," I said as I crossed the apartment and opened the door. He must have followed me because when I turned to close the door behind me, he was there. He cupped my cheek and kissed me. It wasn't slow and sweet. It was passionate, his tongue slipping into my mouth and against mine. By the time he pulled back, I was breathless. "See you in a few."

It took me a few seconds, but I finally moved on shaky legs into the hallway. I heard the door close softly behind me. I touched my lips which were still tingling from his.

I couldn't forget the feel of him, the way he seemed to keep me close this morning. This thing with him wasn't a fling. It felt so much bigger than that. But I couldn't let him in, not all the way. Not until I knew what he wanted out of this. I wouldn't survive another broken heart. I wasn't sure my heart had ever truly mended from last time.

Maybe we could find healing together. As soon as the idea popped into my head, I dismissed it. You couldn't heal with the person who hurt you. That was crazy. My heart was trying to take control of this relationship, and I wouldn't let it. I needed to let logic rule the day.

I might have been the dumbest woman in history, but I took a quick shower, dried my hair, then threw on my warmest winter gear. Then I grabbed my boots just as I heard a knock on the door.

I opened it to find Aiden leaning against the frame with his arms crossed over his chest. "You were taking a long time."

I ran a hand through my hair. "Sorry, I thought I had time to take a quick shower, but it takes forever to dry my hair. I should have texted to let you know."

Aiden hooked a hand behind my neck and pulled me close for a kiss. "Are you ready to go now?"

I lifted my boots in the air. "I thought I'd put these on downstairs."

I closed and locked the door even though no one else was staying here at the moment. He took my hand, and we walked down the stairs and into the lobby. I sat in one of the cushioned chairs by the front door to pull on my boots.

"I'm just going to grab the keys for the snowmobile in case you change your mind." He disappeared behind the counter and reappeared a few seconds later. He shoved a knit hat onto his head and grabbed a jacket he'd left on the counter.

"These boots look new," Aiden said.

"I need you to help me dirty them up," I teased as I went on tiptoe to kiss him.

"Challenge accepted," he said, a wicked grin on his face.

We went outside where there were a couple of shovels resting against the porch railing.

"We should shovel the walk first."

"Should we do that first, or should we make a snowman?" I asked him, knowing what I wanted to do.

"Work first. Then we can play the rest of the day."

I groaned but took the shovel he handed me.

The snow was still coming down, and there was a good eight inches on the ground.

"It's thick and fluffy," I said as I threw the shovelful where I thought the grass was.

"The perfect kind for packing."

We worked in silence for a few minutes.

"Don't you need to plow the lane too?" I asked, remembering what he'd told Heath last night.

"I'll do it after we play for a bit."

"You mentioned a fancy dinner, then a snowmobile ride," I said even as I questioned what I was doing.

"We might need to do the ride first, then go home and get ready for dinner."

"That works for me," I said, shoveling the last bit of snow on the walk.

"Are you ready for some fun?" Aiden asked as he leaned on the handle of his shovel.

I grinned. "I'm more than ready."

Aiden snagged my shovel from my hands and put his and mine on the porch. The lights on the tree and the wreaths were lit since gray clouds covered the sky.

Aiden rolled a big ball that we packed tight. We placed it on the bottom.

"When we're done, we can take a picture for the website," I suggested.

"That would look nice," Aiden said as we got to work on a second ball and then a third for the head. When all three balls of snow were smoothed over and packed tightly, we stacked them on top of each other.

"Now we just need—"

Aiden pulled a carrot and a hat out of his pocket. "I came prepared."

"Once a Boy Scout, always one," I mumbled.

"I wasn't a Boy Scout."

I knew that his upbringing was a source of shame for him. But I said, "You were in the military. I'm sure that taught you to be prepared."

"The military taught me about a lot of good things in life, but not everything."

"Oh, what's that?" I asked. He handed me the carrot, and I placed it in the middle of the snowman's face.

"My commanding officers and fellow soldiers taught me about discipline, loyalty, and hard work. But they didn't teach me about love."

My breath caught in my throat. "Where did you learn about it then?"

He moved in front of me, touching my face with his gloved hand. "From my sister, my grandmother, and you."

He kissed me, his lips cool from the air, the snow coming down stinging my face. When he pulled back, he nodded toward the snowman. "He needs a hat."

He fit the knit hat on top, and we searched on the ground, digging through the snow for smaller rocks for his eyes, mouth, and shirt buttons. When we were done, we stood back and snapped a few pictures for the website.

"Don't you think the owner should be in the pictures?" I asked him.

"I'm just a co-owner."

"Same thing. Get in front."

He moved reluctantly next to the snowman. "Don't you think the picture would look better if you were in it? You're helping me renovate."

"You're right. We can use this picture in our marketing. Rehabbers take a snow break." I moved next to him, and his arm came around me. He took my phone and held it up so that he could snap a picture of us with the inn in the background.

The building itself looked regal in the snow with the columns wrapped in garland and lights, each window sporting a wreath. "This place is beautiful. Your grandmother would be so proud of you."

"I'd like to think so," Aiden said as he pulled off his glove so he could thumb through the pictures. When he got to the last one, he forwarded it to his phone."

"Are you sending it to Marley?"

"I wanted one for myself."

The entire day, I felt like we were a couple.

"Let's go sledding," Aiden said, sounding light and carefree as we searched the garage for sleds. We finally found one and took it to the nearest hill.

He got on first, then gestured for me to sit between his legs. I climbed on without any hesitation. I was committed to enjoying this day to its fullest. For one day, I didn't have to worry about the real world because everything was shut down.

We didn't have anywhere to be or anything to do. We probably should have been working on the basement, but neither of us was in a hurry for that.

We slid down the hill until lunch time. The last time, Aiden turned us so we flipped into the snow, and he landed on top of me. His legs came to rest on either side of my hips, and his gloved hands cupped my face. He lowered his lips to mine, and we kissed until our lips were swollen and our cheeks chapped from the wind and cold.

Then he stood with a grin, holding his hand out to me. I put my hand in his, and he lifted me to my feet. He dragged the sled behind him as we made our way back up the hill. It was the most perfect day.

Inside we took off our gear and let it drape across any available surface to dry. Then Aiden made subs filled with meat, veggies, and cheese. He poured lemonade from the pitcher.

"We should have made hot chocolate."

"I'll do that tonight."

Aiden was committed to making this day nice for both of us, and I was having too good of a time to let any anxieties creep to the surface.

After lunch, he went outside to plow the road, and I went to my room for a nap. A few hours later, my bed dipped. "You always leave your room unlocked?"

I stretched as I considered him. His cheeks were red from the cold, his hands icicles through the thin material of my leggings. "Only when we're snowed in and no one else is at the inn."

He kissed me again softly. Every time he did, it felt good. It was like he knew our time was limited and he wanted to touch and kiss me as much as possible.

When he pulled back, he said, "Are you ready for that snowmobile ride?"

"Absolutely."

We got into our now-dry gear and went outside. Aiden had brought the snowmobile around the house from the garage and parked it in front of the porch. He handed me a helmet and made sure it was buckled correctly before donning his.

Aiden got on, and I slid on behind him. He revved the engine, and then we glided over the snow, through a space in the trees, and into the woods that separated the Matthews' property from the Monroes'.

We didn't travel far before he pulled up to a pond. It was partially frozen, but I could see the lights twinkling underneath.

Aiden turned off the engine, and I got off.

"This is beautiful." I'd never seen anything like it.

We rested our helmets on the seat of the snowmobile and moved closer to the edge of the water. Aiden pulled me back so that I was resting against his chest. There were several layers of clothes between us, but I enjoyed the feel of his arms tightening around me and his chin resting on my shoulder.

Aiden pointed out the ornament shapes underneath the water. "Talon studied how the engineers did this at a garden estate in Pennsylvania. Then his brothers helped make it a reality."

"It's amazing. Do they allow people to come and see it?"

"It's a bit separated from the other light display, so they haven't yet. Or at least I don't think so. Talon keeps this one a bit of a secret."

"I think it's amazing." And it should be shared, but I knew the Monroes didn't enjoy being open to the public. They enjoyed the off-season and their privacy, and they'd only grudgingly accepted Marley's new marketing plan that offered year-round events to increase revenue. Maybe this was something Talon had made just for his family to experience.

We stood there for a few minutes and then walked around the permitter of the pond. It felt good to be outside in the cool air with nothing but the occasional snap of a twig or the clump of snow falling from a high branch. We didn't have anything to do or anywhere to be. And I was fairly positive the Monroes wouldn't be bothering us today.

So when snow flew into my shoulder, I was shocked. "Are you throwing snowballs?" I asked him, just as he flashed me a grin and ducked behind a tree.

I shrieked as I ran for cover and quickly began building an arsenal. Occasionally, a snowball flew by, but I didn't engage until I had a stack. Then I let them fly. He occasionally returned fire but nothing like I was. I pelted snowball after snowball toward his tree.

Feeling bold, I stood to deliver the last few balls. I was momentarily stunned when Aiden came out from behind the tree and barreled in my direction. I ran but it was too late, and Aiden landed on top of me. He quickly rolled me so that I was underneath him and he was straddling my hips.

This was nothing like before when we were sledding. Aiden's eyes danced with mischief, and my body hummed with adrenaline.

He grabbed my wrists and held them above my head in the snow. "You're a force."

I laughed. "You couldn't handle my return fire?"

"I can handle you all right." He lowered his head and kissed me until I forgot we were at war.

Instead of planning my escape, I was distracted by the warmth of my body despite the snow underneath me and the cool air.

Finally, he pulled back, "Let's go home. I have plans for you."

He helped me to stand to brush off the snow. We climbed onto the snowmobile and headed home. The light was beginning to wane, the flurries coming down lighter now.

When we got off, he said, "The worst of the snow is done. We should be able to clear everything out tomorrow."

The thought of going back to reality, to guests checking in and us resuming work on the basement, was disappointing. But I knew this was a brief respite.

"I'll get this in the garage, then start dinner. Why don't you take a bath in my room and get ready there?"

I smiled. "I can do that."

He kissed me, then smacked my butt when I turned away from him. I gave him a look over my shoulder, but he just chuckled. I loved that Aiden was more easy-going with me. I'd noticed that he was more serious since he got out of the military, but it was nice that I brought out the younger version of him.

Inside, I grabbed the dress and shoes I wanted to wear and my toiletries, then headed upstairs to his apartment. He'd left his room unlocked, so I stepped inside and made my way to the large bathroom.

It was gorgeous with a large soaking tub and walk-in shower with several shower heads. The bathtub had a large window that overlooked the back of the property. There were no houses in view, so I turned on the water in the tub and stripped down. Then I pushed play on a holiday song and stepped into the tub.

I sank into the warm water, content to close my eyes. It was relaxing, especially since my muscles were sore from walking in the snow and sledding. I wondered what it would be like to date Aiden. Would we move into his apartment? Would I work with him?

What would I do after the renovation was done? Would I find similar work with nearby hotels and bed-and-breakfasts? Could I make a go of my own business? I wasn't sure there were hotels that would be willing to work with a consultant. The large chains already had in-house people who did that work for them.

Marley made business ownership look easy, but I'd heard the opposite was true. That it took three to five years for most businesses to turn a profit. I didn't have that kind of time. I had some money in savings but not enough to start a new business.

I got out of the tub, disgusted that I was even considering a life with Aiden. He could break things off at any time. Or maybe this was just a fun few days for him. He'd be able to walk away like last time, and I'd be left with a broken heart.

I dried off, taking the time to lotion my body and dress with care. I dried my hair, applied minimal makeup, then headed downstairs where the dining room table was set and candles lit in the center.

"This looks beautiful."

Aiden came into the room in black slacks and a crisp white

button-down, holding a platter of food. His eyes widened when he saw me. He set the platter in the middle of the table, then approached me. "You look gorgeous."

He touched my shoulder, pulling me close.

I looked up at him. "You look handsome yourself. When did you have time to get dressed?"

"I snuck into my apartment while you were in the tub."

"You didn't want to join me?" I asked.

"I didn't want the food to burn, and I knew if I went into that room, dinner would be a bust.

I chuckled. "That's probably true."

A smile spread over his face. "You're too sexy to resist. I liked having you in my room, enjoying my tub."

"I liked it too," I said softly, my throat tightening with emotion. I liked it too much.

"I have a few more things to get ready." Aiden's hand drifted down my arm, and he entwined his fingers with mine. "Would you pick the wine? I think white would work best."

In the kitchen, he'd set several bottles of wine on the counter. I chose a white that looked to be from a local winery and then helped him carry the side dishes and wine glasses into the dining room.

Dinner was chicken parmesan with warm rolls and salad.

Aiden sat at the head of the table, and I took the seat to his right. "I can't believe you went to all this trouble."

"I never got a chance to cook for you, pick you up for a date, or even take you to prom. I wanted to do something special."

"You were there."

Regret filled his expression. "Not in the ways I wanted to be."

"I didn't realize that was important to you."

Aiden nodded. "I wanted to be the kind of guy you'd be proud of showing up on your doorstep. I wanted to meet your parents and know they trusted me with their daughter."

"You know that's not why I kept us a secret. I was never embarrassed by you."

"It's hard not to feel that when you grew up the way I did. My parents never failed to mention what a screw-up I was and how I'd never amount to anything. No one in our family went to college. Not until Marley. My parents told me I couldn't hope for more. But I wanted to be better, to be the man you deserved."

"That's why you enlisted." I'd figured that out a long time ago. I just couldn't figure out why he didn't want me with him.

"I screwed up."

I frowned. "What are you talking about?"

"I turned down your proposal because I didn't want you to give up on your dreams. I knew your dad wanted you to stay at school, to get your degree. He didn't want your mother's death or a guy messing with your plans. I didn't want to be that guy."

CHAPTER 16

AIDEN

Fiona frowned. "You weren't messing with my plans. I could have gotten a degree anywhere."

I gave her a look. "You and I both know that's not true. I moved around a lot. Sometimes to other countries."

Realization dawned on her face. "You were protecting me." When I nodded, she continued, "But that wasn't your decision to make. I asked you to marry me, and you said no."

I could see the hurt on her face. I knew I'd crushed her that day.

"I've apologized before about how I handled everything back then. But that's not enough. I owe you more of an explanation." I reached for her hand, holding it on the table between us.

"I thought you didn't want me." She articulated each word.

"That couldn't be further from the truth. Walking away from you that day, knowing you wanted me by your side, was the hardest thing I ever had to do."

"You acted like you knew better than me. That you were saving me or protecting me or something. That wasn't your decision to make."

"I know that now."

She stilled. "I can't believe it."

"If I could go back, I would have handled it differently, but I can't say I would have let you leave college to follow me around the world."

Her face hardened. "Also, not your decision."

I sighed. "I don't know what I'm doing in relationships. I sure as fuck didn't know it back then either. But I like being with you now. Do you think we can move forward?"

She narrowed her eyes on me. "I can't have you making decisions for me anymore."

"I promise we'll talk about things first." I wasn't sure where this could go since her job and home were in another state. But I was willing to give it a chance.

"Thank you for telling me what you were thinking back then."

"I only wish I'd done it sooner."

Her shoulders lowered. "I forgave you a long time ago, even if I didn't understand it."

"That's all I can ask for."

Fiona's eyes softened. "Now can we eat? The food smells delicious."

I plated her food, then got mine. We sipped our wine and ate.

"I can't wait until the theater is completed, and we can see guests enjoying the movies, and eating the popcorn."

"Me too." I was pleased that Fiona was so invested in the renovation.

"I have a feeling it's going to be huge for you and Marley."

"Have you decided what you're going to do yet?"

Fiona shook her head. "I want to finish the theater renovation, get through the holidays with my family, and then figure it out before the New Year."

I hated not knowing what was going on with us. But it would be selfish to ask for more when she needed to make a decision about her career. I couldn't interfere. "Marley is hoping to start showing movies in January."

"I just hope I'm here to see it."

I squeezed her hand. "You will be."

"Neither of us can predict the future."

"We don't need to worry about it tonight. This is for us. Let's enjoy being together without any more talk of the future."

Fiona raised her glass. "I can get on board with that."

I refilled her glass, and we carried the plates to the kitchen. "I'll clean this tomorrow. Let's take the wine up to my room."

"That sounds perfect," Fiona said as I grabbed the bottle and my glass. We headed upstairs.

"You know what we should do?" I asked as we took the stairs to the third floor.

"No. What?"

I moved toward the double doors. "We should dance. We're already dressed up."

Fiona tipped her head to the side. "You can do that. Just open the ballroom for us?"

I raised a brow. "I own half of this place. I can do whatever I want. And when will we ever be alone here again?"

Fiona smiled. "That's true."

I opened the double doors and flicked on the overhead lights. A decorated tree stood in the middle of the room, and there was a large painting of the inn on one wall. I hit Play on the music app on my phone and set it on the floor before holding out my hand to Fiona.

With a smile, she stepped into me. Her body pressed close to mine, and I curled my hand around hers.

Fiona looked up at me, the lights of the tree reflecting in her eyes. "This is romantic."

My lips quirked. "I told you I could pull it off."

Then we fell silent for a few seconds, swaying to the music and enjoying the lights on the tree.

Fiona paused, pulled back slightly, and touched her hand to my chest. "You should offer dance classes here."

I almost tripped over my feet. "Are you serious?"

"Don't you think it could be something cool to offer? You could have yoga classes here on Sunday mornings, dance classes on Friday or Saturday evenings."

"Would we offer those to just guests, or open it to the public?"

"Maybe the dance classes should be open to everyone to gain interest. If it gets too big, then you could limit it to guests. Or have one for guests, one for locals."

"That's a good idea." I knew Marley would love it.

"You have this amazing space, and you're only using it what? Once a year for the holiday party?"

I chuckled. "That's about right."

"What if you could incorporate this space into your guests' stays. It will make an impression. You don't want to keep it closed up and hidden away."

I pulled her close to me. "You're amazing; you know that? I always thought Marley was the queen of ideas, but you've blown her out of the water since you've been here."

"It's only because I deal with hotels, and a lot of them offer their ballroom space for conferences and dances. The only difference is that this is a true ballroom. You need to show it off."

"The paper did a write-up for the holiday dance, referencing the history of the inn."

"You could print that out and frame the article. Post it on the website."

Even though I appreciated her ideas, I didn't want to talk business tonight. "Can we table any more discussion of inns and newspapers so we can enjoy being together?"

Fiona smiled sheepishly. "I'm sorry."

I lifted my hand from her back to gesture at the room. "This is for you. I don't want to share you or this room with anyone else. I like being here at the inn without any guests."

"Do you have time blocked out when you aren't booked? Have you scheduled a vacation, so you could shut down, maybe do some renovations or updates, and take some time off?"

"We haven't. Mainly because we're new."

I nodded as we swayed around the room. "It's like starting over."

"And it's tough because neither me nor Marley has ever run a hotel. That's why your input is so valuable."

Fiona pursed her lips. "Not everyone listens to my ideas, because change and improvements mean more money."

"You can always tell me." I liked to hear how her mind worked.

She drew her lower lip into her mouth. "You want the guests to feel abundant. That means too many towels, a larger in-room fridge, more complimentary items, like water and snacks. You're already doing some of that." Then Fiona shook her head. "I'm sorry. We weren't supposed to talk business."

"I'm honored that you've shared them with me."

"My higher-ups want us to look for ways to save money. That means less cleaning services, fewer and thinner towels, no toiletries. Or better yet, they offer these items to the guests as a paid service. I just don't agree with that. You want them to love the experience so much that they come back, and they tell their friends. If you're always cutting corners, your guests are going to know that. They won't feel pampered."

"The guests need to feel like they're on vacation. That they have more than enough, and what they have is luxurious," I surmised from her description.

"They want something they can't get at home." Fiona let go of me and gestured around the room. "Like ballrooms, bowling alleys, and movie theaters."

I grinned as I looked down at her, enjoying the feel of her in my arms. "It's like you were meant to pop back into my life."

Fiona raised a brow. "For my advice on how to run a hotel?"

"For being you. For your inspiration. For your enthusiasm. Your wisdom. I could go on and on."

She smiled. "You're sweet."

I lowered my head so that my cheek was against hers. "I'm so lucky to have you in my life. But no more talk about hotels or our history. Tonight is for us."

"For us," Fiona agreed as we continued to dance to the next song.

When the notes finally stopped, I dropped her hand, grabbing my phone, and the wine glasses. "Let's go back to my room."

Fiona slipped off her shoes, holding them in her hands as we walked down the hall. "It's too bad the repairman hasn't come to look at the bowling alley; we could bowl tonight."

"We'll be the first to test out the lanes when they're ready."

"That sounds like a plan, Mr. Matthews," Fiona said as I opened my door and let her precede me inside.

My entire body filled with love for this woman. I didn't think I'd ever stopped loving her. I might have tapped it down, pushed it to the back of my mind, or tried to forget how I felt when she was around me.

But now that she was here, filling every bit of space in my life, it was like my old feelings for her merged with new ones.

I couldn't help but think that we were meant to be together. Were we lucky or unlucky to have met when we were so young and unsettled? If we'd met for the first time now, we would have easily fallen into a relationship. There'd be no past to move past.

I locked the door and toed off my shoes. Fiona dropped hers next to mine. I liked seeing them together, her delicate heels next to my larger shoes.

"I think you're thinking about something that's off-limits,"

Fiona said as she held my hands in hers.

"Oh, yeah? And what are you going to do about that?"

"I have plans to distract you."

"Mmm. I'm interested in that." I pulled her against my body and wrapped my arms around her. Lowering my mouth to hers, I kissed her hard and deep. I wanted this woman in my life forever. I had to do everything in my power to keep her in it.

If that meant a long-distance relationship, than I'd be okay with that. I just hoped she'd have room for me once she went back to work and her old life. From everything I'd heard from her, she worked seven days a week and traveled extensively.

If she decided to quit her job, would she be happy at the inn, farther away from any towns and at least an hour from the cities?

Fiona pulled back, working on the buttons of my shirt. "I see I have my work cut out for me."

I stopped her with a hand on her wrist. "I'm always thinking of you."

Her lips turned into a smile as she tugged my shirt from my waistband, then got to work on my pants. "And I'm going to make sure of it."

All the air rushed out of my lungs when she dropped to her knees on the rug.

She lowered the zipper, pulling my pants down. Then she reached for my cock and squeezed it, hard.

I closed my eyes, letting my head fall back. "Fuck. That feels good."

"You haven't felt anything yet," she said in a husky tone before she sucked me into her mouth.

All my blood went to my cock, making me feel lightheaded. "I'm not going to last."

She pulled off, pumping me. "That's the idea."

"I want to be inside you," I bit out.

She cocked her brow. "We have all night."

"Fuck yes, we do." I groaned when she squeezed the base and sucked hard.

My hand tangled in her hair, and I struggled to keep my touch light. I wished I had the strength to stop her, to haul her up and onto my cock. But the rush of her on her knees for me was too much, and before I wanted to, I was spurting into her mouth.

Fiona swallowed, then licked her lips as she gracefully rose to standing.

"We're not done," I said, trying to sound firm.

"I didn't think we were," Fiona promised as her lips curved into a naughty smile. She lifted her dress over her head, leaving her naked.

"Fuck, you were—"I couldn't even say the word naked over the tightening of my throat—"all night?"

She smiled. "You want to get in the hot tub?"

"I want you in my bed." I lifted her, throwing her over my shoulder fireman-style. In the bedroom, I dropped her onto the bed, watching her bounce. Her skin was flush, her eyes bright.

She wanted this as much as I did. She was in this with me, and there was no doubt in my mind she was feeling everything I was. How could she not be?

We were in this together, and we'd figure it out. We'd work through our dreams and desires. As long as we were together, that was all that mattered. And tonight, she was mine.

I pulled her down the bed until her legs hung over the side, and I dropped to my knees.

Her pussy glistened with her arousal. I slid a finger through her folds, gathering the wetness. "You like sucking my cock."

Fiona bit her lip. "I love it."

"You're going to be the death of me," I said slipping a finger into her slick channel.

Her hips moved, fucking my finger. I loved how responsive she was, how much she wanted me.

No matter what we went through, we found our way back to each other. No one would come between us again. Not my ego or good intentions.

I added a second finger, my thumb touching her clit, and she whimpered. I reached up to cup her breast, rubbing the nipple with my finger. "I want you to fall apart for me."

"Please, Aiden."

I tensed, my muscles pulled taut. "Please, what? What do you need?"

"I need your mouth on my clit."

She didn't need to ask me twice; I sucked on the swollen nub, my fingers moving inside her, searching for that spot that would make her lose her mind. When her muscles tensed, I said, "Come for me."

Her back bowed off the bed as she went over the edge, her muscles spasming around my fingers as I moved through her release.

I stood, shrugging off my shirt. Then I wrapped an arm around her back and lifted her higher on the bed. I covered her body with mine. Her skin was so hot, slick with our sweat and her release.

I touched her face, kissing her, before I sat back on my heels. I lined my cock up with her entrance. "I've never wanted anyone like I want you."

Fiona's hands gripped my forearm that was braced on the bed. "I need you."

"I got you." I slid inside to the hilt, taking a second to let her get accustomed to me filling her.

"I'll never get tired of feeling you inside me, filling me up."

I leaned down to suck on her earlobe. "And you won't have to. I'm yours."

The words *I'm yours* rung in the air between us. But neither of us said anything further. She didn't reciprocate the sentiment. But I figured giving her body to me was enough. Or at least I hoped it was. That I wasn't being naive. That Fiona was holding herself back from me. For once in my life, I was going to hope for the best. I would assume this would work out in my favor. Because it had to.

Not being with her wasn't an option anymore.

I drew out to the tip, every muscle in my body tensed as I slowly eased back inside. I kept my movements slow and steady. I wanted to draw this out. I wanted her to feel every hard inch of me.

When I was on the edge of my release, Fiona's muscles were trembling, and sweat was forming on my skin.

I touched Fiona's clit, circling it with my finger before pressing harder. Fiona moaned as her body contracted around mine.

I loved watching her come apart, basking in the pleasure that only I could give her.

I lowered myself so that my body was pressed against hers, making my moves smaller, seemingly sending her into another mini-orgasm. I gritted my teeth together, wishing I could hold out, but the pressure forming at the base of my spine threatened to be bigger than anything I'd ever experienced before, and I couldn't hold back.

I thrust deep and lost myself in the pleasure coursing through my body, making my muscles weak. I had enough brain power left to roll us to our sides so I wouldn't crush her with my weight.

We were quiet for a few seconds, both recovering from the orgasmic high we'd come down from.

I touched her hip, wishing she could sleep in my bed every night. That we could come home to each other after work no matter what we were doing.

I hoped she was feeling even a fraction of what I was. I should have been afraid of getting hurt, but I was in an open free-fall, and there was no stopping me.

CHAPTER 17

❄

FIONA

The morning after the storm, I woke up to the sun streaming through the windows. The sheets beside me felt cold, and when I finally lifted my head, I could see that I'd overslept.

I couldn't remember the last time I'd slept past seven. I slowly stretched, feeling every inch of my sore muscles after the workout Aiden had put me through.

A few seconds later, Aiden came into the room with a mug.

"Coffee?" I asked him hopefully, my voice sounding rough from sleep.

"I thought you could use some."

I shifted to a seated position, accepting the warm mug from him. I blew across the hot liquid, needing it to cool off so I could drink it.

"I got up early to make sure the road was clear. Guests are scheduled to start arriving later tonight."

"You think the roads are okay?" I was kind of hoping we could be snowed in for longer. It was a nice reprieve from the realities of our lives. Each day that passed was one day closer to me needing to leave.

"Seem to be. We didn't get any ice overnight to complicate matters."

I never wished for cold temperatures and ice more than I did now. "I guess we should work since we took off yesterday."

"Marley doesn't care that we took off. Sometimes you have to take a snow day." Aiden settled onto the bed next to me.

"It felt like we were kids again. We ignored our responsibilities and just played."

Aiden's lips curved into a smile. "It was nice."

My heart ached to relive that day. When would we ever get uninterrupted time like that again? I couldn't help but think that our relationship worked when the outside world stopped. That wasn't a good sign. We should be able to maintain a relationship regardless of what was going on in our lives, where we lived or worked, and who our families were. But that had never been the case.

Aiden's phone buzzed. "Probably someone calling to check on the roads or to book a room. I'm going to take this downstairs. Come down when you're ready. I'll cook you breakfast."

I wished we could stay in his apartment and share breakfast. Then we could wear our pajamas all day, and watch TV, make love, and enjoy his hot tub.

Instead, Aiden kissed me and picked up his phone. "Matthews Inn. This is Aiden speaking. How can I help you?"

I heard the soft click of the front door a few seconds later, and I was alone again. I drank a few sips of the coffee, enjoying the fact that Aiden had brought it to me, before I finally got up and took a quick shower.

I wished that Aiden would join me. That we could make love before we needed to face our day. But until Charlotte arrived to man the front desk, Aiden took on those responsibilities. That would always be the case.

Even if I quit my job and moved here, Aiden had his own work occupying his time. Both of us were busy people.

I dried off, pulled on the dress from last night, and carried my heels to my room where I changed into workout clothes. Downstairs, I could see the sun was shining brightly, doing its best to melt the snow that had fallen over the last few days.

"I was going to come look for you."

I smiled. "I decided to take a shower."

He leaned closer and kissed me. "I'm just going to dirty you up again. We need to hang those shelves today."

He was referring to work, not sexy times. I wished that we had no responsibilities. That we could just take a vacation and work on our relationship. But that wasn't reality. This was our life, working long hours toward the next big accomplishment.

For him, that was his family's inn, and for me... I wasn't sure what it was anymore. Putting everything into a business that would never appreciate what I had to offer? Bosses who would continually overlook my talents to hire someone with less experience?

"We have guests checking in this afternoon, but I want to get a head start on the shelves. Make up for time we lost yesterday."

He slid a plate of eggs and bacon across the counter toward me. There were even strawberries cut up on the side. Emotion clogged my throat as I picked up a fork and forced myself to eat. It would be selfish to ask him to take the morning off, to spend more time together. Yesterday was a gift. I needed to enjoy it for what it was and move on.

Aiden arranged muffins on a platter, then covered them. "These will be ready whenever the guests arrive. Since the roads were already cleared, one family said they might check in early."

"That's good." The eggs dissolved into dust in my mouth. I finished eating and got up to clear my dish.

Aiden took it with a smile. "You're a guest here."

The problem was I didn't want to be. I wanted to be the woman at his side, and that was dangerous. I'd asked him to spend his life with me before, and he'd said no. I couldn't forget the look on his face when I'd naively asked him to marry me.

Aiden put our dishes in the dishwasher, and we took bottled waters downstairs. Eventually, there would be a refrigerated unit behind the concession stand for drinks, but it wasn't ready yet.

We worked on the shelves, putting them together, then hanging them on the wall. This unit would be for bowling shoes. When it was done, we'd build the boxes that would form a table and cubbies for each lane. They would sit between the two couches.

At lunch, I went upstairs to make sandwiches while Aiden continued to work. He was focused on getting the work done since the repairman was coming soon.

Charlotte arrived at lunchtime, coming into the kitchen to snag a muffin and an iced tea from the fridge. "I saw that snowman outside. Did you and Aiden build it?"

Charlotte must have seen something in my expression because her eyes widened. "Are you two together?"

I shook my head. "We're not like that. We just dated in high school."

"Oh. I didn't realize that."

I smiled politely. "You wouldn't. We kept it a secret."

"Do you think you'll get back together?" Charlotte asked, taking a bite of the muffin.

I didn't know Charlotte that well, but she was so friendly, I felt like I could be honest with her. My stomach twisted. "I don't see how it could work. It was the same thing when we were teens. We're going in separate directions. We want different things."

"That's too bad. Aiden could use someone. Marley's worried about him since he retired from the military. I think that's why she stayed in the inn for so long with Heath instead of their cabin."

"She's worried about him? Why?"

"He doesn't talk about things, and she just wants him to settle in here and be happy. She doesn't want him to leave again."

There was a small part of me that wondered if I could ask him to move with me, but Charlotte's words cut off that possibility all together.

Aiden was invested in the inn and getting to know his sister again. I couldn't take him away from his family or his legacy. We were in the exact same position as last time. I could ask him to commit to me, but it wouldn't be fair. I wasn't what he wanted.

We might have had great chemistry, but that didn't mean we could make things work long-term. I got out the lunch meat and cheese to make subs, going through the motions while my mind whirred with the possibilities.

Unfortunately, I couldn't find one that kept us living in the same place. I wasn't willing to give up my job when he'd turned me down last time. I just couldn't take that risk again. My heart wouldn't take another break.

Aiden appeared in the kitchen with his hand on his stomach. "What's taking so long? I'm starving."

I nodded toward the plate of subs and chips I'd prepared. "I was just going to bring this down."

"We might as well eat up here." Aiden washed his hands in the sink, then asked Charlotte, "How were the roads?"

"Clear and dry. I expect guests will be arriving soon." She hopped off the stool, flashing us a smile before leaving the room.

"I'm glad she's here today. I just want to focus on the work downstairs."

He hadn't said anything about enjoying our time together. He seemed to be more worried about the work we hadn't completed.

"Is everything okay?" Aiden asked as he sat on a stool and grabbed a sub, taking a large bite.

"Of course." I ate a chip, looking outside at the sun doing its best to melt the snow.

"We only have a week until Christmas."

"Do you have any holiday events leading up to the big day?" I asked lightly.

"I was hoping we could get the movie theater ready for a small showing for family before the grand opening in the New Year."

I frowned. "You think it will be done in time?"

"We replaced some of the seat covers with temporary ones until they can be reupholstered. Heath ordered new curtains because he couldn't salvage the old ones. The wallpaper is gone, and he painted the walls."

"What's left to do?" I asked, not believing that our work was coming to an end.

"I need to get the projector room cleared of the old equipment while Heath works on the concession stand."

"I didn't realize he'd worked so quickly." The night we watched the movie together the theater was dark, and I'd been so wrapped up in Aiden, I hadn't noticed that so much had been completed.

"The repairman called to say he can come today to work on the lanes. So I'll help Heath with the concessions."

"Do you need me?" I asked, thinking I might have been asking about more than the renovations.

Aiden smiled. "You can help us clean."

"I should probably spend some time with my family." I hadn't seen them much since Daphne's housewarming party. And I needed to distance myself from Aiden. Yesterday was a big deal for me, but I wasn't sure he felt the same way.

I didn't want to find myself in a position where I liked him more than he did me. Did he see this as some kind of vacation fling? The thought sat like lead in my stomach, making it difficult to eat. I twisted off the cap for the water and drank.

Aiden ate quickly, then grabbed a few water bottles to take downstairs with him. "Heath just pulled up. I'm going to get back to work."

I smiled as he left the room, wondering why I was here. He didn't need me. I could consult with Marley on design elements over the phone and via email.

I wasn't needed, and that brought back how I felt after Mom died and then Aiden left. I was adrift. It was why I'd buried myself in classes, then work.

Could I go back to that? That solitary existence where I lived in hotel rooms across the country, making notes, and offering suggestions for improvements no one would take. Instead, they'd cut back on amenities, offering cookie-cutter decor that you could find in any hotel.

I wasn't sure I wanted to go back to my old job, but what else did I have? Marley didn't need me here. Not really. Even though I enjoyed the work I'd done, Marley and Aiden could survive without me.

They had Heath, and they could call in any expert that they needed. Shaking my head, I headed downstairs to clean the display case on the concession stand while Heath and Aiden worked around me, pulling out the old popcorn machine and installing a new one.

The movie theater would be ready to go soon, and there wouldn't be anything for me to do.

Surely, Marley could manage the bar and the game room by herself, even if my heart longed to offer suggestions for improvements and to see the finished project.

Long before Heath and Aiden were done, I said I was going to my dad's house. Aiden barely looked up when I left. He might have been trying to hide what was going on between us from Heath, but it still hurt.

We'd never be able to share our relationship with anyone because we didn't have a future. Aiden already realized that, and I needed to get on board. This thing between us was a fun way to pass the time. It had the added bonus of our shared history. But that just made it more treacherous for my heart.

I showered and headed to my dad's, wishing I could bring Aiden with me. That he wanted to spend time with my family. But he saw what I hadn't. We didn't fit into each other's lives. That's why we'd kept them separate even when we were together as teens.

Daphne and Cole were already at Dad's. I parked next to Cole's red Monroe Christmas Tree Farm truck and went inside.

As soon as I opened the door, Izzy flew at my legs, helping me forget my trepidation about being in my childhood home. "Aunt Fiona. Where've you been?"

I patted her back. "I was helping Marley renovate the movie theater at the inn. You should come see it. It's almost done."

"Can we?" Izzy asked Daphne as she approached us.

Daphne nodded in my direction. "If Fiona says we can."

"I think Aiden was planning on having a few people view a movie before Christmas, and then we'll have a party sometime in the New Year." It felt weird to talk about plans because I knew that I wouldn't be a part of them after I left. Everyone would move on without me. The renovations would be completed. Marley would have another party to celebrate.

Cole held his hand out to Izzy. "Let's go see what Grandpa has to snack on."

My heart squeezed when she took his hand and skipped along next to him as they headed for the kitchen.

"Will you be here for that?" Daphne asked softly.

I turned my attention to her. "I think Aiden wants to have it before I leave."

Daphne's forehead wrinkled. "Are you still planning on leaving?"

"Why wouldn't I be?" I asked brightly even as my heart picked up the pace.

"Heath mentioned that you and Aiden have been spending a lot of time together."

"You know we're working together."

Daphne kept her gaze steady on me. "When we were younger, and I asked why you didn't come home more often, Teddy told me that you were avoiding Aiden because you'd dated, and it ended badly. I was hurt that you didn't talk to me about it until recently."

"First of all, no one knew about it, and you were a lot younger than me. Your age doesn't matter now that we're adults. But back then? I wouldn't have confided in you." There was a divide between us that was only partially about the fact that she was in middle school. She hadn't even gotten crushes on boys yet, whereas I was in love with one.

Daphne sighed. "Why don't you talk to me about what's going on now?"

She led me into the rarely utilized living room. Mom always wanted us to keep this one room nice. It still had all the same furniture but with a lot more dust. We settled onto the couch, and I said, "You just got engaged and moved in with Cole. Your life is moving in a different direction."

"That doesn't mean you can't talk to me. I know there's a gap of years between us, but you're my only sister. I thought we talked over those video calls because you wanted to have a better relationship." She chewed her lip. "Maybe it was only because of Izzy."

I covered her hand with mine. "I do want to have a relationship with you. Our bond is special. It's just... I've been spending a lot of time at the inn, and every time we're together lately, it's a family gathering."

"We obviously need to change that. But in the meantime, what's going on with you and Aiden?"

I let out a breath. "We were snowed in, and he was being all romantic." When Daphne inched closer with a smile on her lips, I continued, "We spent the day in the snow, built a snowman. Then he took me on a snowmobile to see the lights at the pond on the Monroes' farm. He even cooked dinner for me, and we ate in the formal dining room. He insisted we get dressed up. Afterward, we danced in the ballroom."

Her expression filled with awe. "That is so romantic. You and him all alone in that inn? It's a scene from a movie."

I laughed without any humor. "Our relationship doesn't have a happy ending."

Daphne frowned. "Why not?"

"You know he enlisted my sophomore year. After Mom died."

"You think her death prompted it?"

"Honestly? I don't know. He had this inner drive to prove himself, or he thought the military would turn him into a respectable man. He said he didn't want a future with me. We didn't want the same things."

"Are you sure that's what he wanted? You were so young."

"Last night he said that he pushed me away because he didn't want me to quit school and follow him around the world. It's in the past. My issue is that we're in the same situation again. My job is somewhere else, and his is here. I wouldn't take him away from Marley now that he's just gotten her back. And he loves running the inn."

"Are you happy? Will you be when you go back to your job?" Daphne asked.

"I can't just quit my job in the hopes that what Aiden and I have will last. There's no guarantee that he won't push me away again." If anything, he'd held me tighter last night. It had felt different from any other time we'd had sex. Like it meant more to him. He'd said I was his, and I hadn't responded. My throat had gotten tight, and I was scared that the hope in my chest would expand so much that I wouldn't be able to rein it in. It felt imperative that I hold myself back so I wouldn't get hurt.

Daphne's forehead wrinkled. "Oh, Fiona. You're so afraid of people leaving that you won't take a risk to truly be with them."

That assumption sent my mind reeling. "I'm not afraid of people leaving."

Daphne ticked off on her fingers. "Mom died. Then Aiden left. You're scared he'll do it again."

I shook my head. "Well, wouldn't you be?"

"It's been years, and you were so young then. You're not the same people. Aiden's grown up and gotten away from the crap he dealt with when he lived with his parents. And you're different too. You're just starting to see that there's more to life than work. Don't be so quick to dismiss what you have with Aiden. Give him a chance."

"Mommy! Dinner's ready," Izzy called from the doorway.

"Think about what I said." Daphne touched my shoulder as she stood and took Izzy's hand.

I couldn't help but think that despite Daphne's optimism, history usually repeated itself.

CHAPTER 18

❄

AIDEN

*I*t was well after dinnertime by the time we had the concession stand looking better. Fiona cleaned the display case, the counters, and the cupboards. We'd replaced the popcorn machine and removed the old cash register. Now we just needed a tablet and point of purchase to take credit cards. It was so much simpler, and it took up a lot less room.

"You're going to serve popcorn, candy, soda, and water?" Heath asked.

I looked around the space. "That's the easiest. We'll purchase a refrigerator case for the drinks. I don't want to deal with fountain sodas."

"I can create a storage room for you where you can keep extra supplies," Heath offered.

"You've thought of everything."

Heath leaned against the counter, crossing one foot over the other. "You forget I live with Marley. She has a running to-do list for everything."

"I assume you're the one that needs to cross everything off," I said wryly.

"You got that right. But I wouldn't have it any other way. I'm blessed that she came back into my life, and she gave me another chance." Heath had a good energy about him. He was content, happy.

I longed to have what he did.

Heath focused on me. "How are things going with you and Fiona?"

I thought about the night we'd spent together. It had been close to perfect. Fiona hadn't said exactly how she felt, but I hoped they were similar to my feelings. Today, she'd been a little distant. But I figured it was just getting back into the swing of things now that the snow cleared. "Things are good."

"Is she still planning on leaving when we're done with the theater?" Heath grabbed a water bottle, twisted off the cap, and took a long pull.

"As far as I know. She hasn't mentioned it one way or the other." I wondered where her head was at. Had things changed for her like they had for me?

"Are you willing to move to her to make things work?" Heath asked.

That question threw me off. "Why would I move? Everything I want is here. The inn. Marley."

Heath gave me a pointed look. "Fiona might not be."

"We can do long distance." My throat tightened because I wasn't so sure that was the case. We hadn't even tried last time. I'd been certain that I didn't want her to leave school for me. Now I'd be asking her to quit her job, the only career she'd ever known. It was tough for me to retire from the military. I didn't want to force her into a decision.

Heath raised a brow. "Is that what you want?"

I leaned on the counter with my elbow. "In an ideal world, she'd be here with me. I just don't know what she wants. Marley would love if Fiona helped with the rest of the renovation, but what then?"

"That's what you need to find out. You can't pretend the end date isn't quickly approaching."

"It's not until after the New Year." I just wasn't sure of the exact date. "And she said she'd visit often to see her family."

Heath shrugged his shoulders. "You know how it is. Once she gets back into work, she'll be busy. She won't get back as often as she'd like. Can you handle that? Do you have the time to visit her?"

I cleared my throat. "Not really. Charlotte has been working weekdays, and I take the weekends."

Heath shook his head. "It sounds like you have a lot to talk about then. Where is she?"

"She went to see her family. She's been so busy here that she hasn't seen them as much as she'd like to."

"The thing about relationships is that you need to let the other person thrive. If that means opening a new business, going into a different career, or even moving. Are you prepared to meet her where she's at?"

I thought back to how she'd so effortlessly proposed to me when I was nineteen and how I hadn't been ready for that gift. I'd thrown it back in her face. I'd registered the hurt, but I hadn't let myself absorb that, to think about how it might damage her for relationships going forward. I sighed. "I'll have to be."

Heath touched my shoulder. "I want you two to make it."

"It worked out for you and Marley, and her home was in California."

"She hated it here. Initially, she wanted to renovate and sell the inn. But she fell in love with the inn and the farm. She remembered how much she loved me. You have to make it so Fiona won't want to leave."

"Are you saying that I need to show her how great it is to live in an inn?" I'd done a good job of that during the storm, and I was positive she was on her way to falling back in love with me, if she wasn't already there.

"You couldn't ask for a better time of year. There's something about the holiday season. Women can't resist it."

I scoffed. "I'm hoping she can't resist me."

Heath moved toward the theater doors. "Come on. Let's take a look."

The original chairs have been cleaned, the worst of the chairs recovered. The curtains would be in soon. The old ones had already been removed, leaving the space brighter. The walls were a soft gray. There was new red carpet on the floor and the electrical had all been brought up to code.

Tiny lights lined the aisles, and Heath had kept the original sconces on the walls. When he turned on the lights, there was a soft glow to the room.

He hit a button, and the projector screen came down. "We need to fix the projector room. Then we can have a showing."

"You want to do it before Christmas?"

"I think you need to. Invite the Calloways."

"Should I invite the Monroes?" It was as much Heath's project as it was mine and Marley's.

"If you feel comfortable doing that. I'll talk to Emmett, see if he can be slightly less grumpy than usual for one night."

"You do that." I walked around the room, taking it all in. It felt grand for such a small space. "Tomorrow, the repairman for the bowling alley will be here."

"Marley can take pictures of the showing and post it on the website. With the holiday decorations, it will be perfect. I think you're going to be busy soon. How many hotels can offer an onsite movie theater, a game room, and a bowling alley?"

"Not many."

"I'm confident we can utilize the game room too. We'll recover the pool tables, add a few foosball tables and maybe an air hockey table for the kids."

"Do we want to make it more kid friendly? We could add a few basketball-hoop arcade-style games."

Heath grinned. "I love Skee-Ball."

"It has a gentlemen's club feel now with the bar and the grand interior. Do you think Marley will want to change it that much?"

"I think Marley likes the idea of making the entire hotel more kid friendly."

I was pleased we'd planned so much in one evening, but I wish Fiona were here. I'd come to rely on her input. She had a feel for what people wanted. It was too bad her superiors couldn't see how brilliant she was. We were lucky to have her support and advice.

My heart hurt at the thought of her leaving or me not being able to see her because I was tied to this place. I loved it, but I wanted her more.

"When things went bad between me and Marley, I flew to California. I told her I was willing to move there to be with her."

"Were you?" I hadn't heard about this.

"I'd do anything for her. If you feel the same way about Fiona, you'll know what you need to do."

Then he walked out of the room. I heard the clang of his tools hitting the metal storage box as he put them away.

I let my head drop back, and I sighed. I loved her, and I knew I wouldn't get another chance at this. I had to go all out, and if that meant making a contingency plan for the hotel, I'd need to do it.

I'd talk to Marley about what would need to happen for me to be more flexible, whether it was a possibility to manage the hotel from Chicago or wherever Fiona was.

∼

The next few days were busy. I worked on the projector room with Heath since his crew was needed on another project—a kitchen that had to be completed before Christmas.

We cleared the old equipment out of the room, building new shelves and a table. It felt good to work with my hands again.

When it was completed, we set up the new equipment, then stood back to see how it looked.

"You do good work. I think your specialty is custom woodwork," Heath observed.

"I enjoyed it."

"How would you like to do this kind of thing for me? Whenever we have custom projects, whether it's shelving, cupboards, or even a window seat."

I sighed. "I'd love to, but I can't commit to anything right now. Not until I figure things out with Fiona."

Heath nodded. "The offer still stands."

"I appreciate it. You've been nothing but supportive since I got back."

Heath clasped my shoulder. "You're my best friend and future brother-in-law."

His reference to being my brother-in-law didn't bother me like it used to. I was happy for him. "You thought about a date for a wedding?"

"Marley wants to get married on Christmas Eve."

I tipped my head to the side. "This Christmas Eve? You're kidding."

"She's already hired a wedding planning service in town, and one of their wedding planners, Aria from Happily Ever Afters. She wants to keep the guests to family and friends. It will be small."

"Where does she want to get married?" I asked him.

"She wants to get married on the front steps and hold the reception in the ballroom."

"Of my inn?" My brain was trying to keep up with this information. We were planning for a grand opening of the theater which would include a private family showing the day before Christmas Eve. Now we had to plan a wedding for my sister too?

Heath shot me a look. "Last time I checked, it was yours and Marley's."

"I didn't mean anything by it. I'm just feeling a little overwhelmed. This is the first time I'm hearing of it."

"You don't need to do anything except stand by my side at the altar."

"You want me to be your best man?" My chest swelled with pride.

Heath smiled. "You're my best friend, and Marley's your sister. We wouldn't be here without you."

"I'd love to stand up for you," I said, giving him a hug. "And welcome you to the family."

Heath raised a brow as I pulled back. "The Matthews family of two?"

"That's right." I thought about my parents, how they'd left after Marley graduated from high school and hadn't returned.

Marley said they'd made rumblings about the inheritance and said she'd paid them off. I had no idea how much money she'd given them, but we hadn't heard from them since.

I hoped it stayed that way. If my parents knew about the reopening of the inn or Marley's wedding, they might use it as an excuse to pop their heads out of whatever hole they'd been hiding in. But I wouldn't say any of that to Heath. "I'm happy for you."

Heath chuckled. "I never thought I'd see the day where you'd be happy for me marrying your sister."

"I couldn't find a better man for her." Heath took care of her.

It didn't matter that Heath was my friend, or I'd asked him to protect her when I enlisted. Instead, he'd fallen in love with her. I couldn't fault him for that. Not when he made her so happy.

Heath looked away, his eyes suspiciously shiny.

"Are you sure there isn't anything I can do for the wedding?"

Heath cleared his throat. "You can help with the setup in the ballroom. A rental company will be delivering the tables and chairs. We'll need to set up a couple of bars, but we have them in storage. Aria is handling the rest of it."

"Is this what you both want? You don't want to take more time and have a larger affair?"

Heath grinned. "This is exactly what we want. A party with our family and friends."

"But it's Christmas. Won't people already have plans for the holiday?"

Heath shook his head. "That was the idea. Marley didn't want to have a large wedding. She wants to keep it cozy."

Marley appeared in the doorway. "Did you tell him our plans?"

Heath's grin widened as he pulled her into his side, looking down at her. "Sure did."

"I'm happy for you, sis."

Heath let her go so she could hug me.

Marley pulled back slightly to see my face. "Are you really?"

"I just told your fiancé I couldn't find a better man for you. Whatever you want, we'll make it happen."

Marley and Heath exchanged a look. Then she said, "I think Aria has everything taken care of."

Marley returned to Heath's side. "Are you ready to get out of here? Aria wanted to go over some details."

Heath nodded to her. Then asked me, "You can clean up here?"

I waved them off. "Get out of here. You've got a wedding to plan."

Marley grinned as she led Heath out of the room. I put away the tools, then dusted the remaining sawdust from the room. I was happy for my sister, and I couldn't think of a better location for their wedding than the inn. It would be gorgeous even if it was winter. The inn was its best at Christmas.

~

Later that night, I let Fiona into my apartment.

She kissed me, and then I asked, "Did you hear that Marley and Heath are getting married here on Christmas Eve?"

"It will be beautiful," Fiona said with a smile. "Are we still planning on having a family showing of a movie the night before?"

"I think so. We won't be in the way of the wedding preparations, and the kids are looking forward to it."

"With everything going on, this might be the last night we have to ourselves," Fiona murmured as she wrapped her arms around my neck.

"Then we'd better make the most of it." I closed the door and led her to the bedroom, thoughts of how I wanted to spend the night playing like a reel in my head. I thought I'd take things slow, start a fire, maybe light some candles, then pour some wine.

But when we got to my room, I was desperate for her. I closed the door, then pressed her against it, kissing her while my fingers fumbled with the button of her jeans. She helped me shove her jeans down, then off as I sank to my knees, breathing her in.

"You're gorgeous," I said as I looked up at her and slowly lowered her lace panties.

I eased my finger between her folds, her hips arching off the door. "I want to see you."

She removed her sweater with shaky hands, then unclipped her bra, baring her breasts. The nipples were a dusky rose, standing at attention.

I reached up and palmed one, rubbing a thumb over the hard nub.

Her breath hitched as she touched my hair.

I loved this woman, and I never wanted to be away from her. It was clear to me that I'd need to be flexible like Heath said.

I nudged her legs wider as I eased a finger inside her, drawing a whimper from Fiona's throat. I wanted to watch her come apart. I wanted to drive her wild with need.

I pumped my fingers inside her, my other hand tweaking her nipple. When she moved her hips in time with my fingers, I sucked on her clit. She cried out as the orgasm flew through her. Her walls spasmed around my fingers. When her body relaxed against the door, I wiped my mouth, then stood. I lifted her into my arms and carried her to the bed.

I'd never get enough of her, and I wouldn't let her move without me. With that settled in my mind, I lowered her to the mattress and removed my clothes.

When I entered her, I made sure we were touching, my body lowered over hers, our fingers entwined, and our mouths fused. When her body arched against mine for her second orgasm, I swallowed her cries.

I loved her. I just wasn't sure she was ready for the intensity of my emotions, or the thoughts running through my head. This woman was my future, and I needed to do everything I could to show her the possibility of us.

CHAPTER 19

❄

FIONA

We helped Marley prepare for the movie night and the wedding during the day, then fell into bed exhausted. We didn't have much time to talk about us or the future. But I was confident that we were in a good place. We had plenty of time to discuss things after the holidays.

For the first time, I was looking forward to spending them with my family. But first, we needed to make sure the movie night ran smoothly, and everything was ready for Heath and Marley's wedding.

I spent the day of the movie showing vacuuming, dusting, and polishing every surface of the theater. Then I stocked the concession stand with candy and everything we needed to run it, including popcorn bags, butter, salt, and drinks.

Aiden worked in the projection room, testing the projector and the lighting.

When we were satisfied everything was ready, we rushed through showers and met in the lobby to greet our guests, which were essentially our families.

We'd decided to keep tonight casual for the kids and would plan a fancier affair for the official grand opening.

I was more worried about tonight running smoothly. I wanted the kids and our families to enjoy themselves. I'd never been so excited to attend an event at a hotel before. Even though I was just the consultant, I felt as if the theater was my project. This was the first time I was hands-on with a project, seeing it through from consultation to completion.

In the lobby, Aiden pulled me into his arms, making my heart rate pick up.

I braced my hands on his biceps. "People will be arriving any second. We should probably check the room one more time to make sure everything looks good."

Aiden silenced me with a kiss. "Everything looks great, and the room didn't fall down while we were in the shower."

"Are you sure?" I chewed my bottom lip.

Aiden held me tighter. "Relax. It's just our friends and families."

"What if they don't like it? What if the movie doesn't play? What if the popcorn machine won't pop the kernels?" My mind was racing with endless possibilities, each disaster worse than the one before.

"Fiona. Everything is fine. We tested the lights, the projector, and the popcorn machine. Even if a problem arises, we can handle it. Things happen. Life isn't always perfect. But it's the imperfect moments you'll remember." Aiden's voice was firm and reassuring.

I softened into his body. "I like that."

Then he kissed me, slow and sweet; heat simmered under my skin. I almost suggested we go back to his room when the first knock sounded. I pulled away to say, "They're here."

I loved it here. I loved being so close to my family and Aiden. For once, it felt like my life was mine. I made the choice of when and how to work. Staying in one place was nice.

I didn't even want to think about going back to my old

schedule, flying every week to a new city. One I didn't get to tour.

Aiden opened the door to find Sarah, Knox, and Addy. Addy flew past me without a greeting, then skidded to a stop in front of Aiden. "Where's the theater?"

Aiden chuckled as he crouched down to her level. "It's downstairs. Would you like some popcorn?"

Addy nodded. "Yes."

"She's very excited for the movie," Sarah said as they came inside.

"We're hoping everyone is as excited as she is." The next few minutes I stayed by the door, greeting everyone who arrived.

I was pleased that Dad came. I wasn't sure he got out much anymore.

Charlotte manned the concession stand, but we'd need to hire some local kids to run it when we were officially open. When everyone was seated, Aiden said to me, "Let's head up to the projector room and get this started."

Anxious with nerves, I followed him to the stairs and settled in the room to watch him prep the movie.

I didn't relax until he dimmed the lights and pressed play. It was *Miracle on 34th Street*, the version we'd watched. When it was playing for a few minutes without an issue, Aiden stood and held his hand out to me.

"I want to show you something."

I put my hand in his and stood. "Are you sure it's okay to leave?"

"We can come back if there's an issue." He led me down the hall to one of the doors that led to a small balcony. There were two. When he reached for the knob, I said, "We didn't do anything with these rooms."

Aiden flashed me a smile. "Trust me."

"Okay," I said, drawing out the word as he opened it and led me inside. I sucked in a breath. It looked just as new as the theater itself. "What did you do?"

"It made sense to update the carpet and seats when we did the main gallery."

"I didn't know you were doing this."

"I wanted it to be a surprise." He gestured for me to sit in one of the seats. Then he sat next to me.

The Monroes and the Calloways were sitting together, munching on popcorn and candy. Everyone was focused on the movie playing on the screen. We were seated in the dark, and no one knew we were here.

Aiden grabbed two glasses of champagne, handing one to me. He must have prepared this ahead of time.

He raised his glass. "To our movie theater."

"To our movie theater." It felt good to say that. To pretend that this was mine. That the man sitting next to me would always be here. I let myself fall into the fantasy of staying and being with him. We'd renovate the rest of the inn, and then I could take my time to figure out what I wanted to do next and spend time with him and my family. This could be my home.

~

On Christmas Eve, there were dozens of workers on the grounds of the inn, preparing for the wedding. Aiden helped set up the chairs and tables in the ballroom, and I was overseeing everything else.

Aria was here with several other wedding planners on site to help. I wanted everything to be perfect for Marley and Heath's wedding.

After lunch, I went to my room to get ready. I hadn't been in the space for a few days, but someone had been watering the tree, and there was even an angel on the top of it.

Other than watching the movie last night, I hadn't spent

much quality time with Aiden. I knew that would come after Christmas Day, since I was spending it with my family.

Aiden hadn't said what his plans were, but Heath and Marley would still be in town for the day, then were planning to travel to her home in California sometime in the next week for their honeymoon. I figured he'd want to spend time with them, and the rest of the Monroes. Daphne was splitting her time between the Monroes and the Calloways.

I wasn't sure if Aiden was comfortable with us discussing our relationship with our families, much less spending the holiday together.

He didn't have a large family, so he might not have been thinking about it at all. He was used to being deployed over the holidays.

I showered quickly, applied my makeup, let my hair dry straight, and then got dressed. It was the same gown I'd worn for our fancy dinner when we were snowed in. It was hard to believe that was only a few days ago. It felt like a lifetime.

When a knock sounded on the door, I opened it, expecting Aiden, but it was Aria.

"We're seating guests for the wedding. I wanted to let you know."

"Do you need help?"

Aria waved me off. "Your job is to relax and enjoy the wedding."

Aiden was standing up for Heath, and I was just a guest.

I felt a little out of place because I didn't know the Monroes that well yet. Thankfully, Daphne and Izzy were attending with Cole. "I'll be right down."

"I'll finish my rounds to make sure everyone makes it downstairs on time," Aria said as she continued down the hall.

The only people who needed to be there were Marley and Heath. I didn't think they cared if anyone else made it. Their love was all that mattered.

I grabbed my clutch and made my way down the stairs to the lobby where I found Izzy waiting, a winter coat covering her puffy gown.

Daphne smiled. "She's been waiting for you."

"You look like a princess," I said to Izzy as she attempted a curtsy.

Cole took her hand. "I think we need to have a seat. The wedding starts soon."

"When do we get cake?" Izzy asked him as he led her outside, and I didn't hear him answer.

Daphne watched them go, covering her chest with the palm of her hand. "He's so sweet with her." Then she turned her attention to me and lowered her voice, "He's going to adopt her."

"How is that possible? She has a biological father," I said.

"Cole wanted to meet with Trent before we got married. He asked Trent to terminate his parental rights, making way for him to adopt Izzy."

"That's amazing." Cole's love for Daphne and Izzy was undeniable.

"Izzy deserves someone who's present in her life, and that was never her father."

"As long as you're happy."

We hooked elbows and walked outside.

The day was sunny and cool, but there were heaters strategically placed throughout the rows of chairs.

"Have a seat. We're going to make this quick. It's cold even with the heaters," Aria said.

"You got it," I said to her as we sat in the row next to Cole and Izzy.

I hadn't seen Aiden since we'd woken up this morning. There hadn't been time for more than a rushed kiss. I'd hoped to see him again before the wedding, but Marley and Heath must have kept him busy with prewedding activities.

The rest of the guests were seated. Heath's brothers—Sebastian, Emmett, Talon, and Knox—stood on the porch.

A string quartet sat off to the side, and as soon as they lifted their instruments and strummed the first note, the guests turned to watch the flower girls, Addy and Ember, walk down the aisle. One by one, they threw red petals onto the white runner, grinning at people they knew in the crowd. When I looked at the men on the porch, their expressions were soft and full of love.

The bridal party was next: Ireland, Sarah, Hanna, and Holly. They lined up on Marley's side of the porch. When the wedding march sounded, everyone stood.

Marley's hand tucked into Aiden's elbow as she walked down the aisle in an absolutely stunning dress. It had to be a designer creation.

Marley might have wanted something small with family and friends, but she stood out. She looked beautiful with her hair half up, the rest hanging in loose curls down her back and covered by a lace veil.

Marley smiled at Heath with her bouquet of red roses in her hands.

When she reached the stairs, Heath met her and Aiden at the bottom. Aiden held onto Marley's hand, saying something that was too quiet for the audience to hear.

"I will always take care of her." Heath's voice was loud and sure.

Aiden inclined his head, then placed Marley's hand in Heath's. He waited until they were on the porch before joining Heath's brothers on the side.

The preacher stood in front of the grand doors to the hotel. "We are gathered here today to celebrate the union of Marley Matthews and Heath Monroe."

My heart was filled with happiness and joy. Aiden caught my gaze and winked.

We were far away from engagements or even commitments, but I was happy even though I wasn't sure how he felt or what he wanted. He hadn't said he loved me even if it felt like he did.

I listened to the rest of the ceremony, clapping at the end when the preacher declared them husband and wife. After Heath and Marley walked up the aisle, Aria whisked them away to take pictures. The guests went inside for cocktails.

In the ballroom, I stood with Daphne and Cole. When the flower girls arrived, Izzy took off with them.

I sipped my champagne and nibbled on a few of the hors d'oeuvres.

Finally, the bridal party appeared, then the bride and groom. Aiden sat at the main table with the rest of the wedding party, and I was seated with Daphne, Cole, Izzy, Charlotte, and a few other cousins on the Monroe side.

They talked about Sarah and Knox's Valentine's Day wedding earlier this year, and Cole and Daphne's upcoming nuptials. I stayed mostly silent because I had nothing to contribute. I didn't feel comfortable talking about my relationship with Aiden because only a few people knew about us, and I didn't know Sarah and Knox well.

After dinner was served and cleaned up, the dancing started. I waited with the other guests while the bride and groom had their first dance, then the attendants joined them for the next one.

Aiden was an extra attendant. He didn't have anyone to pair with since he'd walked down the aisle with Marley. He rounded the dance floor and stopped in front of me. "Would you like to dance?"

I placed my hand in his. "I'd love to."

He pulled me into his arms, and we swayed in time to the music.

"This is a little different from when we were here by ourselves."

He lowered his head slightly so that his lips brushed against my temple. "That's one of my favorite memories."

"Mine too."

"We haven't had much time to be alone lately." Aiden's voice filled with regret.

"We sleep in the same bed," I said brightly even though it had bothered me too.

Aiden's gaze passed over the room before settling on me. "What are your plans for tomorrow?"

"I'm going to spend it with my family."

"Maybe we can have a lazy morning in bed?" Aiden asked hopefully.

"That would be nice." Some of the tension in my chest eased at his words. He was feeling the same disconnect I was and was interested in making it better. That's all you could ask for in a relationship: good communication, and give-and-take.

After the dance, we refreshed our drinks and mingled with the guests. At some point, there was a commotion at the doorway to the ballroom.

The doors had been propped open because the guests had expressed interest in the wedding, and we had very few for the evening before Christmas. Reservations picked up again on the twenty-sixth.

I saw a couple, not one of the guests I'd seen in the inn the last few days. They were older with faces that were worn as if they spent a lot of time drinking or smoking or probably both.

The woman pointed in Marley's direction. "That's our daughter."

"Shit." Aiden's hand, which had been on my lower back, dropped away.

"Are those your parents?" I asked him, but he was already walking toward them.

I rushed to join him, not sure what I could do but knowing I needed to be near Aiden to support him.

"This is our daughter's wedding," the woman said to Emmett who blocked her entry into the room with his feet planted wide and his arms crossed over his chest.

"I don't believe you were invited."

"You weren't," Aiden added stood next to Emmett, his voice hard and unforgiving.

I stayed back, wanting to be nearby in case Aiden needed me but not wanting to interfere with whatever was going to happen. My skin crawled as Aiden's mother, Shay, pointed one long nail at his chest. "How dare you refuse to allow me into my daughter's wedding."

"You weren't invited. You need to leave." Aiden stepped forward in an effort to back them into the hallway because guests were starting to notice that something was going on.

"You think you're something because my mother left you this place?" His mother gestured wildly around us. "But you're just trailer trash. No military training or dating a higher-class woman will change that for you."

Aiden glanced at me, then stepped in front of me, blocking her from my view. I wondered if he thought he was protecting me.

The woman gestured in my direction, then added, "You're no better than us."

I wanted to argue that he'd been better than her since birth, but it wasn't my place to interfere. I waited for Aiden to argue with her, but instead his shoulders lowered.

My stomach knotted. Did he believe her?

His father—I think his name was Hank—tugged on her arm and then said to Aiden, "She said you'd invited us. I didn't realize we weren't welcome."

Aiden's face softened slightly. "Marley wanted to enjoy her wedding with her family and friends. You've never been that for us. We made our family, and it's not blood."

Hank had the decency to flinch, but Shay's face twisted with rage. "Did you think you can pay us off, and we'd stay away?"

Aiden's jaw tightened. "I didn't pay you a dime. That wasn't my decision."

Marley and Heath appeared next to me. "What's going on? We heard yelling."

Aiden held up his hand as if to ward them off. "Nothing for you to worry about. I'll take care of them."

Marley's eyes widened when she took in the sight of her parents dressed in torn jeans and stained shirts that had seen better days. "You promised never to show up here again."

Shay's face crumbled. "The money's gone. We need more."

"You showed up on my wedding day demanding money?" Marley asked incredulously. Then she shook her head. "I shouldn't be surprised by anything you do anymore."

"Let's take this downstairs," Emmett said with an air of authority, and Talon joined him as they each took one of the interlopers' arms and guided them down the stairs.

Aiden followed them into the hallway and then turned to face Marley and Heath. "You stay here. I'll deal with them."

"You're not going to pay them off," Marley hissed.

Aiden sighed. "I don't have that kind of money anyway."

"Aiden—" Marley said as he turned and jogged down the stairs.

"I don't want him to deal with this on his own," Marley said to me and Heath.

I smiled to cover my concern. "I'll go. Go back inside and enjoy your party."

"Thank you, Fiona," Marley said.

I rushed down the stairs and joined the group in the lobby. Thankfully, there were no guests milling about. The front desk had been empty for the wedding, and maybe that's how Aiden's parents had snuck in. I wasn't sure anyone suspected that his parents would show up.

"How did you know Marley was getting married?" Aiden asked in a cold voice I didn't recognize.

"Yesterday, someone posted pictures on the social media pages for the inn," Shay said.

A chill ran through me. I was the one who'd posted the preparation pictures online. "The inn looked so beautiful, and Marley had said that posting daily photos would be good for business. I hadn't even thought about them seeing it and showing up."

"You didn't think," Aiden said to me, and I swallowed over the lump in my throat. Then to his parents, he said, "You need to leave."

Hank grabbed Shay's arm and tried to tug her toward the front door. But Shay ripped her arm from his grip. "We'll be back. You can't get rid of us that easily."

"You'd be surprised what I'd do to protect my friends and family. Gram didn't want you here, and neither do Marley and I." Aiden's tone was cool.

"Shay. This isn't the time or the place." This time, Shay allowed Hank to guide her out the door.

Emmett and Talon followed them out, probably to ensure they drove off the property.

Aiden ran a hand through his hair as he turned his back to me and walked toward the kitchen. My heart thumped hard as I followed him, wondering if he wanted me to.

He braced his hands on the counter and lowered his head. I wanted to touch him, but I felt the anger radiating off him, and I wasn't sure he'd welcome it.

CHAPTER 20

AIDEN

I couldn't believe my parents had shown up at the wedding. I should have anticipated they'd want to cause a scene. It was what they were best at. We figured out early on that we couldn't have friends or significant others over. Not unless we wanted to be humiliated.

No one else's parents reeked of smoke and alcohol and looked like they hadn't bathed in days.

I wasn't sure I could return to the ballroom. I was embarrassed by their presence. It reminded me of who I really was. I wasn't a man who could be proud of co-owning this inn with my sister. I'd always be the kid from the trailer, the one whose mother berated him and embarrassed him in front of others.

Those were my roots. There was no escaping them. No amount of money would ensure my parents stayed away. They'd always come back, demanding more, ruining everything I'd built.

Maybe it was best if we sold the inn and started off somewhere new, somewhere no one knew my name or who my parents were.

When the feather-light touch landed on my hand, I startled.

Fiona snatched it back. "Sorry, it's just me. I wanted to make sure you were okay."

I pushed off the counter, rage pouring through my body. "I can't believe you thought it was a good idea to post pictures of the wedding on social media. What did you think was going to happen?"

Fiona took a step back. "I was just doing what Marley wanted. I thought your guests would love the images, and maybe you could hold weddings here in the future."

I couldn't even process whether that was a good idea because I was so angry that she'd brought my parents to my doorstep, into the ballroom where my sister's wedding reception was being held. "It was reckless."

"I'm sorry." Fiona's voice was shaky and unsure. "I didn't know that they'd be watching the inn's social media pages or that they'd show up here."

"You had to know. This is what they do." I suspected I was being unreasonable, but I couldn't stop the words from coming out.

"You never introduced me to your parents. You said they were too awful for me to be subjected to them. I know what you told me. But I didn't know them or how they'd react. I promise I didn't know this would happen."

How could she have known? But the logical part of my brain had shut down when I realized it was my parents standing in the entryway to the ballroom. They marred something beautiful. Something I thought was safe from their presence. I didn't expect them to show up here, and I should have. "My mother ruins everything that's good."

I ran a hand through my hair. My mom tried to ruin me and Marley, but we'd survived. We'd come out better than them, but maybe we hadn't.

At least my father had seemed slightly embarrassed by her behavior. Maybe it was seeing Marley dressed up in her wedding gown. She was gorgeous, and I didn't know much about fashion, but I had a feeling her dress was worth a lot of money.

Marley was all class. But I felt like there was this stain on my soul, one I'd never clear away.

"You're not them, you know."

I laughed, but there was no humor in it. "You don't know what you're talking about. You grew up in a loving family. You weren't embarrassed by your trashy parents or picked on because you lived in a trailer."

"Well, no, but you know that says more about those kids then it does you, right?"

I couldn't see anything right now. Every muscle in my body ached. I felt like I'd run a marathon without drinking any water. My heart hurt, my back was tight, and I just wanted to disappear. "You brought my parents here. I can't forget that."

Fiona sucked in a breath, her eyes filling with pain. "You know I didn't do that on purpose."

"Do I?" My voice was cold, but I couldn't bring myself to care. I needed to protect her from me. I needed to push her away before her life was tainted too. "You're just as impulsive as you were when we were nineteen, asking me to marry you."

Her hand went to her chest, and pain flashed across her face. "You can't possibly mean that."

"You need to go. Back to your family and your job."

Fiona had shrunk under the weight of my words, but then she straightened, seemingly gathering courage from somewhere deep inside of her. "I'm sorry about what happened. It was never my intention for them to see it."

I shook my head. "Just go."

Fiona let out a frustrated breath. "I'll leave. But you're going to regret everything you said tonight."

"Don't hold your breath." I forced myself to say and do anything necessary to get her to leave. She needed to be as far away from me as possible. I wouldn't rest until she was gone, until my parents couldn't touch her.

I'd kept them away from her when we were dating as teens, and I wouldn't let them near her now. She was mine to protect. But as she turned on her heels and walked away, I couldn't help but think I'd just lost her forever.

I tried to tell myself it was for the best. We never had a future together. We had moments in time where we could enjoy each other, but we wouldn't work long-term. My family didn't make sense with hers. The inn didn't elevate my worth. I'd always be trailer trash, just like my mom said.

Emmett walked into the kitchen a few minutes later while I was drinking ice water. "You okay? Fiona just walked out with a couple of suitcases."

"You help her to her car?" I asked tightly.

"Talon helped her carry her things out."

My stomach sunk even though it was what I wanted. "Good."

"You don't want to run after her, tell her you're an idiot for whatever you said or did?" Emmett's voice was gruff.

I snorted. "The best thing she could do is leave. She's better off without me."

Emmett sighed long and hard. Then he grabbed two glasses from the cabinet and a bottle of scotch I kept under the sink. He poured two shots, shoving one over to me.

I didn't wait for him to take his; I just threw it back, enjoying the bite of the liquor on my throat. I slammed the glass on the counter. I welcomed the rush.

"You're an idiot. You know that, right?"

"Fuck off." I'd heard he was the asshole Monroe brother. The one who resisted change on the farm and fought his brothers and mother over everything. But right now, I didn't want to talk to anyone.

"I was the first of my brothers to fall in love. When I met

Ireland, she was engaged to someone else, but that didn't stop me from wanting her."

I lifted my head, the throbbing a dull ache now due to the alcohol. "Why are you telling me this?"

"Because maybe you need to hear it."

I gestured at him to continue.

"Ireland wanted to hold her wedding on my farm. I said yes, not because I wanted to see her marry someone else but because I wanted her to be happy."

I scowled. "I don't see how this has anything to do with me."

Emmett gave me a hard look before he continued, "On the day of her wedding, her fiancé's girlfriend showed up to tell her that he'd been sleeping with her."

That had my attention.

"Ireland ran from the wedding, and I found her by a waterfall near my cabin. She was dressed in her wedding dress, and she was crying. I wanted to ease her pain." Emmett threw back his shot, then poured another. "I took her to see the pond, and then it started snowing. She was stuck in my cabin for a couple of days."

I whistled. "You still wanted her."

Emmett nodded. "I won't bore you with the details. But she hadn't loved her boyfriend by the end. They'd been doing the long-distance thing, not well obviously. Maybe she thought what we'd shared was some vacation fling, a break from reality, but it was always more for me. When we decided to give the relationship a real shot, I think I panicked. I wasn't used to having a girlfriend or being committed to anyone. When she got too close, I kicked her out of my house. I thought I didn't deserve her. That I wasn't good enough for her."

"You fucked up."

Emmett nodded. "Just like you. I fell back on old limiting beliefs. But the thing is, you are your own person. You are not the house you grew up in or how your parents act. You define the man you are now."

"I thought if I enlisted in the military, I'd be a man worthy of her."

"You still don't think you're worthy of someone like her."

My jaw ached from grinding my teeth.

Emmett held up his hand. "You may not believe me, but think about it. Until you know you're worthy, you won't be." He walked out of the room without another word.

I poured a second shot and drank it. He hadn't helped me. His situation had nothing to do with mine. The alcohol was starting to cloud my brain. I needed to go back to the reception. I stopped in the bathroom to wash my face, then pat it dry.

Upstairs, the party was still going on. Plates of crumbs were on the tables, so I must have missed the cutting of the cake.

As soon as Marley spotted me, she crossed the room. "Is everything okay?"

"I took care of it."

Marley's hands rested on her hips. "You took care of our parents, or you took care of Fiona?"

"Hopefully, we won't see Hank and Shay for a while, and Fiona is staying at her family, where she should have been all along."

Heath walked up in time to hear my last remark. "Fiona left?"

Marley waved a hand in my direction. "Can you believe him?"

Heath had the audacity to chuckle. "Actually, I can. You always fuck everything up before you can get what you want."

I ran a hand through my hair. "I just had a messed-up conversation with Emmett. I think he was trying to help, but he didn't make any sense."

Heath arched a brow. "Emmett talked to you?"

"Something about a runaway bride and thinking he wasn't good enough for her because Ireland was some socialite."

Heath nodded. "Ireland was a trust-fund baby. I'd forgotten about that."

"I'm glad it made sense to you," I said tightly.

"He thought Ireland was better than him. He didn't deserve her, so he pushed her away. Kind of like how you kicked Fiona out and told her to go home."

The hair on my neck stood on end. Had I done the same thing? "I wanted to protect her from my family."

"By not seeing her anymore? By hurting her? How is that protecting her?" Marley started pacing. "You turned down her proposal for the same reason. You wanted to protect her, make her decisions for her. You thought you knew what was best for her, and it sure as fuck wasn't you."

"You got that right."

Heath shook his head. "You're missing the point."

My jaw tightened. "This is your reception. You should be enjoying yourselves."

Marley paused. "I would be enjoying myself if you weren't being such an idiot."

A fast song came over the speakers.

Sarah approached us with a smile, seemingly oblivious to what was going on. She grabbed Marley's hand. "Come dance with us."

Sarah pulled Marley onto the dance floor, leaving me alone with Heath. "Spare me the lecture."

Heath chuckled.

"And stop laughing at me."

"I have to say it's nice being on the other side."

The tension made the muscles in my neck tight. "What the fuck is that supposed to mean?"

"I messed up with Marley too." Heath moved to stand next to me.

"I didn't mess up," I insisted.

"You just kicked the love of your life out of your inn."

I let out a shaky breath. I turned down her proposal, and now I'd kicked her out on Christmas Eve. "I'm an asshole."

Heath shot me a look. "That's what we've been trying to tell you."

"I thought I was shielding her from my parents. If she's not here, they can't hurt her."

"Is that what you said?" Heath asked reasonably.

I winced. "I was angry about her posting pictures on social media. My mom saw it and took it as her invitation to show up here uninvited."

"You blamed Fiona, when that should have rested solely with your parents."

"She can't possibly want me. Not after seeing that public display. That was the Matthews. Who'd want a part of that?"

"Did you let her figure that out for herself, or did you make that decision for her? The same way you said no to her proposal."

"It would have been stupid to quit school and marry me. What did I have to offer her? She would have resented me eventually."

"The point is that you didn't let her make that decision then, and you're not letting her make decisions now."

That caused me to pause. Was I making the same mistake I had last time?

"That's not how relationships work. You're supposed to communicate and come to decisions together. It's never going to work if you unilaterally make all of them for her."

"I didn't think that was what I was doing."

Heath gave me a look. "That's fairly obvious. And I thought I was an idiot."

"Hey," I said with a warning note in my tone.

Heath held up his hands. "I call it like I see it."

If Heath was right, I'd been pushing Fiona away my entire life. I didn't think I was good enough for her, so I protected her by rejecting her before she could realize it. But what if I was wrong? What if I was good enough? What if I wasn't my parents? The headache was in full force again, and I couldn't reach for any of the answers.

"I'm here if you want to talk."

I gestured around the room. "This is your wedding night."

Heath flashed a smile. "You could have what I do. A woman who loves you despite all your flaws."

Had Fiona loved me despite my history and the fuck-ups in my past? All I'd done was make a bigger mistake. Had I messed up the only person that loved me for me? "I think I fucked up."

"That's what I've been trying to tell you."

"What am I going to do?" The panic clawed at my throat.

"You're going to take some time to think about what you want, and if it's her, and you're willing to do whatever's necessary to get her back, then we can talk about it."

I raised a brow. "You're going to be on your honeymoon."

"I'm around tomorrow," Heath said.

"On Christmas." I didn't want to be apart from Fiona on the holiday, but I was the one who'd pushed her away. She'd already planned to spend it with her family. It would give me time to think.

"What else are you doing? Besides wallowing."

"Marley said I could join you, but you're hanging out with the Monroes. They aren't my family."

Heath frowned. "You're *my* family, and everyone is welcome."

"Even a Calloway?" I asked, thinking about what would happen if I managed to get Fiona back.

With a rueful grin, he said, "We didn't kick Cole out yet. Although at this point, I think the Monroes would prefer to keep Daphne and Izzy and do without Cole."

"We'll see." I had things to figure out, and I wasn't exactly in a holiday mood. I couldn't remember the last time I'd spent it with anyone other than my fellow soldiers.

Heath hooked an arm around my neck and pulled me into his chest. "I'm not letting you spend it alone. So get that out of your head."

I twisted away from his grasp. "Knock that shit off."

"We're brothers now. I get to treat you like one."

"Don't you have enough brothers?" I asked, thinking of the four he already had.

"I could use one more. Besides, I feel sorry for you. You're obviously incapable of getting in touch with your emotions."

"Like you're good with that?" I asked him incredulously.

"I just married the love of my life. I'd say I am," Heath said as Marley returned to his side, and a smile spread over his face.

"Aria said it's time for us to make our exit," Marley said with her hand on his chest and her shoulder tucked under his arm.

Heath grinned. "I'm all for that."

The two of them were staying at their cabin tonight, and Charlotte had checked into a room at the inn so they could have privacy. I had a feeling Charlotte would be living at the inn for a while. She wouldn't want to impose on them.

"Take care of her," I said, my throat tight with emotion.

Heath looked up at me and tightened his grip on my sister's shoulders. "I told you I would."

"Just making sure."

"Are you two good?" Marley asked, looking from me to her husband.

"Couldn't be better. Aiden's going to dig his head out of his ass sometime tomorrow and call us to work on a plan to get his woman back."

A smile spread over Marley's face. "Perfect. I adore Fiona."

"I do too." It just took me a ridiculously long time to figure everything out.

Marley hugged me tightly. "I want you to be happy."

I shouldn't make any promises, even though I wanted to assure her that everything would be okay. "I will be."

The guests lined up on either side of the doorway on the front porch. When Marley and Heath came outside, we threw red flower petals at them. Marley laughed when Heath lifted her into his arms and carried her bridal-style across the porch and down the steps.

I opened the passenger-side truck door for them, and he tucked her inside. When he closed the door, I couldn't help but think that leaving in Heath's truck was perfect for them. Marley adored expensive things, but she also loved Heath for who he was, Christmas tree farm and all.

Surely, Fiona would accept me for who I was and be patient while I worked through the shit from my past.

CHAPTER 21

❄

FIONA

*A*fter Talon helped me carry my bags to my rental car, I called Daphne on my way to her house.

"Hello," Daphne said.

I could barely form words around the tears streaming down my face and the tightening of my throat.

"What's wrong? Did something happen?"

I took a deep breath, then said, "Aiden asked me to leave the inn. Can I stay with you tonight?"

Daphne sucked in a breath. "Why would he do that?"

"It's a long story. Can we talk about it when I get there?"

"Of course. Drive safely, and I'll see you when you get here." Daphne's voice was filled with concern.

When I pulled up, Daphne met me on the porch.

She ushered me inside. "Cole will get your things."

We settled on the bed in the guest room. "Tell me what happened."

I sighed. "Aiden's parents showed up at the wedding."

Cole set my bags next to the dresser, then said, "I'll get you two some water," before ducking out again.

"They made a scene, demanding to be allowed to stay at the reception."

Daphne's forehead wrinkled as she grabbed the tissue box from the nightstand and set it in front of me. "Were they even invited?"

"Nope."

"What did Aiden do?"

"He blocked them from going inside the ballroom, but they still managed to make a scene. Calling him trailer trash and saying he wasn't better than them. Then they asked for more money."

"Why would they show up on Marley's wedding day and act like that?" Daphne asked.

"This is how they are. It's the same reason he never wanted me to meet them when we dated. He eventually got them to leave. But I think them showing up there like that, causing a scene, brought back old memories. He thinks he's not good enough. That he'll always be that kid who grew up in a trailer."

Daphne shook her head. "No one thinks of him that way. He's a good man. He runs the inn. He's retired from the military. He's nothing like his parents."

"I tried to tell him that, but he wouldn't listen. He blamed me for them showing up." I grabbed a tissue and dabbed at my eyes.

"How is it your fault?" Daphne asked.

"I posted the wedding preparation pictures online. Marley said capturing events like that would be good for marketing. I never thought his parents would see it and invite themselves. It was a beautiful moment I wanted to share."

Daphne held my hand. "How could you have anticipated his parents showing up? They haven't been around, have they?"

"Not since his grandmother kicked them out when Marley turned eighteen. She removed the trailer, and they weren't welcomed back. The mother mentioned something about Marley paying her off. Maybe after their grandmother died?"

Daphne shook her head. "I don't see how this is your fault. It sounds like he was upset by his parents showing up like that. He was surprised and took it out on you."

"I think he really believes that his parents will ruin everything, and he can't have a good life."

"So it's better to push all the good out of his life?" Daphne asked.

I closed my eyes. "I don't think he's ever going to move beyond his past."

"So what does this mean for you?"

Opening my eyes, I said, "I have to move on and figure out my life." My break was coming to an end. I needed to make a decision on my job and my future. Now that Aiden wasn't in it, that choice should be easier, but I couldn't even think about that tonight. I couldn't get past the pain. Aiden blamed me instead of seeking comfort. He'd pushed me away instead of holding on tight. "I can't get past the fact that he always does this. When he enlisted, when his parents showed up. He pushes me away. I can't stick around and let him do it to me again."

Daphne frowned. "You don't think he'll come around? That he'll realize he overreacted."

"I don't think so. He was adamant that it was my fault and that we couldn't be together. It was almost like he thought he didn't deserve happiness because of his parents."

Daphne was quiet for a few seconds, and then asked gently, "Are you in love with him?"

The tears fell harder. "We never said it to each other. I'm scared I never stopped loving him. What if he's it for me? I'll always be in love with a man I can't have. One who doesn't think he's good enough for me. Who can't heal from his past."

"It's not your job to fix him or convince him of anything. He needs to figure this out on his own."

"He never said he loved me," I said, trying to think back on our time together.

Daphne touched my hand which was twisting the tissue. "Did you feel his love?"

I thought about the way he'd been lately, how he'd held me tighter after sex, and how it had felt like so much more than a physical act. "I think so."

"He loved you even if he couldn't say the words."

I met Daphne's sympathetic gaze. "I need the words. I need so much more."

Daphne hugged me. "And you deserve that."

"What am I going to do?" I asked when she pulled away.

"You're going to get some sleep, and tomorrow, you're going to watch Izzy open her presents from Santa."

I laughed despite the tears drying on my face. "I'd love to see that."

Daphne smiled. "It's the best day of the year. Then you're going to eat the amazing breakfast I'm going to make, and then we're going to Dad's to see the rest of our family."

"It sounds perfect." This was the reason I'd come home.

Cole set two glasses on the nightstand. "Do I need to kick Aiden's ass?"

I laughed despite the tears. "No."

"I think he's kicking himself right now. He shouldn't have reacted like that." Then to Cole, she said, "His parents showed up at the reception, causing a scene. He blamed Fiona."

"He said I couldn't understand where he was coming from because I grew up with a loving family," I said, trying to get some clarity on what he'd meant by that.

Cole leaned a shoulder against the door jam. "I grew up with an alcoholic father and a mother who enabled him. I was embarrassed by him because he never showed up for anything, and the few times he did, he was drunk. I think he thought he was sober, but he wasn't."

Daphne stood and wrapped her arms around his middle.

"I'm so sorry, Cole," I said.

"I have an idea of where he's coming from. He needs to work through his past before you two can be together."

"He's pushed me away before, and I don't think I can keep coming back only to have my heart broken again."

Cole nodded. "That's something only you can decide."

I didn't want to know if he thought Aiden would change his mind. I had to operate on the assumption that he wouldn't. That he believed he wasn't good enough for me.

Daphne smiled. "No matter what happens, we're going to enjoy the holiday tomorrow."

"Thank you for letting me stay here."

"Get some sleep. Izzy will be up bright and early tomorrow," Daphne said as they backed out of the room, closing the door.

I forced myself to go into the adjoining bathroom to wash my face. It was red and puffy. I just hoped I didn't look this bad when Izzy opened her presents in the morning. I wanted to enjoy the day with my family, even though I knew the scene with Aiden would be replaying in my mind.

I patted my face dry, then opened my suitcases to search for my pajamas. I missed Aiden. I missed the inn. I'd been looking forward to spending the evening with him. It physically hurt to be separated from him, to replay the words he'd said in my head.

The ridiculous part was that it had nothing to do with me. It was all him. He thought he had to pay for the sins of his parents or he wasn't deserving of something good in his life. But it wasn't true.

Unfortunately, I couldn't do anything to fix this for him. He needed to figure it out for himself. I pulled on my softest pajamas and got into bed. I vowed to enjoy the holiday with my family. To not let Aiden's choices get me down. Even though I knew it was a losing prospect.

The next morning, I woke up to bouncing and an excited voice. "Aunt Fiona, get up."

I groaned and rolled back over, pulling the comforter over my head.

Someone tugged on the blanket until it slid off my body. "Come on. I want to open presents."

I rolled onto my back and reluctantly opened my eyes. Izzy was a streak of red-and-green-plaid pajamas as she raced out the room yelling, "She's up!"

Assuming that was my wake-up call, I brushed my teeth, then pulled a brush through my hair before joining Izzy, Cole, and Daphne in the living room.

"Santa came!" Izzy said to me while she posed for pictures in front of the tree by the window. Presents spilled out from underneath the low branches.

I placed my envelope for her on top of one of the packages.

Daphne handed me a cup of coffee. "Are you ready for this?"

"I will be. Thank you." I blew air over the steaming liquid, hoping to cool it. I felt good that I'd taken the time off work to be here.

I sat on the couch and watched while Cole handed Izzy present after present. There would be more at the Monroes house and at my dad's later today. And I had a feeling Cole bought a lot more for her than she usually received.

When she opened a box with a new bike helmet, she looked confused.

"That's from me. You're growing so fast, and you need a good one to protect your head," Cole said.

"I love it," Izzy said before she hugged him tightly. Then she set it aside for another one.

"Cole likes to purchase the practical presents," Daphne said to me, but I heard the warmth in her tone. Izzy hadn't grown up with her biological father, but Cole had stepped into the role.

When all the presents were unwrapped and she was playing with some figurine horses that were in her stocking, Daphne said, "We spoiled her this year."

"You mean Santa spoiled her," I reminded her.

"Nothing but the best for my girls," Cole said as he leaned down to kiss Daphne.

It was so sweet; my heart clenched. I wondered if I should have stayed at my dad's and let them have this morning to themselves. This was their first Christmas together in their new house.

"You forgot my present," I said to Izzy as I stood up and waded through the mounds of wrapping paper to find the envelope. "It's not as exciting as a box, but I hope you like it."

Izzy grinned at me as she tore it open.

"What is it?" Daphne asked from the couch where Cole now sat next to her.

Izzy's eyes widened. "It's a gift card for riding lessons."

"I know you can ride at the farm, but I thought it would be good to have some instruction. That stable also participates in competitions if that's something you'd like to do when you get older."

Izzy flew into my lap and hugged me. "I can't wait. Will you be here for my first lesson?"

I tensed. "I don't know when that will be, but I'd love to catch it."

Daphne shrugged and mouthed, "You shouldn't have."

But I just smiled because it felt good to give my niece what she wanted, and I knew it was expensive for Daphne, especially when she was trying to get her business off the ground.

While Daphne cooked breakfast, I helped Cole clean up the wrapping paper. I was so grateful to be here with my sister's family, but I couldn't shake the melancholy feeling about Aiden.

This morning, he'd texted, *Merry Christmas*, but nothing else since. I wasn't sure how to respond since he'd essentially kicked me out of the inn last night. Was he going to pretend that he hadn't gutted me?

I didn't have the luxury of taking time to think about it because today was for family. I'd have a moment to wallow tonight when everyone was asleep. I wouldn't let myself think about how much it hurt. I kept trying to push those thoughts to the back of my mind, but my heart ached, and my chest felt as if there was a hole in it.

That afternoon, I went to my dad's while Daphne, Cole, and Izzy headed to the Monroes to open presents there.

When I arrived at Dad's, Jameson greeted me at the door. "My favorite sister."

I smiled against his chest. "That's the same thing you tell Daphne."

Jameson stepped away, a grin on his face. "And I usually get away with it. It's rare you two are in the same place at the same time."

I winced. "I guess that's my fault."

"We haven't seen much of you since you've been staying at the inn," Dad said as I walked into the kitchen.

"I was helping Aiden and Marley renovate the movie theater, but that's done now." And I was positive he wouldn't want me helping with the rest of the projects. "I stayed with Daphne last night and got to see Izzy open her presents."

"I bet that was fun," Dad said with a smile on his face.

"It was nice."

"How long will you be staying after the holidays?" Dad asked.

"I'm not sure. I said I'd be back on the second." Now, there was no reason to extend the trip.

"I kind of hoped you would fall in love with this place and stay," Dad said easily.

I shook my head, my heart heavy. "I enjoy being here, but my job is there."

"Are you going to stay there or look for something else?" Jameson asked.

"I'll go back and look while I work. That's the smartest thing to do."

"Do you always do the smartest thing?" Jameson asked with a tone that said he already suspected the answer.

I stiffened. "I try to do the logical thing."

Jameson snorted. "It's more fun to do what you enjoy."

"And you enjoy firefighting, substitute teaching, and driving buses?" I asked.

Jameson grinned. "Those kids are the best. A school approached me and asked if I'd coach the football team."

"Are you serious?" I asked him.

Jameson was good at football, probably good enough to play in college, but he hadn't wanted to. He hadn't taken the college scouts seriously. Dad thought he should have listened to what they had to offer, but Jameson wouldn't. He said he was going to college for an education which none of us believed because he was more of a float-through-life kind of guy.

"You're going to do it?" Dad asked.

Jameson nodded. "Absolutely."

"You should probably be a teacher," I said thoughtfully.

"I like what I do," Jameson insisted.

I wondered if he'd felt pressured by his brothers to do something for the community like they did. I would think teachers are like that, but my brothers might not. Was he embarrassed that he wanted to help kids in this way?

Did Jameson have difficulty deciding because he was worried what we would think of his choices? If so, that changed how I looked at him. And I wished he'd follow his dreams and not worry about what his brothers would say. Surely, they'd be happy for him if they knew?

"You can't go back to school and change your career now," Dad said.

"Why not?" I asked.

"You have to pick a career at some point and stop switching around," Dad said.

It was Dad's typical criticism of Jameson. He couldn't decide what he wanted to do. Somehow, staying in the same career for life would prove something. "He should make the change if it's right for him."

Jameson held up his hands. "Stop it, you two. I said I was going to be coaching a kids' football team. I'm not changing the course of my life here."

Dad frowned. "Are you going to have time for something like this with your hours at the firehouse?"

"I'll make it work. The athletic director said something about an assistant." Then he glanced at his phone. "The school seemed to think it was impressive that I was a firefighter."

Even if Dad didn't realize it, his comment was a dig at this family who'd made it seem like his job wasn't as important as theirs. "It is impressive, Jameson. You do good work."

Wes walked into the kitchen. "Who does good work?"

His best friend, Sutton, followed him, wearing a dress and carrying a bakery box.

"Jameson."

"You mean with his job as a firefighter or a bus driver?" Wes asked.

"Firefighter," Jameson grumbled.

When Sutton set a box on the counter, Jameson dove for them, grabbing two before anyone else could react. "I love you, Sutton."

"Stay away from my friends," Wes said, but Sutton merely laughed.

"I didn't want to come empty handed." Sutton kissed Dad's cheek. "I got your favorite."

"You're always welcome here with or without food." Dad

pulled down plates and set them next to the box. "Try not to eat like cavemen."

"We can't help it," Jameson said as he licked his fingers.

Dad pushed the napkins in his direction.

Sometimes, I wasn't sure he'd ever grow up. I rolled my eyes as I hugged Sutton who'd been at our house a lot when we were growing up.

"Now, what's this about Jameson's job?" Wes asked as he carefully set a donut on the plate and grabbed a napkin.

I sighed. "Stop giving him a hard time. You're going to give him a complex."

"I don't have a complex, and I don't need to be defended," Jameson said grumpily. "I love my jobs."

"Why do you have so many?" Wes asked.

"I like to keep busy," Jameson said.

"Jameson was just telling us that he's going to be coaching a kids' football team," Dad said.

"No shit?" Wes asked, and if I wasn't mistaken, there was a tint of respect in his voice.

Jameson nodded. "They approached me."

"That's great." Wes bit into his donut.

Dad busied himself pouring coffee for Wes and Sutton and milk for Jameson. "I'm happy to have most of my kids home for the holidays this year. That means more help with the turkey."

"Should we wait until Daphne's here?" I asked, knowing she was a better cook than all of us.

Dad looked at the counter where there was a piece of paper with something typed on it. "She left me written instructions."

I stepped close so I could read them. We worked together to follow the steps. Jameson put on holiday music, and we laughed and teased each other. I just hoped the turkey was edible when it was done cooking and not too dry.

When the turkey was in the oven, Wes said, "If it doesn't come out right, it's Daphne's fault. She should be here."

Teddy walked into the kitchen. "Where is Izzy? I want to see my favorite niece."

I hugged him. "They're at Cole's family's house. They'll be here soon."

Teddy grumbled.

"You're going to have to get used to Cole being in Daphne's life," Dad chided.

Teddy shook his head. "Izzy's ours. We shouldn't have to share her with the Monroes."

Dad braced his hands on the counter. "Then you know what you need to do."

"And what's that?" Teddy asked.

"Give me more grandbabies."

The guys groaned, and Jameson said, "Don't be ridiculous. You already have two."

Wes sipped his coffee. "None of us are ready to settle down."

My face heated, even though I knew they were talking about themselves. Whenever Dad gave the boys a hard time for not settling down, he wasn't referring to us girls. He knew we had a better chance of that than them.

Teddy scowled as he opened the box to find one donut left. "I don't want to have kids. I just want to see Izzy. Now that Daphne's not living here, we see her and Iz less."

"That's what happens when you meet someone. You become part of their life, and it includes their family," I said reasonably.

"Well, I don't like it."

Dad cleaned the crumbs off the counter. "What are we going to do with that cottage now that it's sitting empty?"

"You want it?" Wes asked Jameson.

Jameson shook his head. "I prefer the apartment over the garage."

"I'm not planning to stay in town," I said even as my chest tightened at the thought of going back to my old life.

Dad's face fell.

"Should we rent it out?" I asked. "It would mean more money for the farm."

"I don't know if I want a stranger living on the farm," Teddy said.

I racked my brain to think of someone we could offer the space to who wasn't a stranger. "Charlotte Monroe needs a place to stay. She's living at the inn temporarily."

Teddy's gaze narrowed on me. "No."

I placed my hands on my hips. "Are you saying that because she's a Monroe? You know she's a cousin, right? And has very little to do with the farm."

"I don't mind if she lives here. She's hot," Jameson said.

Teddy frowned. "How do you know that?"

Jameson shrugged. "I met her when I was hanging out with Daphne and Cole."

"Now you're hanging out with the Monroes?" Teddy asked him.

Jameson sighed. "Daphne is marrying one. I figured I should get to know my future brother-in-law better."

Dad drew up to his full height. "Cole is adopting Izzy. Whether you like it or not, he's a member of this family. And you need to get over this ridiculous feud."

His words effectively ended the debate on Charlotte living in the cottage. I had a bigger issue. I needed to figure out where my life was going and soon. I was due to go back to work in a week.

CHAPTER 22

❄

AIDEN

I woke up on Christmas morning to an empty apartment. I hated it. I was used to having Fiona in my bed. We usually made love, showered, then cooked breakfast together. Well, I cooked and she kept me company. It was a routine we'd fallen into, and with our busy days, sometimes it was the only quality time we spent together all day.

Now the day stretched out before me with nothing to do. I never thought of Christmas as a lonely day, but it was. Marley and Heath were enjoying their first holiday as husband and wife. My parents were hopefully gone, and my grandmother was dead. I had no one.

I'd pushed away the one person who seemingly loved me. I could have spent the day with Fiona. This was all my fault.

I'd blamed her for my parents showing up at Marley's wedding when it rested solely on them. Fiona had no idea that a few innocent pictures on social media would bring my mother to my door, and I was positive she didn't want that for me.

I remembered the look of concern on her face last night after we'd gotten my parents to leave. She was hurting for me. When had anyone else ever felt pain on my behalf?

I was the one who took care of Marley when my parents didn't. I shielded her from the worst of it. I'd never let anyone else in. Not like I had with Fiona.

She wanted to be there for me, but I shoved her aside and blamed her for my parents' actions. It was inexcusable.

I shot off a text to Fiona first thing in the morning, wishing her a Merry Christmas, but I hadn't heard back. I deserved that from her.

I went for a run, showered, and cooked breakfast alone. At eleven, Heath texted to ask if I was ready to talk, and I quickly responded that I was.

We planned to meet at his cabin. I didn't even care that it was the day after his wedding and he should be with his wife. I was a selfish bastard, and I'd take all the help I could get.

When I pulled up, Heath stood on the porch with a mug, he handed it to me as I approached. "Are you ready to fix this?"

I trudged up the steps, my boots feeling heavy. "I don't know what to do."

"First, you need to apologize for blaming her for what went down last night."

"Fiona's not responsible for my parents' actions. They did shit like that long before she was in the picture. But what if she won't see me or talk to me?" I sat in one of the rocking chairs.

Heath turned and leaned against the railing. "That's a real possibility you need to be prepared for."

I dropped my head into my hands. "How can I make it up to her? How can I show her what she means to me?"

"You're working on a grand opening for the movie theater?"

I lifted my gaze. "That's in a few days."

"Maybe you could do something with that," Heath suggested.

"I don't want to let this go that long."

Heath's brow furrowed. "You might not have a choice. She's probably spending the day with her family. What are you going to do? Show up at her family's dinner and make a public apology?"

"Isn't that what Cole did on Thanksgiving?" I asked, the tension between my shoulder blades intensifying.

Heath nodded. "You can't do the same thing."

I let my head fall back. "I don't know what to do. How can I show her that I love her and want to spend the rest of my life with her?"

"You're on the right track with that question. Whatever it is, it has to be big."

The door opened, and Marley stood there. "Why are you talking outside? It's cold."

Heath gestured toward me. "We're talking about guy stuff."

Marley sighed. "You're going to need all the help you can get, and I'm not standing out here. Come inside."

I followed her inside where she handed me a fresh mug of coffee. Then we sat in the family room where the tree was lit. There were no wrapped presents under the tree.

"I wonder what you bought your new wife for Christmas," I said to Heath.

"Heath's taking me to Hawaii. After the grand opening, we'll go to California to spend some time at my house, and then on to Hawaii."

"That was your Christmas present?" I was impressed.

"Wedding and Christmas present wrapped in one," Heath said as he rested his arm over the back of the couch where Marley sat. "What do you get for the woman who has everything?"

Marley's hand rested on Heath's thigh. "Time together. That's the most precious gift."

Both looked relaxed and happy. As if waking up together was the only thing they needed in life. I wanted that for myself.

Heath kissed her softly, then turned his attention to me. "But we were talking about your situation with Fiona and how you were going to fix it."

"I think it should be the day we open the movie theater. We're already planning a party, and it's her project. She has to be there."

Marley raised a brow. "You hope she's there. What if she goes back home early?"

I hadn't considered that. "It's a possibility."

"You need a reason for her to come back."

"I think we need to make her presence at the grand opening seem mandatory. Like we need her there for some reason. Should we ask her to give opening remarks? Or something else?"

"I think you're on the right track. But I think you should give the speech and use that opportunity to talk to her."

Marley nodded. "You can say it's to thank her. We'll emphasize that this was her project, and it wouldn't have been possible without her."

I nodded. "She's the reason why we're renovating the entire basement."

Marley leaned forward. "I can ask her to stay and help with the basement restoration, but the rest of it is up to you."

"Should we play a special movie? One that speaks to your relationship?" Heath asked.

"She'd probably suggest a holiday movie." We fell silent for a few seconds, thinking about what the best step would be. Finally, I said, "We could have her plan the party even if it's from afar. It was her idea to do Hollywood glam."

Marley smiled. "You play dirty. I like it."

"I know what I want, and I need to use everything in my arsenal to get it."

Heath gave me a pointed look. "If you hadn't fucked this up to begin with—"

I leaned back on the chair. "You screwed up with Marley too. Don't act like you're perfect."

Marley stood with a huff, clearly annoyed with us. "Are you ready for lunch? We have a few more days to plan this out."

I hated that I couldn't fix this now. I wanted Fiona in my bed tonight, but that wasn't going to be possible. I had to plan the right move, or it would blow up in my face. I'd hurt her before. She wouldn't forgive me easily.

～

I didn't want to let things go until the night of the party, so I texted Fiona Christmas evening telling her how sorry I was and that I wanted to talk. She'd said it wasn't a good idea. That she was called back to work and needed to fly to California the next day to deal with a fire in one of the hotels.

I hated that she wasn't here, that she'd already made the decision to go back to work. I felt her slipping through my fingers. Every time I mentioned my concerns to Marley, she told me we were playing the long game.

It was her theory that Fiona would go back to work, hate it, and be ready for a change when she flew back for the party. Marley had taken care of ensuring Fiona would be in town for that.

If Fiona knew what I had planned, she'd stay in California, and that was the last thing I wanted. I needed to see her face-to-face when I talked to her.

I thought about what I needed to do and say to show her that I wanted to be with her forever, and there was only one solution I could come up with. I hoped it was the right one.

The formal invitations were sent. Marley took care of creating the beautiful invitations and getting them hand delivered to our guests. It was one of the times where I didn't protest her using her own money to get things done.

We hired servers to offer champagne and appetizers in the lobby of the basement. It was Marley's idea to create images of each room of the basement that we planned to renovate, and to display them on tripods.

It would serve as a teaser for what was to come. She hoped it would get the public excited about the renovations. I hoped it would entice Fiona to stay and finish what we'd started.

Any time I thought about moving forward without her, there was this crushing weight on my chest. I had difficulty drawing a deep breath. My life played out in my mind as one long, desolate nothingness.

It was hard to watch Marley and Heath together, knowing I might never have that. How many people do you have a connection with? For me, it had only been Fiona, and I wasn't prepared to search for anyone else. I just wanted her.

The day of the party, I paced the theater, making sure that everything worked. I tested the lights, the popcorn maker, and the projector.

Charlotte found me in the bowling alley. "What are you doing?"

"I want to make sure this works right in case someone wants to bowl."

"Marley said this room wasn't ready yet. We're only allowing guests into the theater." There was a part that the mechanic was trying to find for the lane on the end, but the others worked.

"Is there anything I can help you with?" There were a few high tables already set up in the lobby for those who wanted to sip champagne and mingle before the movie started. "Maybe I can run a vacuum through the lobby one more time."

Charlotte held up her hands. "Aiden, everything is perfect. Why don't you take a break, maybe a nap, shower, eat something, and come down when it's time."

"I don't know—"

"I'll take care of things here, and if there's an issue, Marley can help. But you need to relax."

"I don't think I can." I hated being in my apartment alone. Everything reminded me of Fiona.

Charlotte bit back a smile. "Everything's going to work out with Fiona."

I stiffened. "What do you know about that?"

Charlotte's expression shifted to one of sympathy. "I know you two were spending a lot of time together, and she's gone."

"Marley assured me she'd be back for the party."

"Are you planning something?"

"I'm going to introduce her this evening. It's my chance to win her over. I just don't know what to say."

Charlotte smiled. "Oh, you don't have to plan it down to the words. When it's time, let your feelings guide you."

Could I relax and do what felt natural? I wasn't sure I wouldn't screw up again.

"If you go into it with a pure heart, you'll be fine. Don't you love her?"

I nodded. "I don't know if she loves me."

"I'm sure of it. I saw enough of you two interacting to know that much." She put her hand on my shoulder and turned me until I was facing the exit. "Go on. The inn won't collapse while you take a quick shower."

I went to my room without arguing any further because Charlotte was right; I was a nervous wreck. But her words helped me to calm down and to trust that it would be okay. The worst-case scenario was that Fiona didn't love me. Everything else was fixable. If she wanted to continue in her current job, I was prepared to move with her. I didn't want to, but I'd do whatever was necessary to keep her in my life.

I wasn't a nineteen-year-old kid needing to prove myself to the world. I only needed to prove my love to Fiona. That was infinitely easier, or at least I hoped it would be.

I took a shower and risked laying down, positive I wouldn't be able to relax enough to sleep. Hours later, I jerked awake and looked at the clock. I had exactly ten minutes to get dressed and get to the lobby where I needed to greet guests.

Not seeing any messages on my phone, I dressed in a tux Marley had delivered. I was fairly positive she bought it, but I wasn't questioning her tactics. Not when I needed her help.

I took one last steadying breath before I left the apartment and headed downstairs. I could hear a crowd forming in the lobby. I found Marley, who said, "Were you able to take a nap?"

I ran a hand through my hair. "I was."

"Good. You needed it."

I searched the crowd for Fiona.

Marley rested her hand on my arm. "She's not here yet. Her flight was delayed."

"What if she doesn't make it?" It physically hurt to ask.

Marley held her hand up. "We'll figure it out."

I wanted to get it over with now. I felt like I was going to jump out of my skin despite the shower and the nap.

I moved to the door so I could greet the guests we'd invited.

When most of the guests had arrived, Heath said, "I'm going to the projector room. I'll handle that tonight."

"I'll meet you up there."

Heath winked at me. "Hopefully, you'll be busy."

Then he nodded toward the open door where Fiona was just lifting her skirt and stepping onto the porch. I moved toward her without thinking, offering my hand. "You look stunning."

Her hair was swept to one side where it fell over her shoulder in one long ringlet. The emerald dress wrapped around her curves, then flared at her feet. It shimmered underneath the holiday lights and the moon.

Then she lifted her gaze to me as she placed her hand in mine. "Aiden."

"Fiona, I wanted to say how sorry I am—" I began as Marley

pulled her into a hug, then said to me, "Aiden, please get ready to make the announcements. I'll show Fiona to her seat."

I nodded and let go of Fiona's hand. I'd gone off script. My heart was thumping hard, and my hands shook as I shoved them into my pockets. I kept my head down, running through the words I would say to her. I paused at the back of the room, taking in the number of people who'd come out tonight. It was a full house. I wasn't sure I was ready for this.

I patted the box in my pocket for the hundredth time, ensuring myself that it was there and to keep my mind on the end game. I wanted Fiona in my life. The thought of her wearing my ring at the end of the night lit up everything inside of me.

I moved to the backstage area to wait for my cue to thank everyone for coming. When Heath dimmed the lights, Charlotte handed me the microphone. "Just talk from your heart."

I wanted to ask her what she knew about love, but there wasn't time. I took a deep breath, then crossed the stage. I didn't look up until I was in the center. Then I turned to face the audience. They slowly stopped talking and turned their attention to me.

"I want to thank everyone for coming tonight. When my sister, Marley, inherited the inn, she wasn't sure what she was going to do with it. Initially, she wanted to renovate it and sell it. But then she fell in love with this place, the history, our family's legacy, and the contractor."

The crowd laughed, and I relaxed more.

I searched out Fiona who was seated in the front row center.

"I thought I was happy running the inn. Then my high school sweetheart came home for the holidays and rented a room here."

The crowd quieted, as if sensing there would be a big revelation coming soon.

"When I showed her the movie theater, the bowling alley, the game room, and the bar, she convinced me that we had to renovate. That the inn must be restored to how it would have been when my grandmother ran it. Fiona Calloway worked with me to make this a reality." I gestured around at the grand theater, and a few people whistled.

"I wasn't expecting to fall in love with her again, and that's not even what happened." I glanced down at Fiona, her eyes shining. "I realized I never stopped loving you, Fiona. It just increased in intensity. What we have now is so much deeper than when we were kids. And I know I made you promises I didn't keep. But I hope you'll give me another chance to love you. Because this feeling isn't going away, and I want to spend my life with you. Whether that's here at the inn or wherever your job takes you."

We'd talked about the logistics, where Fiona would be seated, whether I should go to her, or whether I should invite her to the stage.

In the moment, it felt right to hop off the stage and make my way to her. The front row was empty except for Fiona. I dropped to one knee. "Fiona Calloway, will you forgive me for the stupid things I said the other day. I didn't mean them. I pushed you away because I love you, and I wanted to protect you. I always have."

Fiona's eyes shone with tears, and she nodded. "I forgive you."

"I'll spend the rest of my life making it up to you. I never want to be without you. I'll follow you wherever you are. You just have to tell me that you feel the same way."

I waited for her response.

Fiona cupped my jaw. "I love you too. I always have."

I forgot about the proposal and the ring and pulled her down so I could kiss her. The room erupted in clapping and cheers.

But I wasn't done yet.

I pulled back slightly so I could extract the box from my pocket. I opened it. "Fiona, will you marry me? Will you love me for the rest of your days, filling my life with happiness and joy."

She nodded. "Yes, I will."

This time I stood and tugged her into my body, knowing that I couldn't pull her into my lap with the tight dress she was wearing. She kissed me, and I felt the tears sliding down her cheeks.

I heard the crowd, but it felt like we were alone in the room. She held her hand out, and I slid the ring onto it. It sparkled in the lights of the theater, and the credits for the movie began to play. It was a song and when a few in the crowd cheered for us to dance, I pulled her into my arms.

When the movie started, I led her upstairs to our balcony and handed her a glass of champagne. "I'm willing to move wherever you are. I just want to spend the rest of my life with you."

"After being back at work and working under the guy with less experience and insight than me, I think I'm going to quit. I want to renovate the basement with you, if you'll still have me."

"Of course." I tugged her hand until she was sitting on my lap, facing the movie screen.

Her lips pursed. "I'm not sure what I'll do after the basement is renovated."

I wrapped my arms around her, content to hold her. "I'm sure we'll need a lot of consulting help. But we'll figure it out together. If you're not happy here, we'll find out what would make you happy."

Her hand curled in the hair at the back of my neck. "I have a feeling that's wherever you are."

"I know I've made promises in the past—promises I didn't keep. But I won't break this one. I promise to be by your side forever."

Fiona smiled softly. "I know. I trust you."

"I can't wait to start our forever." Then I kissed her, forgetting about the movie playing on the screen and the audience below. It was just me and Fiona. Forever.

EPILOGUE

FIONA

Six Months Later

I'd convinced Aiden to hold a Christmas in July theme at the inn. I'd researched different marketing plans with Marley over the past few months, and this one was supposed to be effective. It was ninety degrees outside, but the columns were wrapped in twinkling white lights and the gardens were too.

"I think we should keep the lights on the trees year-round," I said to Aiden as we walked the property, holding hands. He held a picnic basket in his other hand.

We spent a few lunches a week exploring the Matthews' property, getting to know the land and enjoying nature. It was so different from my life in Chicago where I spent my time either in my office or traveling from one hotel to another. But I loved it.

This felt more sustainable. I could enjoy life and work. The best part was that I spent most days with Aiden. With me and Charlotte helping at the inn, Aiden had been taking on more projects with Heath's contracting business.

The three of them—Heath, Cole, and Aiden—had discussed a partnership. Aiden was excited about it, and I wanted him to be happy.

He loved the inn, but he enjoyed working with his hands and creating something too.

We stopped at a clearing in the woods where I could hear the rush of moving water.

Aiden carefully placed the blanket on the ground, resting the picnic basket on top. "What do you think?"

"It's pretty," I said looking around at the tall trees and the light coming through the breaks in the branches to form a pattern on the floor of the woods.

Aiden shook his head. "Come here."

When I reached him, he grabbed my hands and pulled me close. "Let's try that again. What do you think about building our home here?"

My eyes widened. "I thought you wanted to be close to the inn."

"Eventually, we might want some privacy from the guests. Maybe we could hire Charlotte to be the manager and let her move in."

"She needs a place to live now though."

"I can't figure that part out because if we decide to build a house, it will take some time. We'll work on this project along with our other jobs. But if you're on board, I want to break ground while it's warm."

I looked around, trying to imagine living here.

Aiden took my hand. "The lane will continue from the inn to here. The house will go here. It will have an attached garage and maybe even a workshop for me to work on my side projects."

Aiden worked on custom jobs, like cabinetry, shelving, and breakfast nooks. He preferred to build them off-site and then install them when they were completed. Building a separate workspace would allow him to do that.

"I love it."

Aiden cupped my jaw. "But if this isn't what you want, let's talk about that. I want you to be happy."

Warmth flooded my body. Aiden was always in tune with what I wanted. He never assumed the inn would be our focus forever. He was cognizant that our wants and desires could change as we grew together. "This is more than I ever imagined."

I'd assumed we'd live in the apartment at the inn until we decided to expand our family. Aiden was reluctant to have children because he was worried he'd be like his parents. But I knew he wanted them. He adored Izzy. Several times, I'd caught him watching her with longing.

"I can build a deck so that we have space to enjoy the view. Lots of windows to let in the light. It would be private. The guests won't be able to see it, and we can put a gate on the lane so they don't wander."

Aiden looked so unsure it made my heart ache.

I stepped into his body, so that we were touching from our knees to our chests. "I love the idea of building our own place. It's more than I thought we'd do. But now that you brought it up, it's all I can think about. We can build whatever we want. Make it to our specifications."

"I want you to be involved in that process. Let's build our dream house. And if those plans change, we can easily add an addition later."

"I kind of want it now."

Aiden chuckled. "It's a long process, and I want you to enjoy it. Take your time to pick what you want."

"As long as we're together, that's all that matters."

A warm breeze filtered through the leaves on the trees, keeping us cool. Aiden pulled away to unroll the blanket on the ground. Then he was tugging me to the ground next to him so he could kiss me.

I loved being here with him like this. We worked, but we had plenty of time to tend to us. It was the perfect blend of work and love, and I couldn't get enough.

Aiden slowly removed my clothes, the warm air sending tingles across my skin. His forearms were braced on the ground on either side of me as he slowly entered me. It felt like heaven making love in the place where our dream house would be built.

I couldn't think of a more perfect moment. As he moved inside me, I lost track of the rest of the world, our responsibilities, what we were doing later that day. The only thing that mattered was him filling me with an expression of love on his face.

I cupped his jaw. "I love you."

"I've always loved you, Fiona."

Then he kissed me as the orgasm rushed through my body, hot and fierce. When we finally came down from the high, he rolled me so that I was cradled in his arms, my head on his shoulder. My fingers played with the hair on his chest.

"When do you want to get married?"

We'd been so busy with the renovation of the rest of the basement, we hadn't had time to discuss a date. And I was content being engaged.

"I want to get married around Christmas."

Aiden touched my hip. "Should the holiday party be a wedding this year?"

My lips tipped up. "I think so. Is that what you want?"

"I would have married you at the courthouse. I don't care about the food or the music. I just want to be with you. But I love the idea of a Christmas wedding."

"I thought it was fitting since everything started when I came home from the holidays last year."

"You know, your boss passing you over for that promotion was the best thing that could have happened. It brought you to me."

"I feel like I'm living my best life. I have time to drink my coffee slowly and enjoy nature on my lunch break."

Aiden's chest shook under my hand. He was laughing at me. "If you think this is enjoying nature."

I smiled. "Isn't it?"

"It's my favorite way to enjoy nature."

"I love working at the inn. You and Marley listen to my ideas." I never thought this would be my life.

He stroked my hair. "That's because you're brilliant."

I was so grateful that everything happened the way it did. I liked to think it was fate. "You know that pinky promise we did when we were teens?"

"The one where I said I'd wait for you."

I blinked back the sudden sting of tears. "You didn't break your promise. You were still waiting for me."

Aiden's arm tightened around my back, holding me tight to him. "I think you're right. I never stopped loving you."

I preferred to think that our timing wasn't right at nineteen. We both had some growing up to do, and priorities to make before we could be together.

He moved so that he was on top of me. "Want to stay here a little longer?"

I smiled. "I'm fine with that."

Then he kissed me, and I got lost in him and the promise of our future.

∼

Three Months Later

It was the grand opening of the basement area of the inn, a night we'd been planning for months. So far, the movie theater had been a hit. We'd gotten more bookings for families and couples wanting to enjoy what we had to offer.

We were playing around with the idea of opening the theater and the basement area to the public on Friday and Saturday nights.

Tonight was a test to see if people would enjoy the expansion.

I stood next to Aiden, greeting guests as they came inside. When most had arrived, we followed them downstairs where everything had been either replaced or restored to keep with the original look of the space.

The wood in the billiard room and bar was dark and masculine, keeping with the old gentlemen's club feel. Yet we added a few games in the billiards room that appealed to kids, including basketball hoops, foosball, and Skee-Ball.

There was a large cluster of people at the bar, and others were in the billiard room, drinking and having a good time.

Even the bowling alley was open. The Monroe family—including Daphne, Izzy, and Cole—were in the first two lanes.

We stopped to talk to Heath and Marley who held drinks in their hands.

"I think the night is a success," I said to Marley.

"The Calloways and the Monroes are in the same place, and so far no one seems to be fighting." Cole nodded toward lanes three and four where the Calloways were playing.

It was probably too much to ask that they play each other when they were bowling.

"But this is the grand opening. Can we keep people coming back for more?" I asked.

Aiden rested his hand on the small of my back. "Only time will tell."

For a while, we mingled with the Monroes and the Calloways. After bowling, we moved to the billiards room so the kids could play games.

At some point, Cole pulled Daphne into his side. "We have an announcement to make."

Both families were gathered around the bar, the kids not paying any attention to us.

I knew from looking at Daphne's glowing face and the possessive way Cole held her that she was pregnant. They'd gotten married on the Calloway farm in the spring, and I wondered when they'd make this next step.

"We're expecting a baby."

Cheers erupted around us, and I made my way to my sister and hugged her tight. "Congratulations."

"We didn't want to wait too long. Izzy wants a sister or a brother." Daphne exchanged a loving look with Cole.

"You make me want to take the next step," I admitted.

"We have to get married first," Aiden said from my side. Then he shook Cole's hand. "Congratulations. We're happy for you."

We moved aside for the rest of the family to congratulate the happy couple. Then Jameson arrived. His hair was damp, so he must have had time to shower after his shift at the firehouse.

He searched the room, then walked over to me. "I made it."

"Would you like something to drink?"

He waved a hand at me. "Just water."

"Hard night?" Aiden asked him.

"You could say that. We had a call for a fire. Everyone got out." Jameson didn't add any details but I could tell that it had shaken him.

"You need to distance yourself from the worst calls so you can keep doing your job," Teddy said.

Jameson ran a hand through his hair. "I can't do that. Not easily."

My heart swelled because Jameson felt so much. Way more than anyone gave him credit for. He wasn't just a good time guy. "It's hard not to get involved."

"I meet with the homeowners afterward to ensure they have

working fire alarms and fire extinguishers, make sure they know how to use them. I prefer the teaching side."

"You think any more about getting a teaching degree?" I asked him.

Jameson gave me a look, then thanked Aiden for the glass of water. "I'm fine doing what I am."

Not for the first time, I wondered if he was a firefighter due to some pressure from our family when his natural talents rested somewhere else.

Cole and Daphne joined us. "You missed the big announcement. We're pregnant."

Something passed over Jameson's face before he grinned his usual charming smile. "I can't wait to be the favorite uncle of another niece or nephew. It's a tough job, but someone's got to do it."

Daphne laughed. "You're impossible."

"But you love me, and this one will too." Jameson lightly touched her stomach.

The jukebox had been playing all night, and a few people had started dancing in the middle of the room.

Aiden wrapped his arms around me. "I need you to myself for a few minutes."

"I'm on board with that," I said as he led me to the dance floor.

When he pulled me into his arms, he asked, "Are you upset that Daphne's pregnant?"

I frowned. "Not at all. I'm happy for them. I know they want Izzy to be close to any children they have."

"Then what is it?" Aiden held me tighter when the music slowed.

I sighed. "I'm worried about Jameson. I don't think he's happy as a firefighter."

"He's not your responsibility."

I sighed. "He has such a huge heart. I want him to be happy too."

"It seems like he's doing okay from where I'm standing."

Jameson was at the center of our family's circle at the bar, laughing and talking. No matter what things he'd seen at work, he could easily brush it off and be the charming guy everyone loved. "I wonder if he's hiding what he's going through."

"Or you're imagining problems where there aren't any." Aiden's voice was soft and reasonable.

I relaxed in his arms. "Is it wrong that I want all my siblings to be happy like I am?"

Aiden pulled back slightly to look at me. "Your brothers might be a lost cause, but Daphne is settled."

I laughed. "You're probably right. My brothers don't have any interest in what we have."

Aiden fell silent for a few seconds while we swayed to the music. Then he said hesitantly, "I wanted to let you know that I've thought about expanding our family. We have our wedding in December, and we're not getting any younger."

My heart rate picked up. "Are you serious?"

"Our house will be finished in the spring or summer, and we'll be moving. It's the perfect time."

"I wasn't sure if you were ready."

He'd been talking to a therapist about his parents, and Marley attended with him from time to time. But I didn't ask what they discussed. I just knew he felt more confident about himself and the boundary he'd set with his parents.

His gaze rested on mine. "I'm not my parents. I'm going to be a good dad."

"You're going to be great. Should we practice in the meantime?"

"How much longer do we have to stick around?" His hand gripped my hip tighter, and I knew he was anxious to be alone."

"It's our party."

His head dipped, and his lips hovered over my temple. "So not much longer?"

I tipped my head to the side, enjoying teasing him. "The anticipation makes everything so much better."

Aiden's gaze was intent. "I've waited for you since we were eighteen. I can wait a little longer."

I wrapped my arms around his neck, bringing my body flush against his. "That's what I was hoping for."

Then he kissed me, and I didn't care who saw. I was happiest here in his arms, in the inn we were renovating. We were building a future together, and I couldn't be more excited for it.

BONUS EPILOGUE

❄

AIDEN

Two Months Later

I was going to puke. The thought of standing up in front of all those people was terrifying.

Instead of hosting a holiday party, we were throwing a wedding. Mine. I didn't know what I was thinking to suggest it. I should have pushed for a quick ceremony at the courthouse or even a trip to Vegas. But instead, I was dressed in a tux waiting with Heath, his brothers, and Fiona's at the bar in the basement of the inn.

It was dark and cool, but I was sweating.

"Are you feeling okay?" Heath asked.

I swallowed hard. "Not really."

"Have you eaten anything? Marley sent down food for us." Heath led me over to the table where there was a virtual buffet. He put together a sandwich and handed it to me. "Eat this before you pass out."

I shook my head slowly. "I'm not going to pass out."

Heath gave me a look. "What's wrong? Are you worried about your parents showing up?"

"Not at all." We had security at the gate. No one could get in without an engraved invitation, and their name was cross-checked against the official guest list.

"Then what's the deal?" Then Heath stilled. "Are you having second thoughts?"

When I thought about marrying Fiona, the love of my life, I didn't have any. "I want to be married. I don't necessarily want to do it in front of everyone."

Jameson had been filling a plate behind Heath. "I wouldn't worry about it too much. All your friends and family are here to see you exchange vows. It's a happy moment. No pressure."

It was rare for Jameson to give any serious advice. He was the first one with a joke or the one to suggest everyone take it easy. "Thanks. That was a nice thing to say."

Jameson looked affronted. "I give good advice."

When no one agreed with him, he shook his head. "Just because I'm the youngest brother doesn't mean I don't know some things about life."

Teddy gave him a knowing look as he reached for a plate. "I guess we don't see it often."

Charlotte appeared by my side. "You're needed upstairs."

"Is she having second thoughts?" I hadn't even considered that possibility.

Teddy stepped next to me. "You have to relax."

Charlotte blinked at Teddy's hand which rested on my shoulder. "Your bride would like to see you. She wants you to see her for the first time before the wedding instead of in front of the guests."

Teddy nodded approvingly. "It sounds like your bride knows you best."

"We don't have much time before the ceremony begins." Charlotte slipped her arm through the crook of my elbow and guided me up the stairs.

I cleared my throat. "Where are we meeting?"

"Fiona's in the gardens by the fountain. She said it's one of the first places you spent time together when she came home."

My chest tightened at the memory of showing her the maze and the fountain in the middle. I knew then I'd needed a plan to make her mine.

Charlotte led me through the kitchen and out the slider to the backyard. Then we walked around the side of the inn to the entrance to the maze. The ceremony would take place in the ballroom; afterward, it would be transformed for the reception.

Charlotte squeezed my arm before letting go. "This is where I'll leave you. Good luck."

"Thanks, Charlotte."

She patted my hand before she walked way.

I took a deep breath and made my way down the path. With each step, my heart rate picked up. At the end, I'd see my bride in a wedding dress, waiting for me.

My throat was tight with emotion when I finally came to the clearing.

Fiona faced the fountain. She wore a white dress that dipped in at the waist and flared over her hips with tiny buttons running down the back of it. Those wouldn't be easy to remove later tonight, but I looked forward to taking my time.

Fiona turned and smiled. "I wanted to see you before the wedding. I hope this is okay."

"Why wouldn't it be?" I asked.

Fiona shrugged. "Some people say it's bad luck."

Before she'd finished her sentence, I erased the distance between us. "How could it be bad luck? You're breathtaking."

Fiona's lips tipped into a smile. "You look handsome yourself."

I threw a thumb over my shoulder. "How did you know I was freaking out in there?"

Fiona's eyes shone with unshed tears. "When I thought about

the moment you saw me for the first time, there was no one else with us."

"Thank you for making this moment private. I think I can get through the rest of it without passing out." I took several deep breaths for good measure.

"Anytime you feel nervous just look at me and pretend there's no one else in the room except for us."

My shoulders relaxed. I felt like I could do that. "Or there's still time to elope."

Fiona laughed, and I was positive it was directed at me. "It's too late for that. Besides, I want my family here."

"I want that too." I never thought I'd have a family of my own. Not after walking away from Fiona all those years ago. But her brothers were slowly welcoming me into their family, and I was close to the Monroes through Heath. My world was expanding, and I was okay with that as long as Fiona was my home base. The one who grounded me and kept me sane.

Fiona moved close to me, wrapping her hands around my neck. "We're getting married, and then we're moving into our dream house."

For the first time all day, my chest felt light. I'd been worried about all the wrong things. All that mattered was us making the ultimate promise in front of our friends and family. "I can't wait."

"I can't wait to start my life with you."

"I've always been with you. In here." I touched my hand to her chest, over the spot where her heart beat steadily. "The only difference is I'll be by your side forever."

Her lips curved into a smile. "Mmm. I like the sound of that."

"Is it okay if I kiss you right now?" I asked, every muscle in my body tensed.

"I think we have a few minutes before we need to make an appearance," she murmured as she played with the collar of my shirt.

I took that as permission. I'd make the most of these few minutes, then deliver her to her father who would walk her down the aisle. That sounded a little backward, but that was us.

We didn't do things the conventional way. All that mattered was that we'd walk through the rest of our lives together.

Jameson and Claire's story is next in *Every Beat of My Heart*, an opposites attract single mom romance.

BOOKS BY LEA COLL

The Calloways

Cross My Heart

Every Beat of My Heart

The Monroe Brothers

Runaway Love

Finding Sunshine

Reviving Hearts

Trusting Forever

Endless Hope

Forbidden Flame

Ever After Series

Feel My Love

The Way You Are

Love Me Like You Do

Give Me a Reason

Somebody to Love

Everything About You

Mountain Haven Series

Infamous Love

Adventurous Love

Impulsive Love

Tempting Love

Inescapable Love

Forbidden Love

Second Chance Harbor Series

Fighting Chance

One More Chance

Lucky Chance

My Best Chance

Worth the Chance

A Chance at Forever

Annapolis Harbor Series

Only with You

Lost without You

Perfect for You

Crazy for You

Falling for You

Waiting for You

Hooked on You

All I Want Series

Choose Me

Be with Me

Burn for Me

Trust in Me

Stay with Me

Take a Chance on Me

Download a free novella, when you sign up for her newsletter.

To learn more about her books, please visit her website.

SPECIAL EDITION BUNDLES
ONLY AVAILABLE ON LEA'S SHOP

If you prefer to read by trope:

Bestselling Steamy Romance

Blue Collar Steamy Romance

Brother's Best Friend

Childhood Crush

Contractors

Enemies to Lovers

Fake Relationship

First in Series

Football Romance

Forbidden Love

Forced Proximity

Friends to Lovers

Grumpy Meets Sunshine

High School Sweethearts

Hot Heroes

Office Romance

Second Chance Romance

Single Dad

Single Dad/Nanny

Single Mom

Single Parent

Sports Romance

If you prefer to read series:

All I Want

Annapolis Harbor

Ever After

Mountain Haven

Second Chance Harbor

The Monroe Brothers

If you prefer to read paperbacks:

All I Want Series

Annapolis Harbor Series

Bad Girl Redemption

Brother's Best Friend

Childhood Crush

Contractor

Enemies to Lovers

Ever After Series

First in Series

Forbidden Romance

Friends to Lovers

Grumpy Meets Sunshine

Hot Heroes

Lea's Favorites

Mountain Haven Series

Office Romance

Opposites Attract

Second Chance Harbor

Second Chance Romance

Single Dad

Single Mom

Single Parent

Sports Romance

The Monroe Brothers

ABOUT THE AUTHOR

Lea Coll is a USA Today Bestselling Author of sweet and sexy happily ever afters. She worked as a trial attorney for over ten years. Now she stays home with her three children, plotting stories while fetching snacks and running them back and forth to activities. She enjoys the freedom of writing romance after years of legal writing.

She currently resides in Maryland with her family.

Check out Lea's books on her shop.

Get a free novella when you sign up for Lea's newsletter.

Printed in Great Britain
by Amazon

63074807R00150